# PTARMAGEDDON

### A ROBYN DEVARA MYSTERY

# PTARMAGEDDON

## A ROBYN DEVARA MYSTERY
## BY KAREN DUDLEY

RaveN
STONE

PTARMAGEDDON
copyright © Karen Dudley 2006

Turnstone Press
Artspace Building
018 Arthur Street
Winnipeg, MB
R3B 1H3 Canada
www.TurnstonePress.com

Turnstone Press gratefully acknowledges the assistance of the Canada
Council for the Arts, the Manitoba Arts Council, the Government of
Canada through the Book Publishing Industry Development Program,
and the Government of Manitoba through the Department of Culture,
Heritage and Tourism, Arts Branch, for our publishing activities.

Design: Doowah Design
Printed and bound in Canada by Hignell for Turnstone Press.

Library and Archives Canada Cataloguing in Publication
Dudley, Karen
Ptarmageddon : a Robyn Devara mystery / Karen Dudley.

Fiction.
ISBN-13: 978-0-88801-323-1
ISBN-10: 0-88801-323-X

I. Title.
PS8557.U279P83 2006          C813'.54          C2006-905984-5

# PTARMAGEDDON

# Prologue

### March 19

Whenever I read a novel—one that really captures my interest—I find myself speeding through the pages. Sprinting past each cluster of black markings. Past each line and paragraph and chapter. They say it's the journey that matters, not the destination. But I've never been able to read a book like that.

I don't work. Or clean. I forget to eat. I'm completely caught up in the real emotions of fictitious lives. Too eager to reach the end of the story, too impatient to find out what happens to the characters. Clever wordplay and lyrical prose are lost on me. I can't see deeper meanings or hidden connections—can't enjoy the journey—until I read the book again.

Willa always rolls her eyes when I start a book for the second time. "There are so many books in the world," she'll say, "why read that one again?" I've tried to explain it to her. The total submersion of self. The yearning for those last words, even if they aren't "and they lived happily ever after." Most of the best books,

I find, do not end this way. Those are the ones that resonate. The ones that haunt.

I've been thinking about the end a lot lately. And not the end of a novel, though it is the end of a story. Maybe it's this interminable, arctic darkness, or perhaps just the long, dark tea-time of my soul. Does it matter? The story of Selena Barry. It's a narrative with themes both major and minor. Who she was and what she did. Who she loved. And who she hated. The only part missing is the end.

Death. What will it mean? How will it come? Sometimes I find myself eager to rush towards it, to skim past the muddied drudgery and ice-shard pain of existence to discover the end. But once death becomes reality, there is no chance to go back and savor each moment. No second readings. Perhaps, not even a final moment to say, "Oh, so that's how it ends."

Life is not a novel.

I must keep reminding myself of that.

**1**

It was J.R.R. Tolkien who helped me define what was wrong with my life.

I've read *The Hobbit*, inhaled *The Lord of the Rings* trilogy, and I've watched Peter Jackson's excellent film adaptations more times than I'll admit to anyone except Guido the cat (who watches them all with me). And I finally realized that, all my life, I've wanted to be . . . an elf. Tall, slender, ethereal. Great skin. But in the cold, uncolored light of reality, I am a hobbit. Short, plump, and fond of food.

Figures.

Fortunately for me, Kelt Roberson, my friend, work colleague, and—now—lover, seems to like hobbits. You could even say he has a passion for them. Good thing. I've gone through a lot of changes since I first discovered *The Lord of the Rings*, but my height, tendency towards shapeliness, and a marked fondness for food were not among them.

Kelt likes my curves. Likes the way he can tuck

me under his shoulder whenever we walk arm in arm. He also likes my hairy toes—though I suspect he just enjoys teasing me about them.

At the risk of sounding dorky, Kelt is the best thing that ever happened to me. Aragorn to my Arwen (though I must admit nobody has ever compared *me* to an even-star. In fact, when it comes right down to it, I'm not entirely sure what an evenstar *is* except that is sounds like the sort of thing one would like to be compared to). Kelt's got eyes the color of spring leaves, thick raven-black hair, and a brain that's always busy thinking up new ways to save the planet. He loves old sci-fi flicks (especially the bad ones), adores my cat (almost as much as Guido the cat dotes on *him*), and he's a fantastic cook (which really works for my inner hobbit).

Now, all this seems very well and good—and it *is*. Normally. But field scientists do not live what most people think of as a normal life.

Normally, Kelt and I both reside in Calgary in our respective (and tiny) apartments in the Kensington area. We used to work for the same environmental consulting firm, until Kelt decided to go back to school for his PhD. Normally, we hang out at McNally Robinson's together and watch movies together and eat spicy Spolumbo sausages together and go hiking together. Often, we spend the night together. Normally. But we'd been seeing each other for five months now, and he'd been away for three of them. Normalcy was starting to take on a whole new, unwanted meaning.

I *knew* this was part of the whole fieldwork gig. I knew that as biologists, one or both of us could be in the field at any time. For any *length* of time. Still. It felt like far too long since Kelt had whipped up one of his almond waffles for me. Too long since we'd walked arm in arm in the rain, arguing the finer points of recycling. Hell, I'd even welcome the wise-ass quips about fuzzy feet if it meant we'd be together again.

Not having the patience (or, really, any other qualities) of a saint, I was about to do something about it (being apart, that is, not the hairy toes). One could, after all, substitute chocolate chip cookies for companionship for only so long. Or sit in the tub singing off-key renditions of "Mr. Lonely" over and over again before the neighbors started pounding on the ceiling.

I was in the middle of packing when the phone rang.

"Robyn. It's me."

"Kelt!" I almost dropped the receiver in surprise.

Guido the cat reached out from inside my duffel bag and tried to claw the phone cord. I batted his paws away.

"I was just getting my stuff together," I said. "What . . . why are you calling? I know how horny you can get in the field, but jeez, I'll be there in two days, man . . ." My voice trailed off. There was no corresponding chuckle on the other end.

"Um, hello? Kelt? Is everything okay?"

There was a pause. Then, "Not really," Kelt replied.

"What's wrong? You sound funny."

"There's . . . a problem."

Immediately several "problems" flashed through my mind. Kelt didn't want me up there. He'd found somebody else. Someone smarter. Someone taller. Someone who didn't look like an Uruk-hai in the morning.

"What's wrong?" I asked again, forcing the question past a sudden lump in my throat.

The phone line gave a loud crackle.

"Hello?" I raised my voice. "Are you . . ."

"There's been an accident."

An accident?

"I'm okay," he added quickly. "But . . ."

"But what? Spit it out, Kelt! You're scaring me."

"Selena Barry's dead, Robyn. I'm sorry."

Selena Barry? I scrolled through my mental address book. Selena Barry. The name meant nothing to me. Did I know her? Did Kelt know her?

Kelt had paused again. "Are you okay?" he asked, his voice low. Quiet with sympathetic understanding.

I appreciated the sympathy—when his voice went soft like that, it was extremely sexy—but I could use a little more understanding.

"Uh . . . who's Selena Barry?" I asked.

"You don't know her?" His surprise came through clearly despite the now hissing and popping phone line.

"Didn't she contact you?"

"I don't think so."

"But she left you all—" the phone popped again "—field notes!"

"She *what?* We've got a lousy connection here. Did you say she left me her field notes?"

"Yes! They found a letter addressed to you. It was very specific."

I shoved a pile of socks to one side and perched

on the edge of my bed. Guido the cat hunkered down further into the shadows of the bag and glared out at me. He'd been around long enough to know what folded clothes and a duffel bag on the bed meant.

"I think you'd better start from the beginning, Kelt."

I heard him take a deep breath and let it out slowly. It sounded jagged and uneven.

"Who is Selena Barry?" I prompted.

"Another field scientist. She's been in the Yukon for the past couple of years. Living at Willow Creek."

"Where you guys are. Where I'm going to be in"—I glanced at my watch—"about forty-nine hours."

"Yeah."

"Um, okay."

More crackling silence.

"What was she studying?" I figured I'd start with the easy questions.

"Ptarmigan. Climate change stuff, mostly."

"Same field camp as you guys?"

"No." The phone hissed loudly, then "—don't know who funded her."

"Did you know her?"

"It's a small place. Plus I think she might've had a fling with one of my team members on"—*pop*—"days off."

"Oh." I digested that for a moment. "Any trouble over it?"

"Not that I was aware of."

"Okay." I paused. So much for the easy questions. "And now she's dead."

"Yeah." The phone line popped, then went dead for a second. "—found her two days ago. I've been trying to phone you, but we've had a storm and I couldn't get a line out. She was murdered, Robyn. God, it was awful! There was blood everywhere. Soaked right into the floorboards." The words came spewing out now, purging shock and horror in an acid rush of information. "Somebody stabbed her. About twenty times. And . . ." He stumbled to a stop.

"And *what?* Kelt! Hello? *Are you still there?*"

"Robyn, they smeared her blood all over the walls."

**2**

"Tall. Kinda skinny. Blond with those Bruce Cockburn-type glasses." I repeated Kelt's description of the dead woman.

"And you're sure you didn't know her?" Jack was still frowning.

"I'm not sure of anything," I told him. "But I don't think so. Not from that description. Maybe if I saw her picture . . ." I let my voice trail off, then I shrugged. "I just don't know."

My brother poured himself another cup of tea. His frown deepened.

I'd asked Jack over so I could give him last-minute instructions for looking after my cat—put all plants back on top of the bookshelves after watering them; make sure the bag of cat food is in the cupboard with the childproof latch; and never leave sandwiches, especially ham ones, out on the counter (Jack's vegetarian, but if Guido the cat was feeling ornery enough, even one of my brother's vile whole wheat sprout wraps wouldn't be safe). But quite apart from all this, I'd wanted to talk to Jack because I needed to share Kelt's strange and disturbing news with someone else.

I should have picked my friend Megan instead. Even if she was backpacking through Southeast Asia at the moment.

Oh, my brother's a good guy, don't get me wrong. A SoBe-drinkin', Birkenstock-wearin', flute-playin' New Age kinda guy, but every so often, he regresses. The signs are unmistakable. His forehead scrunches together. His eyes start flashing amber fire. Even the tone of his voice deepens as if the surge of testosterone has shaped his skull to more Neanderthal-like proportions.

"It's weird, Turd," he rumbled now. "I don't like it."

"Don't call me Turd," I said automatically. And in vain. Jack had been calling me a shit ever since fifth grade when he'd discovered the Latin name for robin was *Turdus migratorius.*

"I know it's weird, and I don't like it much, either," I told him, "but I'm not going to cancel my trip because of it."

"It might be something to think about—"

"Or not!" I shook my finger at him. "Don't be going alpha on me, Jack. That's not why I brought it up."

"Do they have any idea who did it?"

I picked up one of the oatmeal cookies I'd baked the day before and started chewing on it. "I don't know," I said shortly, nudging the plate of cookies his way.

Jack was quiet for a few seconds. Then, "What's up there, anyway?" he asked, reaching for the plate. He hesitated and put his hand back down without taking a cookie. "I mean, apart from Kelt's gophers."

"Pikas," I corrected him. "He's looking for pikas.

And apart from them, there's basically just a whole lot of wilderness. And wildlife, of course. Grizzlies, waterfowl, moose. Caribou when the weather gets colder. Pika Camp's a four-hour hike from Willow Creek."

"That wilderness retreat?"

I nodded. "Yeah, though it sounds less like a retreat and more like a base camp for scientists. You know, a place where they can go to get a bath. Kick back for a bit when they need a break from field camp. Check their e-mail."

"They're wired? I wondered how you were going to cope with being away for so long."

Jack is under the impression that I have an unhealthy relationship with e-mail. I stuck my tongue out at him.

"Do they get any tourists?" he asked, ignoring the gesture.

"I think so," I nodded. "They've got cabins for them. And one of the owners is a poet, so they get writers and poets staying too. Apparently there's one big cabin where everybody can eat together and hang out in the evening if they feel like it."

I rested my chin on my hand and gazed out the window. "It sounds pretty great," I said not a little enviously. "They've got a hot tub right by the creek and all this incredible, vast wilderness around them. And—"

"How many people are up there?"

I blinked at the interruption. "Uh, I don't know. Depends on the week, I guess. And who's out in the field. Kelt said there were nineteen people in total—the Pika crew and some other scientists—and the retreat staff, of course. No poets this year, which is—"

"Eighteen," Jack corrected me.

"What?"

"Eighteen people now."

"Um . . . right."

"One of whom is a murderer."

"You don't know that," I protested.

"Neither do you."

I gnawed on my cookie for a while longer. "It could've been a tourist," I suggested. "Some total psycho case. It *is* tourist season right now, and Kelt said she was killed at the retreat. Not at one of the camps."

"And how many psycho cases head out to Willow Creek Wilderness Adventures and Retreat to get away from it all?"

"Well . . . Kelt never mentioned any local suspects—"

"Kelt didn't say *anything* about suspects," Jack interrupted. His eyes flashed a warning at me. "The phone line crapped out before you could ask."

"Why don't you have a cookie?" I pushed the plate closer to him.

"No thanks."

"They're not *that* bad."

"You're still chewing on that one."

Good point.

"You know, Turd, for someone who likes to eat so much, you sure are a lousy cook."

"Yeah, yeah. At least Kelt loves me."

"At least Kelt *feeds* you."

Another good point. We sat in silence for a moment. I tried to wash the cookie down with my tea. Jack was drumming his fingers on the table with abstracted intensity.

"I still think it's weird," he said finally. "Smearing her blood on the wall? It's not the sign of a sane mind."

"No," I agreed. "But then, I wouldn't think sane people tended much towards murder."

Jack grunted, still frowning.

I coughed on a soggy crumb and swallowed the rest of my tea. "I'll be fine," I told him, trying to lighten the atmosphere. "Quit worrying so much. You'll give yourself a unibrow. Chicks hate that, you know."

"But what if she was killed because of something she found out? What if whatever she discovered is hidden in her notes? She left them to you. Does that mean *you're* in danger now?"

I couldn't help myself. I burst out laughing. "Jeez, Jack, what the hell have you been reading?"

He scowled at me, the unibrow effectively quelling my laughter. "I think it might be an idea to postpone your trip for a while," he said. "Just until they find the guy. Hell, maybe the RCMP don't even want anyone else going out there right now."

I reached out and patted his hand fondly. "Look, I appreciate the thought, Jack, but I'm not going to postpone my trip. I've already paid for it, and I didn't get flight insurance. And even if I had, I don't think chicken-heartedness is considered a valid excuse."

"I don't think it's considered a valid word."

"Plus," I continued, "Kelt would have said something if I wasn't allowed in. Or if he didn't think it was safe. And besides, apart from that time in May when he was here for all of a day and a half, I haven't seen him *all summer* and, you know—"

"Turd." Jack's tone brought me up short. "You're babbling."

I closed my mouth.

"What's really going on?"

I stared at him for a long moment. It was the look on his face that undid me. My eyes filled with tears.

"I—" I choked off a sob.

Jack was beside me in a second.

"Hey, hey. What's the matter?" he asked, putting a solicitous arm around me. "Is it this woman? Selena Barry?"

I shook my head, unable to speak.

Jack started to rub my back. Easing the tension out of my muscles. "Is it Kelt? Did he say something to upset you?"

"No, no." I waved it off and worked to get myself under control. "It's not Kelt. At least, not like that. It's just . . . " I drew in a shaky breath and took hold of my courage. "Jack, I think I might be pregnant."

The words were out now. Spoken aloud for the first time. Made real for the first time. My hands started to shake.

"Oh." Jack rocked back on his heels. "Oh." His cheeks puffed out as he let his breath escape in a slow exhalation. He didn't say anything else at first. I stared down at my trembling hands.

Then, "Are you . . . are you sure you're not just, you know, . . . late?" he asked.

Late? Oh yes, the thought had occurred to me. More times than I could count. I've never been what you might call regular, so when I missed my period after Kelt had come home for that May long-weekend visit, I hadn't thought much of it. It wasn't the first time I'd missed a period. Stress could do that to a person. So I hadn't been too worried. Not until last week, when the date for my next period came and went without any sign of it.

"Two months late?" I said to Jack now, my mouth twisting from the effort of keeping my emotions checked.

There was another pause.

"Did you try one of those test things?"

I shook my head once. "Too chicken."

His breath gusted out again. We sat in silence for a long while.

"Would it . . ." he ventured. "Would it be so terrible if you were? I mean, you guys seem pretty solid."

My eyes threatened to fill up again. Gods, I was weeping at anything these days. "I don't know," I said, trying not to sound as lost as I felt. "I don't know if he wants kids. I don't know if he *likes* kids. I don't even know if *I* want kids. I just don't know."

Jack didn't say anything.

Fiercely, I scrubbed the wetness from my eyes. I was *not* going to cry. "All I do know is that I have to go see him," I told Jack. "And it doesn't matter what's going on up there or who died or who did it. I just . . . I need to talk to him face to face. I *need* to."

Jack looked at his feet as he considered my words. I was expecting an argument. Maybe even a fight. But when he looked up at me again, his sherry-colored eyes—the mirror image of my own—were bright with acknowledgment.

"Be careful, Turd," he said finally. Softly.

I really hadn't expected him to understand—hadn't

expected *anyone* to understand except Megan and she was on the other side of the world right now. In that instant, I forgave Jack every harsh word, every childhood argument, every occasion he'd called me Turd. My eyes threatened to fill up again. The moment was in serious danger of becoming mushy.

I pasted a cocky smile on my face that wouldn't fool him for a nanosecond. "Always," I assured him. Shakily. "It's alpine tundra, Jack. You can watch your dog run away for a week up there. If anyone's coming after me, I'll see them."

**3**

The North has a lot of things we lack further south. Long-tailed jaegers. Caribou. Northern lights. A sky that goes forever. What the North did not have, at least at the moment, were pikas. Where had all the pikas gone? It sounded like a mystery (or a song, depending on your frame of mind).

Snowshoe hares, lemmings, and marmots experience cyclical and, often, drastic fluctuations in their numbers. So does every other small mammal shacking up in the North. It's all part of life on the Big Alpine Tundra. Part of life in an extreme environment.

Pikas are no different. Their numbers ebb and flow with the best of them. But two years ago, the pika population hadn't just fluctuated. It had crashed. Big time. And nobody really knew why. "Long time passing" wasn't what most would consider a satisfactory explanation.

Climate change seemed to be the culprit of choice these days, nudging out the usual suspects of predation and parasites. The increased frequency and severity of storms and floods and forest fires in recent years had transformed the concept of a warming planet into something less theoretical. Something all too real. As a result, governments and other interested groups were frantically throwing money at any research study even remotely related to global warming. The Ogilvie Mountain Pika Project was one of these.

Fortunately (or unfortunately, depending on your view), all this had coincided with Kelt's decision to leave Woodrow Consultants and seek fame and . . . well, fame in the circles of academia. He'd been itching to start his PhD for a while now, wanting to get out of the hit-and-run, quick-answer sort of work that environmental consulting firms carry out.

"I want to study something *properly*," he'd explained to me one evening. "Like they did in the old days. You know, build my career around the study of a single species. Learn its biology. Try to understand its place in the ecosystem."

I sympathized with his feelings. Consulting work was, out of necessity, superficial and sometimes that frustrated me too. But I *thought* Kelt would study bats. After all, he'd done his master's thesis on them, he was always talking about them, and he had little bats (fake ones) hanging from the ceiling in his bathroom. Most importantly for me, there were bats here in Alberta.

But instead of "building his career" around his little flying mammal friends, Kelt decided instead to study *Ochotona collaris*. The collared pika. A buffy, brownish, little creature found only in the rockslides and talus slopes of the northern mountains.

In other words, *not* in Alberta.

They were cute little beggars, I gave him that. And there wasn't much known about them, so it was an important study. But the Yukon was just so damn far away. Nevertheless, collared pikas were what Kelt had chosen to study, which explained why he had gone up north and why I had been left behind singing "Mr. Lonely" in the bathtub.

One week into the field season, it was already old. Three months later, it was unbearable.

"Go north," my boss, Kaye Woodrow, advised me one blistering late July afternoon. "You've finished your section of the Drayton Valley EIA, haven't you?"

"Pretty much." I nodded. "Just waiting on the tox report."

"Well, the lab called twenty minutes ago to say they're backed up and we probably won't get the results for a few more weeks."

"Oh."

"Oh, indeed," Kaye said, imitating my tone. "And with the marvels of technology, a toxicology report can always be faxed to you when it comes in. Go on, get out of here. Ben's not back for three weeks and I certainly don't have much of anything for you to do. Besides, don't you have overtime banked?"

I nodded again, feeling myself start to perk up.

"Go!" Kaye made shooing motions with her hands. "Air North has a seat sale on right now."

I raised my eyebrows. "How do you know that?"

Kaye put her hands on her hips and gave me a stern look. "I checked the Web, didn't I? Something you could've done all by your mopey self if you'd thought of it."

"I'm not mopey," I protested.

Kaye made a rude noise.

"It's been three months," I said in my defense.

"Go north," she ordered again. Kindly. "See Kelt again. Have a little break. You'll feel much better for it. Trust me, I've been married to a field biologist for thirty years now. And besides, the Yukon is gorgeous in August. You'll love it."

"But how will I make employee of the month if I'm not here?"

"Go!"

I went in to work the day before I left for the Yukon. Part of me wondered if I should tell Kaye about the gruesome murder at Willow Creek (surprisingly, it had not made the news in the South). But I had a nasty suspicion that if she knew about it, there would suddenly be some task for me to do that couldn't possibly wait till I got back. An urgent need to confirm a rare bird sighting, or to determine the breeding grounds for an endangered population of Loggerhead shrikes. Kaye's like that sometimes. Understanding and kind, yes, but a bit overprotective.

With my own worries eating away at my peace of mind, an overprotective boss was the last thing I needed. So I cleaned off the last few papers from my desk, said my goodbys over afternoon coffee, and kept mum about the troubles up north.

I flew to Whitehorse on a clear Sunday night pumped full of Gravol and anticipation and, once we were airborne, several cups of Yukon Midnight Sun coffee. Not that they *grow* coffee in the Yukon, the flight attendant gurgled happily, as if the information was still new and fresh to her, but rather the beans were *roasted* under the midnight sun.

I wasn't sure how this was supposed to brew a superior cup of joe, but I had to admit the stuff was pretty tasty.

With a large cup of it nestled comfortingly on the tray in front of me, I rummaged around in my backpack for some reading material. No work reports or industry magazines for this hobbit. If I had to be in a thin metal tube thirty thousand feet above the ground, I needed hardcore distraction. I'd brought a copy of *The Two Towers*.

With two empty seats beside me I was comfortable enough and I had a couple of Tim Hortons sour cream glazed donuts to fortify myself while Aragorn, Gimli, and Legolas chased Orcs through the fields of the Rohirrim. But rather than losing myself in Middle-earth, I found my eyes constantly straying to the tiny window beside me. As we moved steadily northwards, I pressed my nose against the glass, watching as endless evergreen forests buckled into Ent-covered mountains, which, in turn, gave way to gray, wind-scoured peaks. It got cloudier too, but every so often, the clouds parted to reveal dark, emerald-rimmed lakes shimmering below like pools of black crystal opal.

By the time we began our descent into the White-horse evening, the clouds had started to break up but the sun was still high in the sky. The plane banked, following the curve of a weathered, rounded mountain. I returned my chair to its original upright position and helped the pilot land by gripping the armrests firmly. It worked. There was the gentlest of thumps, and then we were coasting to a stop on the runway. I breathed a sigh of relief. Now I could start thinking about tomorrow.

Tomorrow I would see Kelt again.

My mind shied away from the more troubling ramifications of that—namely, how to broach the subject of missing periods and parenthood. I'd decided the night before to take a tip from Megan. Ever since she'd traveled through Nepal, my friend's e-mails had become progressively more Zen-like. The universe, she was now fond of writing, would unfold as it should. So this was me trusting the universe to unfold. I would let it figure things out by itself while I focused instead on the other, less complicated, reasons for my trip. Tomorrow I would see Kelt again, but tomorrow I would also enter the realm of gyrfalcons and red-throated loons and collared pikas and caribou. Tomorrow I would climb into my rented vehicle and go north.

Canada's North.

They say the most dangerous thing about it is that it captures your soul. They also say that it's made up of ninety-five percent characters. I'd have to wait and see about the state of my soul, but I got off to a good start on the character thing. I met my first one at the Hide-on-Jeckell hostel.

It made sense to spend the night in Whitehorse. Despite the bright sunshine, it was too late to start a long road trip and I'd be fresher after a good night's sleep. The hostel was located on Jeckell Street, hence the name. It was a clean, hobbit-friendly sort of place with a cozy common room, an eclectic library, twenty-four-hour Internet access (woohoo!), and several rooms full of comfortable bunk beds. It also had a large, fully equipped kitchen, which, when I arrived, was being filled with a most tantalizing aroma. I collected my keys, dumped my gear on my assigned bunk, then, resisting the urge to check my e-mail (despite what others might say, I am *not* obsessed), I made like Toucan Sam and followed my nose.

"Hooo! That smells incredible!" I said, inhaling deeply as I stepped into the kitchen.

It was a long room with two fridges, a generous number of cupboards and shelves, and a recycling depot at one end. Framed copies of Far Side cartoons hung on the walls along with handwritten signs politely advising guests that their mothers did not live here and they should clean up after themselves.

A small, fuzzy man was standing at the stove stirring a large pot. He turned around and gave me a wide smile.

"Lamb stew," he said, smacking his lips noisily. "Reckon there's nothing like it to warm your middle on a cold night."

He was a short, stubby character with a strong Australian accent. The fuzzy part came from a head of mad professor hair, a couple of caterpillar eyebrows and a wild beard that looked more like a shredded SOS pad than facial hair.

I rubbed my hands together and suppressed a shiver. "It *is* a mite chilly out there," I agreed. In fact, Whitehorse was fully twenty-five degrees colder than Calgary. "Is it always this cold at this time of year?"

"First time in the Yukon?"

I nodded.

"It can get nippy, mate," he said sagely. "Hope you brought some warm woolies."

"Warm fleecies," I told him. "And a parka."

"Ah, good! Skivvies"—he gestured towards my sweatshirt—"won't do piss-all if the weather decides to turn nasty." He gave his stew another stir and turned the heat down. "I'll just let that simmer for a while," he said. Then he held out his hand. "Ed Farrell," he introduced himself.

I shook his hand. His fingers were rough, the handshake as hard as the calluses. But up close he smelled oddly pleasant. Like . . . I struggled to place the scent.

"Robyn Devara," I replied. "Nice to meet you."

"Got a pot of herb tea on the go," he was saying. "You want a cuppa?"

If a hot drink didn't have caffeine, I couldn't really see the point of it, but I didn't want to be rude. "That'd be great," I said. At least it would help warm my hands.

Ed smiled and turned to the counter. A waft of familiar scent drifted over me again. Lavender! That was it. Ed Farrell smelled like my grandmother's soap.

Weird.

At the far end of the kitchen, there was a good-sized table with a bench on either side. I slid onto one of them while Ed poured me a mug of something that smelled like dried berries and manure. I'm sure he thought he was being hospitable.

"So what brings you to the Yukon, Robyn?" he asked as he passed the mug to me. "You here for your hollies?"

I smiled my thanks and wrapped my cold fingers around the warmth. "Sort of," I told him. "My partner's up on the Dempster studying pikas."

"Pikas? He must be one of those cobbers up at Willow Creek, then."

I blinked. "Uh . . . as a matter of fact, that's exactly where he is."

He nodded. "Thought so. Just came down from there myself. You must be Kelt's sheila."

"That's right," I said, letting the description slide for the moment. "Small world."

"Small territory," he corrected. "Only thirty thousand people up here, you know. Twenty-three thousand of 'em live in Whitehorse."

I hadn't realized the Yukon was quite that empty.

"Not even enough people to fill a stadium back home," Ed said. "I met Kelt last month. Good man. Likes his little rodent mates."

"He does," I agreed. "Are you part of the Wilderness Retreat, then?"

Ed shook his head. "No. No. I just rent tent space from 'em. I'm a geologist by trade—and an Aussie by accent."

"Just by accent?"

"These days." Ed shrugged. "All my rellies still live there. Me, I bounce around the world. Right now I'm up here doing a bit of fishing back o' beyond."

"Salmon?"

He chuckled. "Not that kind of fish," he told me. "Diamonds!" He winked at me. "'Course, just about any kind of gem would be alright with me, mate."

I frowned a little. "Didn't I hear something about a blue beryl in the Yukon?"

He leaned back and stroked his beard thoughtfully. "Ah, yes. The famous True Blue." His tone had turned envious. "Nice piece of mineral, that. Corker. I'd settle for a few of those fair dinkum."

"Are they hard to find?"

Bushy eyebrows rose up to touch his tangled hair. "Gem-quality blue beryls?" He gave me a rueful smile. "You could say that. First ones found were down in Brazil. Maxixe beryl, they called it. Then they found a few of 'em up here. Rarer than emeralds, they are—and emeralds are even harder to find than diamonds. Fetch a nicer price too, depending on their color and clarity."

Fascinated, I propped my elbow up on the table and rested my chin on my hand. "I didn't know that."

"Lot of people don't." He slurped his tea noisily.

"So why are diamonds supposed to be a girl's best friend?"

Ed shrugged. "Marketing, mostly. Diamond cartels were good at that one from the get go. Tricked people into thinking diamonds are rare when in fact that's not the case at all. You looking for a best friend, take a tip from an insider and pick an emerald."

"Why are you after diamonds, then?"

"Supply and demand, mate," he said with a lopsided smile. "Canadian diamonds are highly in demand. Very popular on account of not being blood diamonds."

"Blood . . .?"

"War diamonds. Conflict diamonds. Call 'em what you want. In places like Angola or Sierra Leone, bandit armies fight for control of the diamond fields. Lotta innocent people get caught in the crossfire. But Canadian diamonds, they're clean. People aren't dying because of them."

I conceded the point. "But if emeralds are rarer than diamonds, wouldn't it still make more sense to look for emeralds instead?" I asked curiously.

Ed slanted me an amused look. "Oh, emeralds are truly rare," he assured me. "At least, gem-quality emeralds are. They're beryls too, you know. Just like your True Blue. Beryllium. But the green color comes from chromium. Or vanadium. Could be either. Problem is, the places you might find beryllium aren't generally places you find the other two. So—" he took another loud sip of his tea—"the elements have to be there and the conditions have to be just right. Doesn't happen too often, mark my words. Makes 'em hell to find."

He leaned back and stretched his arms across the back of the bench. "Not that diamonds are a dime a dozen, either. Truth is, finding anything—diamonds or emeralds or precious metals—is a lot of yakka, but then"—he smiled, his eyes twinkling—"that's half the fun of it, right?"

"I don't know. Depends what yakka is."

Ed laughed. "Sorry, mate. The Aussie coming out in me. Hard work, that's what yakka means. Haven't a clue where the word came from, but that's what it means."

I grinned, liking this rough geologist who smelled like flowers.

A group of young people came into the kitchen then. All blond. All extremely fit-looking. They were carrying white plastic bags of groceries and laughing, speaking loudly in another language. German, I thought. They unloaded their food quickly before crowding back out the door. One of the women gave us a brightly curious look before she left. Her eyes were the color of sapphires. Ed watched her leave with an appreciative glint in his eye.

He turned his attention back to me. "I wouldn't mind stumbling over one of those blue beryls," he said wistfully. "Or a nice fat kimberlite pipe." He drifted away for a few moments, caught up in his sparkling fantasy. Then he shook himself and offered me a boyish grin. "You know what a kimberlite pipe is, don't you?"

"Sort of. I know you find diamonds in them."

"That's right." He nodded "'Course, my chances of finding a high-grade pipe aren't what you'd call great. And my chances of having a developed mine are even lower."

I ventured a cautious sip of my tea. It tasted as vile as it smelled. Surreptitiously, I spat it back in the mug. "Really?" I asked, hoping to distract him as I slid the mug to one side. "Why's that?"

Ed rested his back against the wall. "The diamond world's a highly speculative one," he began expansively. "It's really all about getting people to buy your company's stock. You find yourself a pipe, get some publicity, and"—he stuck his thumb in the air—"stock prices go up. The company makes money and everybody's happy as a dog with two tails. And so long as the money keeps coming in, everybody can keep doing what they're doing. Investment. It's the name of the game, mate." He paused. "Remember the Bre-X scandal a few years back?"

I nodded.

"Damn near destroyed the mining industry. All because of investment. Well, the lack of it, really. The scandal broke and suddenly, nobody wanted to invest any money in mining. And with no money, you have no surveying. And with no surveys, you have no strikes to publicize. And with no publicity, you have nobody buying company stock."

"And so you have no money to keep doing what you're doing," I finished.

"Too right, mate," Ed nodded.

"But what about the diamonds you find? They just stay there? You don't dig them up?"

"Most times," Ed shrugged. "Mines are right expensive. Building and operating and all that. Usually there aren't enough diamonds to justify it. Or the market price is too low. Or the diamonds aren't a high enough grade. I tell you, Robyn, more money's spent on looking for minerals than the minerals are worth."

"Huh. That seems . . . a lot less romantic than I've always imagined it to be."

Ed chuckled into his bristles. "Oh, I don't know," he said. "Prospecting's always seemed fairly romantic to me. Take me, for example. I get to spend my summers up here. I'll drink to that any day." He held up his mug. "Cheers, mate."

Quickly I reclaimed my mug and clinked it with his. He tipped the rest of his tea down his throat. I pretended to take another sip.

He smacked his lips and wiped off his beard. "So, enough about me. What do you do for a crust?"

"Biology," I answered after deciphering the question. "Same as Kelt. But I'm birds instead of mammals and I work for a consulting firm."

"Both of you in the field? Crikey, that's gotta be hard on a relationship."

"It's hard yakka," I agreed. "I'll be glad to see him again. I've got almost a whole month to spend at Willow Creek."

Ed's expression turned pensive. "Nasty business up that way. I suppose Kelt told you about it?"

I nodded slowly.

"If nothing else, Paul and Jocelyn'll be happy to see you," Ed was saying. "They run the place. I guess people have been canceling ever since news got out. Can't be helped and you can't really blame 'em, but it's tough on business."

"Did you know the woman who was killed?" I asked.

He dropped his eyes and shook his head sadly. "Not really. I mean, we'd say 'g'day' if we happened to bump into each other, but . . . " He shook his head again. "Terrible thing to happen. Just terrible."

"My brother was worried about me coming up here," I said, a little surprised to find myself confiding in Ed. "He thinks it isn't safe."

"Ah, she'll be right, mate," Ed assured me. "The RCMP have their RV parked there for now."

"The RCMP have an RV?"

Ed nodded. "Yeah. A little camper-type thing. Generally they use it to patrol the Dempster during tourist season, but now they've got it sitting at the retreat. Maintaining a strong presence and all that."

"I take it they haven't arrested anybody."

"No," Ed shook his head. "Odds are on a group of hikers from the States—one bloke in particular—but as

far as I know, coppers are still trying to track 'em down."
He patted my hand. "No worries, mate. Don't your
Mounties always get their man? Besides, everybody's
keeping an eye peeled for everyone else now. She'll be
right." He drained his mug and stood up. "Hey, how'd
you like a nice bit of tucker?" he asked.

"But that's *your* dinner," I protested. Insincerely. I
was starving (I always seemed to be hungry these days,
which worried me). Plus I needed to get the taste of the
tea out of my mouth.

He waved off my objection. "I always cook more
than I need," he said. "Comes from growing up in a large
family. Besides, I'm off to Vancouver tomorrow morning
and stew isn't exactly takeaway, is it?"

"No," I agreed. Selflessly. "In that case, I'd love some.
Thanks."

Ed dished up generous bowls of his lamb stew along
with huge slabs of Yukon sourdough bread on the side. It
was delicious and I told him so.

"Helps to know your way around a stove when you're
in the field," he said around a mouthful of bread. "A body
can't go very far on those little packages of freeze-dried
suppers."

I mumbled something noncommittal. When I was
in the field by myself, I lived on those freeze-dried suppers. Better than "living" on my own pathetic attempts
at cooking. Just thinking about it gave me the willies. I
took another huge bite of stew.

"You done for the season, then?" I asked after I finished chewing.

"Nah," Ed shook his head. "Just going to check in
with the cobbers at the office. I'll be back in a few days."

"Hmm . . . checking in at the office, eh?" I narrowed my eyes and stroked my chin thoughtfully. "You stumble over a few blue beryls you're not telling me about?"

I was only teasing him, but suddenly I saw Ed's eyes glint with . . . something. Dismay? Anger? He blinked and the moment was gone.

"Don't I wish, mate," he said with a rueful snort. "That'd be ripper, wouldn't it?"

His tone was easy and relaxed. I laughed, and the conversation turned to other topics. Field science. The Yukon. And the characters who peopled both.

I told Ed about my other boss, Ben Woodrow, who had come out unscathed from attacks by both alligators and alligator poachers in Florida, only to be shot in the bum by poachers in Alberta. Ed countered with the story of a local chopper pilot who had hacked off a piece of glacier and strapped it to his helicopter because the field party he was attending had no ice for their scotch. He also told me where to buy the largest cinnamon buns on the Klondike Highway (and, therefore, in the world), adding that the locals never bought from the place as it was reportedly run by a former biker. We chuckled over the idea of a biker with a beer gut rolling out dough for cinnamon buns. And we slapped our knees at the thought of a club bake-off.

Ed was fun and informative—and he smelled good. But throughout the evening I kept thinking about that odd flash of . . . something.

And wondering if I'd imagined it.

# 4

It was overcast when I left Whitehorse the following morning. I'd picked up my rented suv the night before to get an earlier start, and I was up and out of the hostel before anybody else was stirring.

I loved this kind of morning. Soft and gray. Quiet. The clouds clinging stubbornly to the tops of the mountains like fledglings afraid to take that first plunge. For the first couple of hours, mine was the only vehicle on the road and I hummed softly, enjoying the solitude as I sipped Midnight Sun coffee from my travel mug.

I passed a sign advising me that I was now leaving the 911 emergency area. Not exactly the most reassuring of road signs. But I forgot all about it when I stopped at the marge of Lake Lebarge.

I was in the *Yukon*.

The Klondike Gold Rush. Call of the Wild. Robert Service and Jack London. Sam McGee. Dan McGrew. The list went on and on. I set up my camera on a rock and used the delay function to snap a picture of myself where Sam McGee from Tennessee had finally felt warm.

I was in the Yukon.

My stomach rumbled hungrily and I suddenly remembered the Yukon was also supposed to be home to the largest cinnamon buns in the world. I got back into the vehicle and consulted the road map. It was just a bit further to the little restaurant by Carmacks where I could fill my thermos with more coffee and buy one of the famous buns. I could also scope out the place for Harleys. (Hey, someone had to confirm it).

The Bun was enormous, more than worthy of the capital letter. Larger even than my cat. A pastry with a pituitary problem. I estimated it would take me a week to get through the sucker. But I could see no sign of bikes or leathers, and the young man at the cash register was disappointingly free of tattoos. That part of the Yukon legend would have to go unsubstantiated for now. I clambered back into the truck and the Bun and I continued happily up the Klondike Highway toward The Corner (otherwise known as the turnoff for the Dempster Highway).

It was a long drive to Willow Creek—anywhere from eight to twelve hours from Whitehorse, depending on the weather (and including gawking time). But I figured the midnight sun (both the coffee and the real thing) would help keep me awake. And besides, I'd come prepared. I had The Anonymous Four's moody *Voices of Light* for cloudy weather, *Music from the Coffee Lands* for sunnier hours, and the tunes from the Broadway show *Hairspray* for when I felt like singing on those empty stretches of highway. I also had all three soundtracks to *The Lord of the Rings* in case I started to get sleepy. Nothing like Orc-makin' music to get the ol' blood pumping.

As it turned out, these last proved an excellent choice. Howard Shore's powerful music suited the Yukon perfectly. Monumental music for a truly monumental landscape. Four hours into the trip, my eyes and neck were aching from the effort of trying to take it all in.

At first, the countryside seemed much like that of Alberta. The same kind of vegetation, the same kind of mountains covered in the same dark green Velcro of conifers. But it didn't stay the same. This northern wilderness was vast. Weighted with the knowledge that behind this mountain or beyond that valley there were still more mountains and meadows. Unknown. Unnamed. Too numerous to count. It was both powerful and humbling. Stunning and awe-inspiring. The sort of place where one quickly runs out of superlatives.

The views were not all colossal in nature. There were smaller moments, too. Fragile yet equally beautiful. Fallen trees whose exposed roots looked like pale squids with too many tentacles. Fields of purple fireweed incandescent in the sunlight. A hawk owl preening on the blackened branches of a fire-charred pine. I pulled over frequently, first in an attempt to capture it all on film and then, realizing a photo could never do this place justice, I stopped the vehicle just to listen to the sound of my breath in the ringing silence.

It was early afternoon by the time I turned on to the Dempster. According to my well-thumbed guidebook, driving the Dempster Highway is not for the faint-hearted. One of only two roads in the world to cross the Arctic Circle, the Dempster is more reminiscent of a narrow back-country road than a highway. It winds through willow-lined valleys and across a series of mountain ranges. The road is bad (to say the least), alternately obscured by dust or made treacherous with muck and shattered shale. There are few, if any, signs of human presence. The guidebook suggested bringing along several spare tires as well as extra food and clothing. Be prepared, it advised, to wait twelve or more hours if you run into any difficulties.

I passed a sign telling me the next services were 370 km away. The Yukon, I reflected, was not big on comforting signage.

A series of rain showers led the way north, paving the road in silver. I could see gray clouds ahead of me, misting the distant mountains into ghostlike outlines. The Dempster sits on permafrost, so rainwater, instead of soaking into the ground, pools on top, leaving the road slick and slippery. It forced me to slow down. I didn't mind too much.

Subarctic forest had gradually given way to the alpine tundra of Tombstone Territorial Park. The land was thinly clad here, cloaked only in the sheerest of fabrics. Rocky outcroppings and fantastically shaped tors poked through the fragile cloth of lichens and mosses like weathered, broken bone. The black granite cliffs of the Tombstone mountain range snatched my breath away with their beauty. Jagged, harsh, and wild. I could almost imagine the Dark Lord Sauron setting up shop in between the crags. Peter Jackson, I decided, could have easily filmed *The Lord of the Rings* in the Yukon. I cranked up the volume on the stereo and the haunting theme of the Riders of Rohan filled my ears.

Perfect.

I was so involved in imagining the Yukon as

Middle-earth that when I heard the loud bang I half-thought I was being attacked by Nazgûl.

But then the vehicle lurched to the right.

*What the hell?*

Suddenly the steering wheel fought my control.

"*Ah, shit,*" I swore, grabbing at the wheel with both hands.

A blowout.

I gripped the wheel firmly and eased my foot off the gas.

The SUV shuddered and bucked, but started to slow down. I checked the rearview mirror automatically. Nobody behind me. In fact, I hadn't seen a single vehicle since I'd turned off the Klondike Highway. As the SUV bounced to a stop, I pulled over to the side of the road. I could feel the tire flapping against the gravel.

I was at the bottom of a gentle dip in the landscape. The rain had left the road pocked here and there with puddles, the whole thing slick with pale gray mud. I pushed the door open. A cold wind blew a smattering of icy raindrops across my cheek. I walked around to the other side of the vehicle, my hiking boots squelching in the muck. The SUV, I noted, was now the same color as the mud. I could see bits of black rubber lying along the road behind me. The tire was toast.

Three hundred and seventy kilometers to the next services.

"*Son of a bitch,*" I swore again. More heartfelt this time.

I had a spare tire. That wasn't the issue. And I was perfectly capable of changing a tire by myself. The problem was, the new tire was bolted in *underneath* the vehicle. I chewed my lower lip and eyed the slivers of rubber resentfully. I'd hoped to arrive at Willow Creek in reasonably kissable condition. Attractive, desirable… clean. Now it looked like I'd be covered in mud (which could be considered desirable in some places, but was somewhat less so where showers and other such amenities were hard to come by).

*What bright spark thought it was a good idea to put the damn spare underneath?*

I cursed and muttered under my breath as I opened up the back and dug out the tools.

*Probably get engine oil all over my hands.*

I yanked a windbreaker over my fleecy. It was starting to rain again.

*Not to mention my pants and jacket.*

I was crouching down in the mud, preparing to slither under the suv, when I heard a rhythmic thumping in the distance. The sound deepened and grew louder.

I stood up just as the helicopter sailed over a hill. It dipped and lurched, bucking the strong tundra winds, before touching down some thirty yards from my suv. The spinning propellers blasted the rain outwards. I had to squint against the wind-whipped droplets to see clearly. A figure hopped from the cockpit—did helicopters even have cockpits?—while I watched with my mouth hanging open, the forgotten wrench still clutched in my hand.

The man sauntered over to me. Casual and unhurried. He was dressed in old blue jeans and a heavy plaid shirt. Reddish hair was shot through with silver, cut short in a just-out-of-the-army sort of style. His face was ruddy and weathered, liberally freckled from the northern sun. His mustache was several shades lighter than his hair.

"Need a hand?" he drawled, hooking his thumbs on his pockets.

His expression was serious, no smile peeked out from behind the mustache. But pale eyelashes did little to hide his eyes and I could see a bright twinkle in them. He was enjoying this.

"That'd be nice." I imitated his laconic tone.

I caught his eye and we started to grin. Then we both burst out laughing.

"Do you always do this?" I demanded, gesturing toward his helicopter with my wrench.

He continued to grin in delight. "You shoulda been here when I picked up a hitchhiker," he told me. "Thought he was gonna crap himself when I landed."

"You pick up *hitchhikers* with your helicopter?"

"And stop to help out damsels in distress." He sketched a bow, then held out his hand. "Dwayne Hicks, at your service."

"Robyn Devara. Thanks for stopping, Dwayne."

"No problemo. Got yerself a blowout, eh?"

"Yeah." I nodded, but he was already crouching down to peer under the suv.

"Not surprised," he said over his shoulder. "Happens all the time around here."

"So my guidebook said. I thought it was exaggerating. I mean, I brought a couple of things of that spare-tire-in-a-can stuff, but . . ."

"Doesn't help much with this." Dwayne gestured at the bits of rubber on the road.

"No," I agreed.

We gazed at the burst tire for a moment.

"Well," he said finally. "You won't get far on foot. Lemme give you a hand."

"I'd sure appreciate it, Dwayne." I frowned in thought. "Dwayne Hicks . . . now, why does that name sound familiar?"

"*Aliens*, man."

"Excuse me?"

Dwayne stood up and brushed at the mud on his knees. All this did was smear the gray goo in even more. He didn't seem to notice.

"*Aliens*," he said again. "You must've seen it. Best film ever made. Dwayne Hicks is the only marine to make it outta there alive. Or least un-cocooned."

I snapped my fingers. "Right," I said. "The guy that has a thing for Ripley."

"That's right. Huh." He shook his head thoughtfully. "Chicks always remember that part. Dunno why."

I was still holding the wrench. Dwayne took it from my hand and crouched down again.

"James Cameron is a god," he said as he wriggled his way under the SUV. "The man's incredible! I mean, *Aliens*? *The Abyss*? The *Terminators*? I'm talking T1 and T2, of course. Cameron had nothing to do with T3."

"Of course."

"His films work on so many different levels, man. Brilliant stuff! Cutting edge."

Praises for the filmmaker continued to issue out from underneath my vehicle. Dwayne had clearly accepted JC as his personal savior—JC, in this case, standing for James Cameron. I considered bringing up *Piranha 2: The*

*Spawning*, but decided it might be too cruel. Cruel and stupid. The man was, after all, fixing my tire.

"Got it!" he grunted. "Bastard was bolted in there good. You know, I've always thought it was a kind of sign. Me having the same name as Corporal Hicks. Sort of gave me a direction for my life, if you know what I mean."

"Uh . . . not sure I follow that, Dwayne," I said, crouching down beside the vehicle. "You wanted to join the army and fight aliens?"

"If it comes down to it, man, I'd answer the call," Dwayne assured me. "But I'm talking more about the way he sees the world." He slid himself and the spare tire out from under the SUV. They were both uniformly gray.

"Here, hang on to this for a sec," he said, passing me the muck-covered wrench. "Y'know, Hicks is one tough mother, but he likes kids and he's not intimidated by strong women. Same with Bud."

"From *The Abyss*?" I guessed. Correctly.

Dwayne's eyes lit up and he threw me an admiring glance. "Yeah! That's the beauty of Cameron's heroes. They're just regular guys doing what they gotta do in unusual situations. They rise above their place on the food chain—which is, as you know, pretty low down. I mean, we're talking a tool-pusher and an army grunt. But the point is, they go beyond what they do for a living and become heroes."

"What do *you* do for a living?" I asked in the pause that followed this. "I mean, apart from rescuing DIDs and scaring the crap out of hitchhikers."

He shrugged and started jacking up the vehicle.

"Anything that comes around," he said over his shoulder. "Used to fly for the mining companies in my younger days. Made a lotta cash and . . . c'mon you bastard . . . seeing how I was never one for pissing away money, I got enough so's I don't have to worry about it too much these days. But I love flying, so I take on the odd job now and again. I get the hikers and wilderness nuts . . . there, she's going good now. . . . Lotsa roots 'n berries types come up here, y'know. 'Specially in the last few years. Lookin' to get into real backcountry. Places where no man has gone before and all that. Mostly, though, I hire out to scientists. Biologists, geologists. Even gotta guy who comes up here every so often to core ice so's they can see what the climate was like when the ice formed . . . pass me that wrench, would you? Thanks. Can't pack all that gear in themselves, y'know. Not if they're settin' up for a season. Need a chopper to haul it in for them, and that's where yours truly comes in."

"Ever take any of the Willow Creek folks out?"

Dwayne frowned. His hands dropped away from the tire and he stared up at me, his blue eyes suddenly flinty. "You're not a reporter, are you?" he asked, his voice as chilly as the wind.

"Gods, no!" I said hastily. "Of course not. I'm heading up to Willow Creek myself. I'm a biologist."

"Oh." Dwayne sat with that for a moment. His face cleared and he turned his attention back to the tire. "That's okay, then."

He worked in silence for a minute, smacking the wrench sharply to loosen the bolts. His hands were callused and scarred. The fingers thick and strong-looking, stained black around the fingernails. A tool-pusher's hands.

"Uh . . . are they getting a lot of press up there?" I asked tentatively.

He nodded once. Curtly. "Media's been all over it like a bunch of maggots on a dead marmot. It's disgusting."

"You knew the woman who was killed?"

Dwayne pried the old tire off and started bolting on the spare one before he answered. "I did," he said finally. "Took her up once in my plane. She was studying birds, you know. Ptarmigan. Needed to track their radios. I had to put brackets on my struts for the antennas."

He fell silent again.

"I'm sorry," I said. "I heard she was nice."

He nodded without looking at me. Then he cleared his throat. "So what are you going to be studying up at Willow Creek?" he asked.

"Oh, I'm not going there to study," I said. "My partner's up there. Kelt Roberson."

"Kelt? I know Kelt."

"You do?"

"'Course. The man knows his *Aliens*."

I grinned, remembering the many evenings we'd spent watching the film so Kelt could catch all the nuances. "That he does," I agreed.

"Hauled in all their gear for them at the beginning of the season," Dwayne said. "And I did their resupply drop a coupla weeks ago. Even brought 'em a few tubs of ice cream as a treat. Kelt arranged it. Shoulda seen them all running up the mountain with spoons in their hands. Hilarious. Huh." He grunted as he tightened the last bolt. "Kelt's partner." He sounded a little disappointed.

"Hey, that looks great," I said, gesturing toward the tire. "I really appreciate it, Dwayne. Oh man, look at your pants. I'm sorry."

He stood up and slapped ineffectually at the muck on his pants. "No problemo," he told me. "Gotta do laundry anyways. 'Sides, always glad to help a fellow Cameron fan."

I smiled and was about to respond when Dwayne's gaze sharpened.

"Robyn Devara." There was recognition in his voice now. "You're the one Selena left her notes to, aren't you?"

"Yeah," I said, suppressing a sigh. "Yeah, that's me."

"I didn't twig on the name right away."

"It's me," I confirmed. "But don't ask me why she did it. I have no idea. I didn't know her." I shrugged. "I wasn't even familiar with her work until I googled her when I got the news."

"Maybe you can find out why she had her pantyhose in a knot about those birds."

"She was worried about the ptarmigan?"

Dwayne nodded. "Never said why. Told me I didn't want to know. But the truth of the matter is, it's been buggin' me." He lowered his voice. "Y'know, ever since she passed away."

"You don't think she was killed because of it, do you?" I asked, trying not to sound incredulous.

But Dwayne was already shaking his head in denial. "No, no. Of course not." He rolled his shoulders back as if sloughing off tension. "It just feels like . . . unfinished business," he explained. "Y'know. Loose threads. I hate that. Cameron never does that."

But sometimes life did.

I touched his arm gently. "I'll let you know what I find out," I promised.

I thanked Dwayne profusely and, lacking anything more appropriate, I offered the rest of the Bun as payment.

"Hey, those things are great!" he enthused, eyes lighting up when he saw it. "Haven't had one in ages."

I handed it over gratefully. My stomach had stopped growling long before the Bun had shown any sign of slimming. The thing was still three times larger than a normal cinnamon bun and I had no desire to be three times larger than a normal person.

I stood and waved to Dwayne and the Bun as they took off and headed south toward Dawson City, shading my eyes and watching until the helicopter was just a glint on the horizon. The break had done me good. I felt refreshed, a little less stiff. And, thanks to Dwayne, I was still mud-free. I looked at my watch. Late afternoon. Willow Creek was just on the flip side of the Park. If I could avoid any more blowouts, I'd make it there well before dinner. I rubbed my hands together and prepared to get underway.

I continued up the Dempster past the braided rivers and black mountains of the Tombstone range and out in to the Blackstone Uplands. The terrain was different again here, studded with willow-lined lakes, bisected by the Blackstone River to the east. It was dry along this stretch of the highway, the rain trapped further south by the Tombstone Mountains. A dust cloud billowed out behind my vehicle like a bushy white tail.

The tourist guide said the Blackstone Uplands was the richest area for birdlife along the highway. Despite a definite eagerness to reach Willow Creek, I found myself slowing down. There were birds up here I'd never seen before. Gyrfalcons. Long-tailed jaegers. Hoary redpolls. New birds for my list. I swiveled my head back and forth, keeping a sharp eye out for any fluttering movements.

I paused at Two Moose Lake, which boasted six red-necked phalaropes but no moose. I spotted a couple of harlequin ducks and a single whimbrel, which looked so much like its virtually extinct cousin, the eskimo curlew, that my heart almost stopped until I saw the telltale speckled wing lining. Despite this avian activity, the land seemed strangely quiet. Few birds were calling, and even the whine of insects was drowned out by the steady wind. There was no distant rumble of traffic, no jet trails crisscrossing the sky. In fact, there was scant evidence of human presence here at all. A small camp-ground back at Tombstone. An old miner's cabin. An RCMP truck speeding past me, heading south—the first vehicle I'd seen on the road besides Dwayne's helicopter. In terms of humans, the Yukon was an empty place. As Ed had observed, there weren't even enough people to fill a stadium.

In a place like this, I mused, community would be everything. Would mean much more than it does in the south. More than just nodding to your neighbors. More than handing out candy to little Harry Potters on Hallowe'en. It was something people like Dwayne understood, something they lived by. Up here, in a land that was all about harshness and adversity, community was essential for survival.

The thought was an uncomfortable one. This didn't seem like the kind of place where murder was committed. A crime of passion, I could see. A shooting or a stabbing in a bar. But a killing like the one Kelt had described? It seemed out of place here, though I wasn't sure where exactly I would expect such a thing to happen. Just not here. Not in this empty, empty country.

I watched the RCMP truck in the rearview mirror. It disappeared into the hills, a moving cloud of dust the only sign that marked its passage. I wondered where they were going. What they were looking for.

*Tall. Kinda skinny. Blond with those round Bruce Cockburn-type glasses.*

Kelt's words started cycling through my mind like an unwanted dish on the Sushi Train. Selena Barry. Had I met her before? Maybe at a conference? I tried to recall the last few conferences I'd attended. I didn't remember speaking to a ptarmigan researcher. What had possessed this woman to leave me her field notes? And why had she been worried about the ptarmigan?

I was distracted from these unsettling thoughts by a pair of birds winging overhead. I craned my neck out the window to get a better look. Loons? As I drew closer, they veered down, heading toward a small, silvery lake by the side of the road.

They landed with a splash and I pulled over to watch as they paddled across the lake, the ripples of their wake breaking up the mirror-smooth waters. Definitely loons, from the shape of them. I rolled down the passenger window and peered through my binoculars. Yes! Red-throated loons! The first ones I'd ever seen. I drew my breath in with a low whistle and settled my shoulder against the seat to watch them.

They were pearly gray birds with blood red throats. Incredibly beautiful and somehow achingly lonely at the same time. Symbolic of the very land they lived in. I wished Kelt were beside me to share the sight.

I sat with them for a long time, captivated by their aquatic grace and their tremulous, falsetto wails. I found myself reluctant to leave—seeing a bird for the first time can take you like that—but the loons had reminded me why I was here. The real reason. The one that had nothing to do with Selena Barry or her tragic death or even my own, more personal, worries. The universe was undoubtedly unfolding as it should, and I wasn't going to let anything spoil my first trip to the Yukon. Or my reunion with Kelt.

The North was a big, empty place. But it had community. And RCMP. And Kelt. And besides, I could take care of myself.

## March 31

Finally. The end of a long, long winter, or at least the promise of the end. It can't come fast enough. The dark months didn't affect me this much last year. Why were they so unbearable this time around? After all, it's not exactly pitch black, there is moonlight and starlight enough to see by. And everyone seems to make an extra effort to socialize—not in a desperate kind of way, either, but with a warm, genuine feeling of fellowship. When the temperature starts to plummet, you can actually feel the community pulling together, uniting against the winter. I've never experienced quite the same thing anywhere else. And yet, this winter still bothered me. Too many black days filled with too many black thoughts. Maybe next year I should get a light visor. Diana swears by them.

Winter is all about survival up here. Physical and spiritual. On the latter front, Jocelyn proved herself essential once again. Constantly surprising us with spur-of-the-moment festivities. A lavish dinner in honor of the first snowflake that stayed. A contest to see who could make the most snow angels in one minute. A midnight toast to the northern lights. I can still see the steam from our rum toddies curling up to partner with the dancing lights. Magical. How does she come up with these ideas? Reminding us of the need for celebration in the midst of adversity. It certainly makes it easier to put up with her the rest of the time.

This year, Paul took it upon himself to introduce my poor ignorant Aussie self to the Bard of the North. Strange things done in the midnight sun and all that. I countered with Banjo Paterson's The Animals Noah Forgot. New for Paul. A trip down memory lane for me. Shades of more innocent times.

In some ways, we're like a little family out here on the Dempster. Jocelyn works very hard to make it so—part of her overwhelming need to be needed, I think. She doesn't seem to realize that not all of us need to be mothered. God, it took me thirty years, a divorce and traveling halfway across the world to get away from my mother. I, for one, do not appreciate Jocelyn's constant solicitude (though, like the arctic night, it didn't bother me as much last year). Terry is the only one who seems to be able to avoid her maternal tendencies. Not sure how he does it. Maybe because he's like the patriarch of our small group? No, that's not right. He's more like the older, bachelor uncle. The one who's knocked around the world a bit. Quiet, wise, savvy enough to let Jocelyn have her way. Paul, who should be the patriarch in this scenario, is more child than partner—or at least Jocelyn treats him as such. It would drive me crazy.

I go into Dawson when the walls close in too much. And Willa and I go down to Whitehorse when we need to see a movie or eat at a restaurant or remember that we're part of a much larger world, (or, in my case, when I need to get away from Jocelyn for longer than a day).

I wish Willa didn't need Jocelyn quite so much, but they've known each other for years, the pattern was set long before I was in the picture. And given Willa's family history, I suppose it was only natural for her to seek out a mother figure. In a strange kind of way, I guess it works for both of them. So, I bite my tongue. I'm not stupid enough (or brave enough) to force Willa to choose between us.

Sometimes we're more like a real family here than Jocelyn might wish to admit—with all the messy, mucky resentments, the fluid alliances, the misunderstandings. And the secrets. Ah yes, the secrets. We all have them. Big ones, small ones. Some, out of necessity, guarded more closely than others.

As I think back on the past three years, it seems strange that I never once went out to Regent. That I was able to forget my ghosts—my secret—in the pleasure of life with Willa. I suppose I just wanted to pretend it hadn't happened. Three years. I'm surprised they let me have that long. Ghosts do not suffer oblivion easily. And last fall, when I finally saw what they wanted to tell me, I couldn't blame them.

I think I always knew this would happen. The possibility was always there. It's why I've obsessed about the place for so many years. Why the memories still burn.

Enough. I don't want to go down that path. Not tonight.

The nights are shorter now, the days are warmer, and the ptarmigan begin to stir from their winter's sleep. Every spring it seems I fall in love with the Yukon all over again. It is an aching, wild place. But even the Yukon, like our little family, has its dirty secrets. And maybe, I tell the ghosts, I'll be able to do something about one of them.

It'll feel good to be back in the field. To give in to the lure of Service's lonely Little Voices. Terry picked up my Holohill transmitters yesterday along with a fresh supply of notebooks. I'm equipped and ready to go, waiting now only for the weather to clear.

It would help if I were a fish biologist. If I had the strength of the Fisheries Act behind me. I don't. I don't know anything about fish, but I know my birds. My ptarmigan. I'll gather enough evidence that someone, somewhere, will have to pay attention.

**5**

The turnoff for Willow Creek was just past Chapman Lake—in a deep valley populated by subarctic forest. Ahead of me, I could see the mountains of the Taiga Range, home to both bald and golden eagles.

The road to the retreat was well marked, if not particularly well maintained. Narrow, deeply rutted and soupy with reddish-brown muck, it led through a dense tangle of spruce and aspen before squelching to an end in a muddy clearing beside a large wooden cabin.

I hardly looked at the place at first. Hardly saw the honey-colored logs of the cabins, or the white canvas of the old mining tents beside them. Hell, I barely noticed the sign for the cedar hot tub over by the creek.

Kelt was reading on a bench in front of the cabin.

*Gods, he looked good!*

He was wearing a long-sleeved T-shirt that had faded and shrunk, nicely setting off both tan and muscles. His black hair had grown past his collar and he needed to shave. He was looking more like Aragorn all the time.

I glanced at my reflection in the rearview mirror.

Despite the long and tiring drive, my eyes were bright and sparkling—abstinence and anticipation'll do that to you. My hair, on the other hand, looked like I'd been hiding out in Helm's Deep for a month. I tried to pat the auburn curls in place, but they weren't having any of it. I hoped Kelt would only notice the eyes.

The wind was gusty so he hadn't heard me drive into the clearing. He didn't look up from his book until I stopped beside an orange pickup truck. I could see him blink against the sun.

"Hey, little boy," I leered out the window.

He stood up and raised a hand to shade his eyes.

"An SUV? *You rented an SUV?*"

I turned off the engine and scowled at him. Three months apart and *this* was the greeting I got?

"Look, Pika Boy," I said, "it was the only thing they had with four-wheel drive. You wanted me to drive the Dempster Highway—by myself, I might add—with some lousy little city car?"

He pulled his mouth to one side. "Nooo, I guess not. It's just that—"

"They're a cancer on the face of the earth," I finished for him. "I know, Kelt. I know about the lousy fuel efficiency. I know they release tons of crap into the air. *I know about axles of evil.* Okay? It's not like I bought one to drive to the golf course. And, I might add, if I hadn't been driving an SUV, the little blowout I had earlier might have been a lot worse and your friend Dwayne would've had to fly me here in his chopper."

"You had a blowout? You met Dwayne?"

I eyed him. "Yes and yes. He very kindly changed my burst tire for me which is why I'm still nice and clean and not covered in gray muck. Now, are you going to give me a kiss, or what?"

His expression cleared and he grinned at me sheepishly. "I'm sorry, sweetheart, come here."

I got out of the SUV and stretched, stiff from too many hours of driving. Kelt's arms slid around my waist. The kiss was enough to mollify me.

"That's more like it!" I said, a little breathlessly.

"Mmmm. You feel good," he mumbled into my hair.

He didn't feel so bad himself.

"Where's everybody else?" I asked when we came up for air again.

"Still at camp." He grinned and wiggled his eyebrows at me. "I told them they all had to stay there till Thursday."

"You didn't!"

He squeezed me again and gave me another kiss. "Damn right. You really want anybody else hanging around now?"

Good point.

"No." Decisively.

He caressed my cheek. "I didn't think so," he chuckled. Despite the bright sunlight, his green eyes were dark. "I don't feel like sharing you just yet."

I grinned up at him. "I see."

He slid his hand under my shirt and around my waist.

I jumped at the feel of his hands on my bare flesh. "C'mon, Pika Boy," I said, pulling away. "First help me get my gear out of the Satan-mobile and then you can show me where we're staying. But don't take too long. I feel a serious need to play 'mating season.'"

"So how's it really going?" I asked Kelt later as we lay naked and pretzeled on the bed.

He leered at me sleepily. "Much better now."

"Pig!" I poked him in the side. "I meant with your work."

"Oh, that."

I smiled and snuggled closer.

We were in an old mining tent—our home away from Pika Camp. Sewn from heavy white canvas and supported by a metal frame, it had a moldy air of permanence about it. Despite the odor, it wasn't bad, as tents go. In fact, it seemed more like a small cabin than a tent. Wooden door on the front, window in the back. Tall enough to stand up in and spacious enough to accommodate a few sticks of furniture. These consisted of a wood-frame bed with a foam mattress, a small table and chair and assorted red Beatrice milk crates, which served as shelving or dressers, depending on the need. Right now, they contained piles of neatly folded clothing and carefully lined-up rows of books.

I'd noted this last with a certain amount of dismay. This was Kelt's tent for the summer, which meant that Kelt was a bit of a neat freak when he was in the field. I, myself, tended to slob out whenever I got into a tent (or a cabin . . . or a hotel . . . and I guess my apartment wasn't exactly *Better Homes and Gardens* . . . ). Tents were the worst, though, and we'd be sharing one at Pika Camp. I hoped it wouldn't be a problem.

Throughout our reunion, I had been vaguely aware of the distant sound of voices outside. I'd been under the impression that Kelt and I were the only ones staying in the tents, but I could hear people moving around outside now. The thunk of someone splitting firewood, an occasional laugh or quiet remark. The retreat staff, perhaps, or maybe even an unexpected scientist in from the field. It didn't really matter. The mesh window faced out onto the forest rather than the central clearing, and the tent door effectively kept the real world at bay. Personally, I was in no hurry to rejoin it.

"It's going well," Kelt answered my question. "Slowly. But that's to be expected at this time of the year. The crunch time—at least for pikas—won't come for another week or so. Not until they start accumulating their hay-piles. That's the best time to trap them."

"So there *are* pikas up there?"

Kelt nodded. "A few small colonies. Not nearly as many as there should be. Rachel and Michele have been looking at the plants to see if the pikas are responding to poor growing seasons, but I don't think that's the answer—at least, not the whole answer."

"Why not?"

"Masculine intuition," he told me without cracking a smile.

"Is that along the same lines as male hygiene?"

"Meaning what?"

"An oxymoron."

"Ha, ha." Kelt gave me a playful poke. "Seriously," he said, "when Gerard first set up Pika Camp, he did it primarily to look at the biodiversity of different alpine communities. Especially those with different glacial histories. It was really more of an ecological study than anything else. Pikas were just a part of it."

He propped himself up a little higher, settling me against his chest.

"After the first three years," he continued, "all indications were that pika populations were stable. Fluctuating according to regional weather patterns, of course, but still relatively stable."

"So what happened?" I asked. "I mean, Pika Camp's been here for what? Five, six years?"

Kelt nodded. "This is the sixth season," he confirmed. "But as the study progressed, it became increasingly obvious that pikas were, in fact, extremely sensitive to variations in climate system patterns. This whole region"— Kelt flung out his arms—"is experiencing some of the greatest warming trends in the last four decades. Mostly because of where it's situated. North. Close to the Pacific. Surrounded by tall mountains."

"And this is affecting the pikas how?"

Kelt laced his fingers together thoughtfully. "Lots of ways," he said. "The vegetation mix is changing, and warm winters mean less snow cover, more rain and more frequent freeze/thaw events."

"Pikas den up under the snow?"

Kelt nodded. "Yeah. No snow means no nice warm burrows for pikas. The freeze/thaw thing's pretty hard on the plants, too. Pikas are dependent on the vegetation that grows each season. You have a bad growing season or a different mix of vegetation and . . . "

"You have hungry pikas," I finished for him.

He nodded again.

"Is that what's happening now?" I asked. "I mean, with this population crash."

"I think so," Kelt said. "I suppose it could be some weird-ass virus, but nobody really believes that. The thing about the North is that climate change isn't just a theory up here. It's happening and it's happening now. Honestly, a person could spend years up here studying the effects."

My heart sank at his words—*years!*—but I tried to not to show it. "How's the camp panning out?" I asked instead.

"Not bad." His tone before had been relaxed, if a little sober. But now he sounded odd. Somehow strained.

I raised my head and looked at him. "But not great?"

"No," he replied slowly, "not great. There's one person—"

"Michele," I guessed.

"How did you know that?"

"Feminine intuition," I said airily.

I wasn't being entirely honest with him. There was only one phone at Willow Creek, a satellite phone in the large cabin. These last three months had been frustrating not only because Kelt and I had been apart, but because we'd had a grand total of one private phone call the entire time. Between the retreat staff, the tourists, and sundry scientists, there always seemed to be someone hanging around. Nothing like people wandering in and out of the room to put a damper on your phone sex. Problem was, it effectively put the kibosh on a lot of conversation too. I could smirk about feminine intuition all I wanted, but the truth was, I'd gotten very good at reading Kelt's tone of voice.

"You always sound strange when you talk about her," I explained. "All tight and uncomfortable. So, what's the trouble?"

He took a deep breath and blew it out noisily. "She

gets my back up," he admitted. "And I'm not sure if it's serious enough to do something about it."

"What would you have to do?"

"Ask her to leave."

"Oh." I was surprised. "That bad, eh?"

"She's a good worker," Kelt said. "And she pulls her weight around camp. Most of the time. But the woman sees everything in terms of sexual politics."

"Hmmm." I wrinkled my nose. "That gets tired pretty quick."

"*Very* tired," Kelt agreed. "She never gives it a rest. I'll give her credit, she's not nasty about it, but she's always in your face. Rachel's talked to me about her. So has Jim. Stavros hasn't said anything yet, but I can tell he's getting pissed off."

"Shouldn't Gerard be the one to worry about this?" I asked, naming Kelt's advisor and Pika Camp's project manager.

"He's not here," Kelt told me. "He came for three weeks at the beginning and it doesn't sound like he'll get back till just before we close down for the season. You, Ms Devara, are currently snuggled up to Pika Camp's acting CEO. So, if there's a problem with one of the junior grad students . . . "

"You're the one that has to deal with it," I finished, giving him a sympathetic pat. "Bummer. So what exactly has Michele been doing?" I asked.

Kelt curled his lip and made a sour face. "It's hard to explain. You almost have to experience her. Right now she's got a thing about the alphabet and how, because it was invented by men, she can't properly express her love for another woman."

"I see."

"Plus, she'll jump all over you if you use certain words."

"Like?"

"Like 'guys' as in 'hi, you guys, how's it going?'. She even has a thing about 'ladies and gentlemen.'"

"Really. Why?"

"Too 'gendered,' to use her word."

"Puh-lease!" I made retching sounds.

Kelt grinned. "I'll be interested to see what you think of her."

"Hmmm," I said again. Doubtfully. "I don't have a lot of patience for that kind of thing."

"Me either," Kelt said. "Though I have to say, we're all trying to be nice and understanding right now. Because of Selena Barry."

"What does she have to do with Michele?"

"They were pretty close. Maybe even *very* close."

"He said mysteriously."

He shrugged. "It might just be camp gossip, but rumor has it Michele had an affair with her."

I stared at him. "*Michele* was the one you were telling me about?"

Kelt gave me a crooked smile. "Sorry, I guess I forgot to mention that part."

I considered it for a moment, then smiled back and shrugged. "Serves me right for making assumptions."

He lifted his shoulders again. "Who knows whether it's true. And it doesn't really matter. They were, at least, friendly and it was . . . a terrible thing to happen."

I put my head on his chest and absently started

tracing circles on his stomach. Kelt has a nice stomach, not washboard, but still flat and hard. But I wasn't thinking about his abs at the moment.

"Did the Mounties find whoever killed her?" I asked in a quiet voice. "I met a guy at the hostel. He said they were looking for a bunch of hikers."

"You met a guy at the hostel?"

I nodded. "Ed Farrell."

Kelt's mouth quirked up in a half smile. "Ah, you met Ed, did you?" Then the smile faded as he considered my question. "They *are* looking for a group of tourists. Well," he amended, "they found most of the group, but the guy they really wanted to talk to—Lance—left to go hiking backcountry up by Inuvik."

"By himself?"

Kelt nodded.

"So, why do the cops think it was him?"

Kelt was quiet for so long, I didn't think he was going to answer me. "He had some kind of a fight with Selena," he said reluctantly.

"A fight? About what?"

I felt him shrug. "I don't know. I wasn't here when it happened."

"Did you meet this guy?"

"Yeah."

"And?"

"And, what?"

I sighed inwardly. Kelt's dislike of what he called nosiness and gossip (and normal people called curiosity and information) could be very irritating at times. "And what was he like?" I pressed.

Another shrug. "Youngish. Kind of an asshole. I really didn't have much to do with him."

I waited, but that was all I was going to get.

"Incidentally," Kelt said after a moment. "The RCMP want to see you."

"*Me?* Why—oh. Because of the notes."

"They asked if you could come in after you're rested."

I was silent for a minute. A vehicle rumbled and coughed in the distance. It sounded like it was missing a muffler.

"They said after you're rested," Kelt assured me, misinterpreting my silence.

I sat up and tucked the sheet around me.

"You know, this whole thing creeps me out," I told him. "Those field notes? Why would she even make arrangements for them? That's just weird. Did she know someone was after her? And why leave them to me? I'm pretty sure I didn't know her. And I can think of several people right off the top of my head who are more qualified than I am when it comes to ptarmigan."

His green eyes were troubled. "I don't know, either. Maybe you met her somewhere?"

"Have you got a picture of her? I tried googling, but I couldn't find one."

He started to shake his head. "No—wait. Maybe. Hang on, I think there's a copy of *The News* somewhere around here."

He rolled off the bed and padded over to the table where papers and notebooks had been neatly stacked. His body was silhouetted against the soft glow of the sunlit canvas walls. He had to rummage around a bit, but he finally unearthed a folded newspaper. He climbed back into bed and passed it over to me.

Selena Barry's picture was on the front of *The Yukon News*. She had been an extraordinarily good-looking woman. Mature—maybe ten years older than me—but still a definite elf. A sort of female Elrond. Her eyes were partially hidden by the reflection of the flash in her glasses, but she was smiling at the camera. She looked pleasant. Friendly.

I shook my head. Even more puzzled now. I didn't recognize her at all. "I don't know her," I told Kelt.

He had propped himself up on the pillows again. He was gazing out the window, his eyes far away. Sad.

"She seemed nice," he said quietly. "I barely knew her, but she seemed nice. She didn't deserve . . . that."

I waited, sensing there was more.

"I found her, you know."

"*What?*"

"She lives—lived—over in the cabin by the creek. The old miner's cabin from back when this was a claim site. Anyhow, I needed a bird book so I went over to see if I could borrow a field guide. The door was closed but not latched, you know? When I knocked, it opened and . . . well, she was already dead."

"Oh, Kelt! Gods, are you okay?"

He shrugged one shoulder and didn't say anything. He didn't look okay.

"I'm so, so sorry," I said, putting a gentle hand on his chest. He covered it with his own. "Why didn't you tell me?"

"I did. But we had a bad line and I knew you hadn't heard me." He ran his fingers through his hair and shook his head. "I was going to try calling again, but there was always someone around. It's so damn hard to get any privacy around here. And besides . . ." he trailed off.

Chilled, I wrapped the sheet around me more tightly and waited.

"I was afraid," he admitted after a moment.

I blinked. "Afraid? Of what?"

"I don't know." He pulled his mouth to one side and gave me a strange look. "Afraid you wouldn't come. Afraid you would."

My heart lurched into my throat. "You . . . don't want me here?"

"No! That's not it."

"Then what?"

He shrugged uncomfortably. "It's just that I *know* you, Robyn, I know you like to nose around stuff like this."

Offended, I drew myself up and opened my mouth to reply.

"I worry about you," he said.

I closed my mouth and eyed him, chewing on my lower lip.

"You kind of have a history, you know. It would be just like you to get involved in this!" He flung his arms in the air. "Poking around. Asking questions. Trying to find out who killed her. All because the woman left you a bunch of notebooks."

"I have no intention of poking around," I argued. "But you have to admit, the field note thing *is* a little strange."

"It is," he conceded. "But it may not have anything to do with why she was killed."

"I never said it did," I pointed out. "And give me some credit, here. You told me how she died. With her blood *smeared* all over the walls. How stupid do you think I am? Do you really think I want to go anywhere near that?"

He held my eyes for a few seconds. "No," he admitted, the tension in his face easing a little. "No, I suppose not."

There was a moment of awkward silence.

"So, where are these notes, anyhow?" I asked.

"Her partner left them with the RCMP. I think they'll make arrangements for you to access them when they talk to you."

I felt suddenly uncomfortable. As if a cold shadow had ghosted through the tent. I wasn't at all sure I *wanted* to access Selena Barry's notes.

"Wait a second . . . you said her partner left them with the RCMP? Her *partner*? I thought she had a fling with Michele."

"Yeah."

"At the same time?"

"Yeah," Kelt said again. Flatly.

"I see," I said, though I didn't. "One of those things, eh?"

"I wasn't about to get involved."

"No," I agreed. My mind puzzled over that piece of information. Selena Barry, it appeared, had led a somewhat complicated life.

"I'm sorry," Kelt said softly.

I looked back at him.

"I didn't mean to imply that you're nosy."

His eyes had gone deep and dark again. I was still annoyed with him, but I had to admit, he *was* very sexy.

"Or stupid?" I suggested.

He chuckled and offered me a lopsided grin. "Or stupid," he assured me. "You're far, far from that."

I pretended to think it over for a moment. "Well, in that case . . ." I slid down the sheets till I was lying against him again. He tucked me under his arm.

"And of *course* I wanted you here," he chided. "More than anything else. Are you kidding? The nights get cold this far north. I need those furry hobbit feet of yours to keep me warm."

"Ha, ha."

What with one thing and another (and another and another), the last of the afternoon passed by quite pleasantly. Kelt had stockpiled egg sandwiches and a thermos of tomato soup in case we got hungry. Jocelyn, one of the owners of the retreat, had apparently promised us a five-star breakfast the next morning. We didn't plan on getting out of bed until then.

The RCMP, however, had other ideas.

## 6

He arrived without any warning. Rapping sharply at the tent door, causing the canvas to shiver. He called Kelt's name, his booming voice out of place in the wind-whispering quiet. He could have picked a better moment. Actually, he could have picked a worse moment, I suppose. Like five minutes ago. But still.

Kelt rolled out of bed and snatched up his jeans. "Hang on a second, Frank," he called out.

I burrowed under the covers resentfully. "Who's Frank?" I hissed. "And why the hell is he bothering you *now*?"

Kelt yanked his pants on and started looking around for his shirt. "RCMP," he said tersely.

Oh. Crap.

I threw off the covers and began the hunt for my own clothes.

It took us a few moments to make ourselves presentable. Before he opened the door, Kelt gave me a brief, apologetic hug.

"Sorry," he mouthed silently.

I gave him a crooked grin and shrugged. It wasn't his fault.

The officer was standing just outside our tent. A little too close for courtesy. It didn't endear him to me.

He seemed short for a cop—he must have had to stretch to meet the height requirement. His upper body was an inverted triangle. Wide and bulging with muscles at the shoulders and chest. He stood stiffly, as straight as the proverbial ramrod, crisply ironed shirt tucked tightly into his pants, navy tie precisely centered on his massive chest. Even his close-cropped hair was achingly neat. Not a single strand out of line with the others. His mustache was pencil-thin, carefully clipped to stop just shy of the corners of his unsmiling mouth. An overwhelming sense of power and tight control emanated from him.

He was intimidating as hell.

"Frank," Kelt greeted him easily. "Sorry about the wait."

All of a sudden, the officer—Frank—looked uncomfortable. His eyes slid to my face, taking in my heavy-lidded eyes, lingering on my thoroughly kissed lips. I suppressed an urge to smooth my hair.

He cleared his throat. "Uh, sorry to bother you, Kelt," he said. The words were awkward in his mouth, as if apologies didn't come naturally to him. He turned toward me and offered a tight smile. "You must be Robyn Devara," he said, holding out his hand. "Constable Frank Matas."

"Hi." I shook his hand. His grip was firm, but not as crushing as I'd feared.

"Is everything okay?" Kelt was asking.

"Fine," Matas said. "No new developments. But I heard Ms Devara had arrived and I wanted to bring these boxes over."

My gaze flickered past him to the boxes that had been stacked on the ground. There were four of them. Brown cardboard boxes piled neatly on top of each other. According to their labels, they had once contained Unico tomatoes. Silver duct tape sealed them shut.

"Selena Barry's field notes," Matas said by way of explanation. "Willa Groot, Ms Barry's, uh . . . partner, brought them over the day before yesterday."

"Um, okay," I said. "Thanks."

I took a closer look at the pile. Those were pretty good-sized boxes. "Jeez, how much stuff did she leave me?"

"Approximately two and a half years' worth," Matas said. Then he stood there, arms crossed, looking at me as if he expected me to start going through them this instant.

"What do you want me to—" I began.

"We need you to go through it," he interrupted. The words were more order than request. "Kelt says you didn't know her."

It was phrased like a statement, but sounded like a question. As if Matas hadn't believed what Kelt had told him. I sensed Kelt stiffening beside me.

"That's right," I confirmed. "He just showed me a picture of her a little while ago. From the newspaper. I didn't recognize her. I don't know why she left me"—I gestured toward the cardboard boxes—"all that."

Matas took a small notebook out of his breast pocket

and flipped it open. "I understand you're a biologist," he said. "A bird specialist."

I nodded, wondering why he needed to consult his little notebook for that.

"You know a lot about ptarmigans, do you?"

"I know a little," I corrected him. "I've never worked with grouse before."

"Grouse?"

"Ptarmigan are members of the grouse family," I explained.

Matas appeared unimpressed by this bit of knowledge.

"Do you think you'll be able to understand Selena's notes?" he asked.

It was a stupid question, given that I hadn't even *seen* her notes yet. But it seemed unwise to point this out.

"I can certainly try," I said instead.

Matas nodded once. "We'd appreciate that," he said. "They don't make much sense—at least to non-biologists. Just a bunch of numbers and codes. A few descriptions." He seemed annoyed by it.

"I'll do my best," I promised him.

Kelt bent over and picked up the top box. "Maybe we should get them inside the tent," he suggested.

Kelt and I each hefted a box, leaving Matas with the remaining two. He didn't seem to have any trouble lifting them into the tent. I saw his eyes take in the rumpled bed, the general disordered appearance of the tent. My bra, a black lacy one I'd bought just for this occasion, hung over the back of a chair. I set my box on the floor beside the table and tried not to blush.

But Matas didn't say anything about the state of the tent or the presence of frilly underthings. "You understand these papers are evidence in a crime investigation?"

I nodded.

"Sign this, please." He handed me a sheet of paper. "It states that you are now in possession of this evidence as of today's date."

Wordlessly, I scrawled my name on the paper. Evidence in a crime investigation. All of a sudden, this whole thing seemed very real and very serious.

"We'll need a report as soon as possible," Matas was saying. "And we're going to need you to keep it to yourself. If you find anything strange, anything that might have something to do with why she was killed, don't go noising it about. Come and see us. We're set up in the RV right now. The white Bigfoot camper in the parking lot. The logo's on the door."

"We?"

His mouth tightened almost imperceptibly. "Inspector Chesnut," he said. Unhelpfully. Then, with a curt nod that included both Kelt and myself, he exited the tent.

"What the hell is *his* problem?" I demanded, as soon as I made sure Matas was no longer within hearing distance.

Kelt smiled ruefully. "He's a bit much," he admitted.

"A *bit*?"

"Okay, a lot," he amended.

"I thought he was going to bust us for having

pre-marital sex. And speaking of which . . . why the hell couldn't he have waited? At least till dinnertime. That's just rude!"

"Um, it *is* after dinner, honey. It's almost eight o'clock."

"What? But it's so light—oh, the midnight sun."

"It won't get much darker here," Kelt said. "Not for another month or so."

"Well, he could've waited until tomorrow morning," I grumped, unwilling to let him off the hook. "I mean, I just got here."

Kelt enfolded my indignant self into his arms.

I opened my mouth to say something else, but he kissed me into silence.

"Mmmm," I said.

"Feel better?"

"No," I lied.

He kissed me again. More thoroughly.

I sighed and relaxed against him.

"Look, I know Frank can be a bit of a hardass," Kelt said, "but think about what they're dealing with."

My face clouded and I turned to where the boxes had been piled. "I know. I am." I took a deep breath and let it out slowly. "I'm sorry. I take it the investigation isn't going well."

"That's my impression." Kelt made a face. "For whatever *that's* worth. Frank's pretty close-mouthed."

"No kidding."

Kelt gave me a half smile, acknowledging my tone. "Yeah, well, I'm not sure he'd say anything even if he *were* friendlier. Pretty much the entire Pika Camp was here when it happened, you know."

"I thought you guys only came out one or two at a time."

"Usually we do, but we'd just had a big dump of snow, so most of us had nothing to do. Jim and Trina stayed behind—Trina's not here anymore, she finished collecting her data early and left a few days ago. Anyhow, they'd stayed to fiddle around with some equipment that had been giving us a hard time, but the rest of us were here."

"And therefore considered suspects."

"And therefore considered suspects," he agreed.

I pondered that for a moment. "So what about this hiker they're so interested in? What's your theory?"

He sank on the edge of the bed and scrubbed at his face. "You know, I really don't want to go there," he said. Firmly.

"Go where? It's a natural question."

He frowned, his expression darkening.

"But I take your point," I added hurriedly.

I started fingering the topmost box, picking at the edge of a piece of duct tape. "Do they seriously think I'm going to find evidence in these?"

It was more a rhetorical question than anything else, but Kelt shook his head.

"I don't think so, sweetheart," he told me. "They're just covering all the bases. If they thought there was something relevant in there, I don't think they would have released them to you."

It made me feel a little better.

"Come here." Kelt patted the mattress.

I sat down beside him and he put his arm around me. It was difficult to take my eyes off the boxes.

"Let's not think about it right now," he suggested softly. "Not tonight."

I looked up at him, those green eyes of his had gone all sexy again. Gods, I'd missed him. Now that we were together again, I wasn't sure how I'd ever survived being apart.

I touched his face gently. "I really missed you," I told him.

The smile he gave me banished all thoughts of crime investigations and disturbing boxes and rude police officers.

Kelt was right. The field notes could wait.

At least till tomorrow.

## April 11

How do we live? How should we live? More sustainably. That goes without saying. Consuming less. Caring more. Leaving a smaller footprint.

It all seems so hopeless in this new century. Environmental problems seemed more solvable in the 1980s. People seemed to care more. I wonder if they did, or if I'm just remembering it that way. The back-in-the-good-old-days syndrome. Still. There seemed to be a bright feeling of empowerment back then. These are the problems, but we can fix them. So full of confidence. Bursting with the conviction that we could solve any problem, no matter how messy.

But then we started to study what we'd done. To really look at the problems we'd created. We began to glimpse the scope of it all, and out of this was born bitter hopelessness.

Regent is worse than I thought. Worse than we could have predicted or even imagined twenty years ago. Hindsight, as they say, is 20/20, but how could what seemed like an ideal solution back then, turn out to be so very, very wrong? Now it isn't just the past that haunts me, but also the future.

I'll never get to sleep tonight.

# 7

"*How did you know her?*" She spat out the words furiously.

I recoiled at the woman's tone. The friendly smile I'd offered shuddered and died on my lips. "Uh, excuse me?"

"How did you know Selena?" she demanded "Was it you? It *was*, wasn't it? *Bitch!* I knew you were the one!"

I opened my mouth and closed it again. Unsure how to respond to this bristling fury. My eyes darted around, automatically searching for Kelt. But he'd gone looking for Jocelyn and our promised breakfast.

I was guessing this wasn't Jocelyn.

I'd been lounging at one of the tables in the main cabin. It was a cheery sort of space with several south-facing windows and a larger picture window looking westward to Willow Creek. The chairs were mismatched and worn, but the tables had been oiled to a soft shine and there were several blanket-covered couches clustered around a black woodstove in the corner. The place felt comfortable. Homey. But what had seemed so light and spacious a moment ago, now felt cramped and confined. The air suddenly seemed chilly.

I was alone here with this strange, enraged woman.

She had the sort of figure tabloid journalists would call statuesque (if they could spell it). Features anyone would describe as beautiful. High cheekbones, cream-smooth skin. Wide-set gray eyes with an unusual, almost silvery, sheen to them. An elf, if I ever saw one. But her generous lips were pulled tight with emotion. And her silver eyes, red and puffy from crying, seared the air between us with cold fury. She might be an elf, but she was an angry, unhappy one. It didn't take many little gray cells to identify her. What I couldn't figure out was what she thought I'd done.

"I'm Robyn Devara," I introduced myself, holding my hand out politely. Trying to defuse the situation.

She ignored the gesture. "I know who you are," she said bitterly. "What I want to know is how the *hell* you knew Selena. Where did you meet her? Jesus, just look at you! I can't believe it was you!"

"Willa." I kept my voice calm and even. "I'm sorry about what happened to Selena. Really I am. But I'm not sure what you're asking me. Please,"—I gestured to the chair across from me—"why don't you sit down and we can talk about it."

Willa stared at me for a long moment. A moment that teetered on the razor edge of chaos.

*Son of a bitch, she's going to hit me.*

I sat utterly still. Pinned by those odd metallic eyes.

*Where was Kelt when I needed him?*

I held my breath. Adrenaline started coursing through my veins. My body tensing into fight or flight mode.

"Please?" I said again. Softly. Cautiously. Half-afraid it would provoke an assault.

Her eyes flickered. Once. Twice. Then they filled with tears.

As I watched, she seemed to collapse in on herself like a used-up star, leaving a black hole where only rage had been. With a strangled gasp, she sank into the chair and covered her face with her hands.

I let my breath out slowly, willing myself to relax. My muscles were slow to respond.

Willa put her head down on the table and began to cry. Someone—probably Jocelyn—had set the table for breakfast with sunny yellow placemats and matching linen napkins. Wordlessly, I passed one of the napkins to Willa.

Just then, Kelt poked his head into the room. His happy grin disappeared as soon as he saw Willa crying beside me. Concerned, he started into the room. I frowned and shook my head. He hesitated and I gave him a quick, reassuring smile. He nodded and disappeared out the door.

Willa sobbed into the yellow napkin. Noisy, snot-drenched, soul-tearing sobs. A minute ago, I thought I'd have to fight her, now part of me wanted to hug her. You couldn't look on grief like this and not want to help. Couldn't hear such lost, desperate cries and not be moved to tears yourself. I sat there, clasping my hands uselessly.

Eventually, the aching cries diminished, quieted into soft gasps.

I gave her a few more minutes, then, "I never met Selena," I told her quietly.

She sat up and stared at me. Even the soft morning sunlight was too harsh for her grieving features. Her face was swollen and splotched. Her eyes were shot through with tiny blood vessels, but there was no anger in them anymore. Nothing but wrenching loss drowning in bottomless pupils.

"I never met her," I said again. Keeping my voice low and soothing. "I didn't even know who she was until Kelt phoned with the news."

Willa kept staring at me. Uncomprehending. "But . . . then why . . . ?" she stuttered and stopped.

"Why did she leave me her work stuff?" I guessed. Then I shook my head slowly. "I truly have no idea. I've never corresponded with her. I didn't even know anybody was doing a ptarmigan study up here."

Willa was silent for a moment, then she drew in a long, shuddering breath and gulped audibly. "She had an affair," she explained tonelessly.

Her voice was flat. Devoid of emotion. I didn't trust it.

She scrubbed a hand over her forehead. "I don't know who it was with. I thought it was you. But . . . I don't . . . I don't know why she did it." Her voice started to rise again. Hurt and anger tangling together with grief. "I don't understand! *I don't understand anything!*"

I passed her another napkin.

"She said we were soulmates. *Soulmates!* I thought

we were good. I thought we were happy . . . " She choked on a sob. "It's not bad enough that she died? How could she do that to me?"

I couldn't tell if she meant the affair or death. Maybe both.

"I don't know," I said after a moment. "I only know that she left me her field notes. And I don't understand that myself."

"Willa." A woman's voice interrupted our conversation. She swept into the room. A tiny whirlwind of a person. She spared a brief glance and a smile for me. From the lines on her face, she smiled widely and often. But when she turned her attention to Willa, her expression was grave and sympathetic.

"Jocelyn." Willa stumbled to her feet. "I thought . . . I . . . I didn't know . . ." She started to cry again. Weak, wounded sounds.

"I know, hon." Jocelyn reached up to embrace her. "I know. It's all right."

I stood up, banging my shins painfully against a chair in the process. Wanting to help. To utter the perfect words that would somehow make everything better. But there was nothing I could do. And there are no such words.

They turned away from me as Jocelyn led Willa from the room. Willa's back was bent, her shoulders slumped down. Though she was at least a foot taller than Jocelyn, she seemed much smaller. Crushed and diminished. Beyond broken.

It seemed like an eternity before Kelt came back to the cabin, though it was probably only a few minutes later. As soon as he opened the door, I jumped to my feet again, needing the comfort of a hug. But Kelt hadn't returned alone. A much shorter man preceded him. The stranger's face was dominated by large, soulful, brown eyes, and he began apologizing as soon as he stepped into the room.

"Robyn, I'm so very sorry about what happened— and on your first morning here too." His voice was soft and deliberate. He reminded me of the elves of Lothlorien whose ponderous speech made them all sound a bit slow on the uptake. Like they weren't the freshest lembas breads at the bakery.

He floated towards me and took my hand in both of his. "Are you all right? I'm so sorry. I . . . um, I hope she didn't upset you too much. Willa's just so fragile right now—even more than usual."

I raised one eyebrow at that.

"Not that she makes a habit of yelling at strangers," he hastened to add. "I mean, I've never known her to do something like that, and I've known her for ten years. It's just the circumstances."

His puppy dog eyes pleaded with me for understanding.

"I'm fine," I assured him. "And it's nothing to apologize about. I just wish there was something I could have done for her."

He nodded sadly. "I think we're all wishing that."

Kelt came up behind me and put a warm hand on my back. "Robyn, this is Paul Lattimore," he introduced us. "Jocelyn's partner and co-owner of the retreat."

"Ah yes, the poet," I said, managing a smile. "And a successful one too, from what I hear. A rare animal in these parts."

"In almost any part, I think," he said, meeting my smile with a tentative one of his own. "Half of me still expects to get a polite letter from my publisher saying it was all a mistake and would I please send a cheque for all the overpaid royalties."

"Really?"

"Of course. Terry goes in to Dawson for the mail, I don't drive." He gave me a surprisingly boyish grin. "And he's under strict instructions to lose any envelopes that come from Toronto."

I chuckled.

"But never mind all that now. Welcome to Willow Creek, Robyn," Paul said. He was still holding my hand, but now he shook it warmly. His grip was soft, just short of squishy. "Jocelyn and I have been looking forward to your visit. Though, um, not nearly as much as Kelt has, I think." He beamed at me.

In a lot of ways, I am a child of popular culture. So whenever I think about poets, I always imagine them to be dark, brooding characters. Prone to wearing black turtlenecks and out-of-fashion head apparel. Angry. Intense. Jagged up on caffeine and the injustices of the world. Paul seemed nothing like this.

His slow baritone was like warm cocoa. Rich and smooth. Physically, he was pale and slender, his dreamy expression perfectly suiting the mass of spectacular curls that sprang from his head. A throwback to the Romantic era, if I ever saw one. The little tuft of hair under his bottom lip was, however, *très* modern-day coffee house.

It had been partly the success of his poetry collection *do birds have walking dreams?* that allowed him and Jocelyn to purchase Willow Creek seven years ago. They had built it up into a thriving wilderness retreat, though, after meeting them both, I suspected Jocelyn had been the driving force behind the venture. Paul seemed far too ethereal to be described as a force.

"I think Jocelyn will probably be occupied with Willa for a while," he was saying apologetically. "And here you are waiting for your breakfast. I guess I should do something about that, although, um, I'm afraid I'm not much of a cook." He wafted over to the kitchen and started opening cupboards at random as if expecting to find plates of breakfast prepared and ready to eat.

The kitchen was nestled in the northwest corner of the cabin, open to the rest of the room. Cupboards had been built out of the same honey-colored wood that lined the walls and floors. A well-provisioned spice rack took up much of the available wall space. Paul opened and closed another cupboard. To the right, there was a tall counter with a couple of comfy-looking stools tucked underneath it. I pulled one out and slid onto it, leaning my elbows on the counter. This might take a while.

"Got any eggs?" Kelt suggested.

"Uh . . . I think so." Paul pulled a drawer open, then slid it closed again. "And there's some homemade granola . . . somewhere." He opened another cupboard hopefully.

Kelt joined him in the kitchen. "May I?" he asked, indicating the cupboards.

Paul stepped back with some relief. "Please do. Just help yourself to anything you want. Jocelyn made some cranberry orange biscotti yesterday. They should be around here somewhere. They're very good. She dips them in white chocolate."

Kelt found the biscotti on the first try. Paul seemed impressed.

Kelt set the jar on the counter, then he started rummaging through the cupboards, pulling out items as he named them off. "Let me see . . . ginger marmalade . . . nectarines . . . grapefruit. We could have a fruit salad. Oh, and here's the granola."

"Sounds marvelous," I said. "As long as there's some sort of caffeine involved too."

On cue, Kelt slapped a bag of dark roast coffee beans on the counter.

"It's even Fair Trade," he told me.

"I knew I fell in love with you for a reason," I said.

He grinned.

"Do you have any milk or cream?" he asked Paul.

"Oh, uh . . . yes, Jocelyn keeps it in the cold storage out back." He hesitated as if trying to recall which door led to the cold storage. Then he drifted towards the back door. "I'll just be a minute," he told us.

"Thanks."

Kelt waited until Paul was out of the room, then he stepped around the counter and slipped his arms around my waist. I turned towards him for a kiss, but he held back. He smoothed the curls away from my temples, examining my face intently.

"You okay?" he asked.

I considered the question and nodded. "Just in need of some caffeine."

"What happened with Willa?"

"She thought I'd had an affair with Selena."

His green eyes blinked in surprise. "What? Why?"

"Because of those damn notes, I think. I wish she'd never left them to me." The words surprised me with their bitterness.

Kelt looked at me gravely, then he put his hands on my shoulders. "Here, turn around," he said.

I did and Kelt started massaging my neck, his fingers digging deep into the knotted muscles. I hadn't realized I was so tense.

"Kelt . . . mmmm, that feels good . . . you did . . . ouch, not so hard . . . you did tell the RCMP about Selena and Michele, didn't you?"

The fingers stopped.

I turned my head. Kelt looked defensive.

"*You didn't tell them?*"

"It wasn't my business."

"What do you mean, it wasn't your business?"

"It's camp talk, Robyn. You know how I feel about that kind of thing."

"*Camp talk!* Selena is dead, Kelt. She had an affair with Michele and now she's dead! Don't you think there might be a connection there? I mean, I know they're looking for that missing hiker, but they haven't put out a warrant for his arrest. It's possible he has nothing to do with any of this. We have no way of knowing, we're not exactly 'in the loop.'"

"I *think* she had an affair with Michele," he corrected, his voice tightening.

I waved off the distinction. "That's sort of beside the point," I said. "Look, Selena had an affair with *somebody*, even Willa knows that much. If you think you know who it was—even if you're not sure—you should tell the RCMP about it."

Kelt didn't say anything.

"I don't see why this is a problem," I told him. "I'm sure they'll be discreet."

"Fine! I'll tell them."

"They need to know," I insisted.

"I said I'd tell them. Okay? Give it a rest! You said you weren't going to get involved. You *promised* me you wouldn't get involved."

"I'm sorry," I snapped. "But, like it or not, I *am* involved. Selena Barry made damn sure of that."

He started to respond, but at that moment, Paul stepped back into the room. A green and white carton was tucked under his arm.

"I can't quite find any cream," he apologized. "But I did find some soy milk and . . . " He trailed off, suddenly aware of the tension in the room. "Um, I know it's not really the same thing."

I stretched my lips into a smile. "It'll be fine," I lied.

Paul smiled uneasily, his feet rooted in the doorway.

"Soy milk?" Kelt remarked after a moment. Despite

an obvious effort, his tone didn't quite come off as relaxed. "That must be hard to find up here."

"Oh, um, it is," Paul stuttered. "But Selena . . . is . . . was lactose-intolerant so we always ordered it in for her. Nobody else even likes it. I tried to find some milk, but all I could see was some yogurt. I . . . um, I thought that might be weird in coffee." He inched into the room uncertainly. "Uh, I guess Terry'll have to go in to Dawson today. He always picks up our milk. As . . . as well as the mail."

"We can cope," Kelt assured him.

"Well, I guess I should really go and talk to him about that. Here." Paul handed the carton to Kelt and beat a quick retreat. For someone so seemingly ethereal, he was awfully fast on his feet when he wanted to be.

"Thanks, Paul," I called out.

He waved as he shot out the door, leaving an oppressive hush behind. Kelt went into the kitchen and started laying out our breakfast. His lips were tight and he refused to meet my eyes. I knew it was up to me to break the silence.

"I'm sorry," I told him. "I didn't mean to jump all over you."

"It hasn't been easy around here, you know?" He slapped a few biscotti on a plate.

"I know."

"I've had problems at the camp. Selena gets murdered." He started slicing savagely into a grapefruit. Juice squirted across the counter. "And then you come and start telling me I should have done this. And why didn't I do that?"

"I'm sorry," I said again.

He drew in a deep breath and let it out slowly. He finished sectioning the fruit. "Me too," he said after a moment. "You're right, I need to tell someone about Michele—even if it's only a rumor. I just hate to get involved in that kind of thing, you know? It's none of my business."

"Under normal circumstances, I'd agree with you, but these are hardly that."

Glumly, he started spooning coffee into the percolator. "I know. But I still feel like the camp gossip. How many cups of coffee do you want?"

"That depends on if you're going to make me drink it with that stuff."

He smiled crookedly. "Not a soy milk fan, eh?"

"It's *vile*," I told him, screwing up my face. "Have you ever tried it?"

"It's not that bad," he said. "But it's not that great, either. Maybe we should've gone with the yogurt."

I laughed and Kelt came around the counter and gave me a long hug.

And, for the time being, life was back to normal again—as normal as it could be, given the circumstances. I could wish that Kelt wasn't so touchy. So stressed. It left me wondering just how and when I'd be able to bring up the infinitely more sensitive subject of pregnancy.

**8**

I was contemplating the pros and cons of a fifth biscotti when Jocelyn came looking for us. A black and rust-colored tortoiseshell cat followed closely at her heels, trying its best to trip her up.

"Oh good, you found something to eat," she said with a relieved smile. "I'm so sorry about . . . well, everything, I guess."

She had a wide mouth that spoke quickly and precisely. Each word was carefully enunciated as if English was not her first language. Her hands spoke too, rapid, controlled gestures emphasizing her words. Very French Canadian. My first impression of her as a whirlwind appeared to be accurate. There was a controlled energy about Jocelyn. She seemed the sort of person who had dozens of things going on at once—and who knew, at any given time, exactly which stage each was at.

"No need to apologize," I told her. "How's Willa?"

Jocelyn's smile disappeared. "Not great," she shook her head. "But she is calmer now. And she feels terrible about what she said. I promised her I'd talk to you about it."

"No worries," I said. "After everything she's been through, it's understandable."

"Why don't you join us?" Kelt nudged a chair toward her.

Jocelyn sank down on the edge of it. A hummingbird pausing to rest. Her smile peeked out again.

"Coffee?" Kelt asked.

She nodded gratefully. "Thanks, Kelt, I could use one."

The cat jumped up into my lap, startling me. "Well, hello," I said to it. "And who are you?"

"That's Karma," Jocelyn told me. "A bad kitty."

"Bad Karma, eh?"

Jocelyn nodded. "Most of the time. Occasionally—very occasionally—she's good Karma. If she's bothering you, just push her off."

Karma looked at me, her gold eyes daring me to try.

"She's fine," I said, stroking her. "I like cats. I've got one at home. I've only been gone a couple of days, but I already sort of miss him."

Karma dug her claws into my leg. "Just like home," I said, wincing.

"We've got four," Jocelyn told me.

"Four." I tried to imagine four Guidos. Shuddered.

"Paul and I are trying to have kids," Jocelyn explained with a crooked grin, "but somehow we just kept getting more cats instead. There's a black and white one—that's Edgar. Flynn's our stripey one. And Murf's the big orange boy. He's with Willa right now." Jocelyn took a sip of her coffee and sighed. "It seems to help her."

"Cats are good therapy," Kelt agreed.

"You don't worry about predators around the retreat?" I asked. "I mean, aren't there wolves in the area?"

"And wolverines and grizzlies and lynx and fox," Jocelyn said. "But we keep the cats in at night and they don't wander too far during the day. Generally, predators don't come very close. There's too much activity around here—not that you'd be able to tell at the moment." Her tone was dejected.

"I heard people are canceling their reservations," I said sympathetically.

Jocelyn passed a hand over her eyes. She looked tired. "I can't blame them, really I can't," she said. "But we've only been up and running for four years now—and for the first two, our only guests were family and friends. This year was *supposed* to be our breakthrough."

She made a face. "Listen to me! Complaining about cancellations, after what happened." She put down her coffee mug on the table, wrapping both hands around it as if to warm them.

"The truth of the matter is, I really didn't know Selena very well," she said slowly. "Willa brought her to the retreat, let me see, it must be close to three years ago now. I tried to make friends with her—after all, Paul and I have known Willa for almost ten years. She's like a sister to me. But Selena was a very different animal. One of those people who keep to themselves. She seemed . . . driven. I guess that's the one word I'd use to describe her. Very dedicated to her work. She never really had much time for the rest of us." A note of disapproval crept into her voice. "Not even Willa sometimes." She paused and seemed to give herself a shake. "I was shocked by her death—we all were—but as the days go on, I'm starting to realize that I really didn't know her at all."

I wondered if this was an oblique reference to Selena's affair.

Jocelyn heaved a sigh. "And now I sound like I'm making excuses for myself!"

"For what it's worth, I don't think you're being callous," Kelt told her. "Life has to go on, and this retreat *is* your life. It's natural to worry about it."

She smiled at him fondly. "And there's you being so nice and understanding." Her tone had lightened. "And happy! Look at you, all pink and glowing. Glad your Robyn is finally here with you, I think."

Kelt grinned at me, his cheeks flushing a little.

"Hmmm," I said, stroking my chin as I pretended to examine his face. "You *do* look all pink and glowing. Just like a little cherub."

Kelt stuck his tongue out at me. Most uncherub-like.

"You know, he missed you terribly," Jocelyn told me. "I'm glad you were able come up."

"Me too," I said. "I was missing him something fierce myself and"—I gestured around the room—"you really have a lovely place here."

Jocelyn looked pleased. "If you're finished with breakfast, I could give you the grand tour," she offered.

I nodded eagerly. "I'd like that."


The Willow Creek Adventure and Wilderness Retreat was much larger than I'd originally thought. A sprawling rather than a dense development. The largest cabin sat on a hill at the southwest corner of the property, overlooking the muddy clearing that served as a parking lot. The creek cut across the property, angling past the main cabin and passing within twenty yards of its northeast corner. Five smaller cabins, each the size of a small room, were scattered to the west. One of the smaller ones had a distinct greenish tinge to it.

"Why is that one green?" I asked Jocelyn, pointing to it.

"Oh." Jocelyn wrinkled her nose. "That was the first one Terry built for us. We'd decided to use pressure-treated wood. It's supposed to last a lot longer than any other wood. But Terry ended up getting a terrible rash on his hands from working with it. And then we started hearing about treated wood and how the arsenic in it leaches out into the environment and . . . well, Paul and I decided to have Terry build the other cabins the old-fashioned way."

"They're a much nicer color," I told her with a smile. "That one looks sort of . . . seasick."

Jocelyn grinned back.

The other cabins sported brandy-colored logs. Black stovepipes poked up from slanted roofs, and large windows looked out on to the forest or the creek, depending on where each cabin was situated. Whoever Terry was, he'd done a nice job on them.

We followed a well-flattened path around the big cabin and down into the woods behind it where the smaller residences were situated. White spruce and quaking aspen dominated the area, the vegetation providing a screen of privacy for the occupants—when there were any.

The Yukon had seemed like a quiet territory right off the bat, but the silence around Willow Creek had a distinctly unnatural quality to it. It wasn't just that the place was devoid of guests; rather, it was like the land itself was aware of what had happened here. As if the psychic stain lingered on. Fouling the ground. Polluting the very air. A fanciful notion, maybe, but one that wasn't easy to shake—especially after I spied the RCMP's camper standing somber watch in the parking lot.

The scientists' tents were along the east side of the retreat. Eight of them, all sunbleached white. All lined up like a mini-garrison.

"The geologists left early this morning, so you two have the place to yourselves for a while. I've got a group of entomologists scheduled to arrive tomorrow." She made a face. "At least, I think they're still coming. They haven't called to cancel."

I hoped for her sake they wouldn't. A bunch of rowdy, bug-lovin' academics would really help liven up the joint.

"Come on, I'll show you the creek," Jocelyn said, leading us down a dirt trail.

Here and there, patches of horsetail ferns softened the lines of the forest floor with their frothy green fronds. Karma had decided to follow us and she skulked through the knee-high ferns like a jungle cat. Although the air was warm, there was still a faint bite of coolness. An ever-present reminder about the dangers of letting your guard down in a place where it can snow in July.

"Willow Creek feeds into the Blackstone River," Jocelyn explained over her shoulder. "And gives us our drinking water."

"No giardia?" I asked.

Jocelyn shook her head. "No beavers this high up. Also, the creek's fed by glaciers." She stopped at the creek bank and gestured toward the water. "This is some of the cleanest water in the world."

It looked it. Willow Creek was clear of sediment and—I bent down and dipped my fingers in the water— very cold. It gurgled and burped, flowing past deposits of rounded, weathered rock. The only sound in the place besides the soft susurration of wind in the trees. A stubby-tailed American dipper hopped along the edge of the creek bed, probing the shallow water for invertebrates. There were more trees on the opposite bank. Aspen and spruce with the odd tamarack poking up among them. Beyond the trees, the Ogilvie Mountains provided a backdrop of faded blues and pale mauves.

"The hot tub's over that way," Jocelyn said, pointing to the west.

I turned and saw a small, round cedar hot tub nestled in a stand of white spruce beside the creek. There was a sign hanging from the tree beside it. I squinted to read it. *Next hot bath 150 km.* I chuckled.

"We use the creek to fill the tub," Jocelyn said, answering my smile with one of her own. "And then there's a wood-fired stove on the far side, which heats it up. We charge fifteen dollars a tub. I wash it out after each use, and then, of course, Terry has to cut the wood." She seemed tentative about the price. Almost apologetic.

"Sounds like a heck of a deal to me," I said.

Jocelyn smiled again. Relieved. "Kelt said you'd probably like to have a dip before you head out. There's another path from the tents. And a privacy sign you can hang up at the trail head."

I glanced back at him and he wiggled his eyebrows at me suggestively. I grinned and mouthed the word *pig*. Then, suppressing my smile, I turned my attention back to Jocelyn.

"Sign us up," I told her.

We followed the path by the creek for a while, past several of the smaller cabins. Each had been named after a Yukon animal. Caribou, ptarmigan, moose, lynx, bear. Wooden signs on the front of each cabin were painted with black silhouettes of the appropriate creature. The larger structure—the one with the dining area and common room—was known simply as the Cabin. It had been, Jocelyn explained, their home until Terry had built the others.

"Paul and I live in the Bear now," she said. "Unless we have a really big group, then we move to a tent. Terry still lives on the top floor of the Cabin. You should see his room some time. Such a tranquil space. Willa and I call him the feng shui master."

"Robyn hasn't met Terry yet," Kelt told her.

"Oh. Well, I'll take you to meet him then. He's a real sweetheart, very easy to talk to."

"And he's your builder?"

"Our jack-of-all-trades, really. And much appreciated he is too. I love Paul dearly and he's a brilliant poet, but he's hopeless when it comes to the kind of basic skills you need to run a place like this."

Kelt and I exchanged an amused look, remembering Paul's feeble attempt to make breakfast.

As we hiked past the Bear cabin, I spied a

decrepit-looking structure leaning off by itself in the woods. The windows were small, miserly. The logs, once warm and vital, were now nothing but ancient silvered bones. Various plants and grasses sprouted from the sod roof like a bad haircut. I didn't have to ask who lived there. The bright yellow crime scene tape that stretched across the door and windows was a dead giveaway.

"That's where Willa and Selena lived," Jocelyn confirmed, following my eyes to the pale gray cabin. "Willa's staying in Moose Cabin for the time being." She paused and lowered her voice. "Her family disowned her years ago. She doesn't have anywhere else to go. But she couldn't stay . . . there." Her mouth trembled. She pressed her lips together and looked away quickly. An awkward silence followed.

"The building seems pretty old," I said, sensing Jocelyn's need to change the subject.

She shot me a grateful look. "It *is* old," she agreed. "It was built back in the sixties, when this was as far as the Dempster went."

"Sixties? It looks older."

"Yes, I know. I don't think old Jake was ever much of a builder." She smiled crookedly. "He'd certainly never heard of a plumb line."

"He was a hell of an amateur naturalist, though," Kelt said.

I turned to look at him.

"The guy lived here for over thirty years," Kelt explained. "One of those back-to-nature types. But he left incredibly detailed notes. You wouldn't believe some of the stuff he was looking at. Winter survival rates, reproductive success, dispersal patterns. For all kinds of animals. And this was way before anybody else was doing it."

"Aldo Leopold of the Yukon, eh?"

"Something like."

"No wonder Pika Camp was set up here."

"Not too many places up here can boast data sets like that," Kelt agreed.

"It was the reason Selena wanted to work here," Jocelyn said pensively. "She always said it was a bit of luck that Jake had had such an interest in ptarmigan. It made her study possible. All that information on climate over the years."

"Still no word on that hiker?" The question was out of my mouth before I could stop it. I winced inwardly, knowing Kelt would probably have a word with me later about it.

But Jocelyn just shook her head. "No," she shrugged wearily. "I hope to god they find him soon. It's hell to think he might still be around."

"I'm sorry," I told her.

She looked at me and I saw that her eyes were bright with tears. I felt terrible for bringing it up.

"It's not your fault," she said, sensing my guilt. "I think about it all the time whether somebody asks me or not. We all do."

Kelt and I didn't say anything.

After a minute, Kelt caught my eye and we turned to continue along the path, but Jocelyn didn't move. She stood silently, still gazing at the old cabin. I paused to wait for her.

Jocelyn sighed. Her eyes were sad. "I don't know what's going to happen to the old place now. Willa came up here with us, you know. Seven years ago, when we first bought the place. She fell in love with the old cabin as soon as she saw it. All that weathered wood and leaning lines. The artist in her, no doubt."

"I didn't know she was an artist," I said.

But Jocelyn was too lost in her own thoughts to hear the comment. "I don't know if she'll ever be able to go back," she said. "I don't know if any of us will." She turned her back resolutely on the cabin. "If it was up to me, I'd burn it to the ground."

I wondered if she realized how angry she sounded.


We met up with Terry toward the end of the tour. He was climbing into a mud-covered green pickup truck at the far end of the parking lot. Jocelyn called out to him to wait.

"I'm going for milk and mail," he told her as we came up to the truck. "Did you need something else?"

Up close, he was younger than I'd first thought. A thatch of salt-white hair lent his features a maturity beyond his years. He was wearing a faded blue sweater that was unraveling at the sleeves. The color did little to enliven his sallow skin. He was slender, neither tall or short. Physically, an unremarkable man. But he had the softest voice I'd ever heard. Timid. Whispery. You almost had to hold your breath to hear what he was saying.

"No, no, I'm fine," Jocelyn assured him. "But I thought you'd like to meet Kelt's partner. Robyn Devara, Wayne Theriault. Better known as Terry in these parts."

Terry offered me a gentle smile. His eyes met mine briefly before slipping away in a blink. "It's very nice to meet you, Robyn," he said softly.

At least I think that's what he said.

He must be horribly shy, I realized as I tried, and failed, to make eye contact again. He had that deer-in-the-headlights sort of look to him.

"Nice to meet you too," I told him. "I understand you built all these lovely cabins."

His eyes flickered up to mine again. "That's right," he said with another tentative smile. "Well . . . to be fair, I did have a lot of help."

"You did a beautiful job. Jocelyn and Paul are lucky to have you here."

He looked at the ground and bobbed his head shyly.

"How are things at Pika Camp?" he asked Kelt after an awkward moment.

"So far, so good," Kelt replied. "We're heading into crunch time, so my answer might be different in a week or so."

Terry smiled at the ground again.

"Well," he said after another long pause. "I should really be on my way. Are you sure you don't need anything?" This last to Jocelyn.

She paused and tilted her head to one side. "Tomatoes," she said finally, "but only if they're nice. Otherwise, don't bother. Will you be back for dinner? It's bison stroganoff tonight."

"I'll be back by six," he told her, bobbing his head again. Then he jumped into his truck with a distinct air of relief. He didn't look at Kelt or me again.

The three of us stood and watched him drive off. Clouds had started to pile up overhead, blocking out the late morning sun. The air was noticeably cooler and I found myself wishing I'd brought a fleecy with me.

"Well, that's about it for the grand tour," Jocelyn said, rubbing her hands against the chill. "Why don't we go back and get another pot of coffee on?"

She turned back toward the main cabin, and Kelt and I trailed after her like baby grouse. Karma had long since disappeared into the ferns.

"Why does Terry go by his last name?" I asked as we followed the path.

"He doesn't like his first one much," Jocelyn answered. "Says every time he hears the name 'Wayne' it sounds like whoever's saying it has a nasal problem."

"Wayne." I tried it out, dragging out the *ay*. "I guess you could make a case for that," I conceded. "Is he from the Yukon?

Jocelyn glanced back at me and shook her head. "No. Actually you'll find that very few of us are."

"Really?"

"Strange but true." She took a few more steps before continuing. "Everybody in the Yukon has their story," she explained. "Some come up here just to get away from the crazy bustle of life down south. Others come to escape an unhappy life. Or the memories of one. And some of us just want to start over."

Her eyes were far away and there was a whisper of something odd in her voice. Old pain, perhaps. She brought herself back to the present with a shake of her head.

"The Yukon is big enough to absorb most people," she told us. "And empty enough so your chances of finding peace are better here than they are just about anywhere else. It can be a harsh land, but there's *room* here. You can breathe deep when you have to. Or lose yourself if you need to. I'd never go back south now. Not willingly."

## April 13

Liane e-mailed again. Sounding depressed as usual. I'm tempted to phone—I know she's hoping I will—but I'm trying hard to resist the urge. I feel sorry for her, I really do. But she's got to figure it out for herself. I did. Willa did. It makes us stronger. She's hardly the first person to be estranged from her family. We all have demons. How we wrestle them shapes who we are. Willa thinks I'm being harsh, though I don't see her offering a helping hand.

Okay, maybe that's unfair. I'm sure if Liane had bonded with Willa the way she did with me, then Willa would be only too happy to be on the phone with her for hours every night. I can't do that—and I don't think I should. I can't fight Liane's battles for her. I'm not Jocelyn. And besides, I have enough demons of my own at the moment—not the least of which is depression.

I keep telling myself that what I've seen out at Regent would depress anybody, but I can't afford to be less than functional right now. Not with so much work ahead of me. God, I thought my mood would improve when the sun came back. Some days are better than others, of course, but the bad days are pretty bleak. And Liane keeps e-mailing for help. How can I be positive for someone else, when I can't even do it for myself? I'll wait a day or so and e-mail her back. I know she'll be disappointed, but it'll have to do. It's really all I can manage right now.

## April 23

Willa is feeling neglected again. Read "artistically uninspired." It seems to be happening more and more lately. The blank canvases. The black depression. The volatile temper. Abandoned by her Muse, she expects me to make up for it. To replace it somehow. I don't remember it being this bad before.

Jocelyn doesn't help, of course. Everything Willa does or says—no matter how outrageous—is always justified and, naturally, my fault. If I didn't spend so much time in the field, Willa wouldn't be so anxious. If I were more supportive, Willa would feel more secure. Etc. etc. Jocelyn never actually comes out and says these things, but they are oh-so-gently (and not very subtly) suggested. It drives me crazy!

I do have an ally in Paul. Not surprising, I suppose. Ever since I saw him coming out of the clinic in Whitehorse, he's been going out of his way to be helpful. I've told him not to worry. I may not agree with his decision—or at least his decision to do it without Jocelyn's knowledge, but it's not my place to say anything. Least of all to Jocelyn. I don't think he believes me but if that's why he's trying to help me out now, then I can't really complain, can I? God knows I appreciate the intervention.

Between Willa and Jocelyn, I sometimes feel like I'm getting it from all sides. Yesterday Paul tried to temper Jocelyn's overprotective instincts. Kudos for the effort, but it was all for nothing. He committed the grave error of criticizing Willa for her bouts of temper. He should have known better. You can't fault Willa, not around Jocelyn. She told him she didn't appreciate the "interference," and today when Paul and I were laughing over something,

Jocelyn pursed her lips tight and gave me a look that would peel paint. Message received. Loud and clear. Grrr.

Deep breath. Yoga breath. This isn't about Jocelyn, is it?

Willa. My beautiful, artistic, exciting, loving, and utterly frustrating soul mate. I don't know, maybe I haven't been understanding enough. Maybe I have been neglecting her. Caught up with my own obsessions. God knows, my work has occupied much of my psychic space lately. Oh, it's unfair of her to blame me for her creative blocks, I'm under no illusions about that, but I suppose this is the artist personified. The bad with the good. I'm certainly not about to throw in the proverbial towel. She puts up with my demons, the least I can do is put up with hers.

I hereby resolve to be less preoccupied and more supportive.

## May 2

Despite Willa's uncertain temper, I managed to get out and collect a few samples. Enough, I think, for my purposes. The birds are still winter-weak and easily caught. It'll be much more difficult in a few weeks when courtship begins in earnest. The males haven't started calling yet—it's far too early. They need more time to build up to performance level, to replenish diminished stores after the long, harsh winter.

It's still very cold up in the higher elevations and it started snowing again early this morning. Nothing too heavy, but the ptarmigan have wisely retreated to their snowy burrows to wait out the weather. I decided to follow their lead and came back early—both to avoid the snowstorm and to spend some quality time with Willa (I do worry about her when I'm gone). Willa, however, left earlier to go into Dawson for the day. So I will sit here toasting my toes by the woodstove and waiting for her to come home. Fervently hoping she'll have found her Muse again.

## May 5

Hallelujah! The creative juices are flowing, the paint is flying, and Willa is happy. Suddenly everything is not my fault anymore. She was happy to see me, of course, touched by my concern for her and charmingly repentant for her earlier behavior. But now that I've been home a few days, she is suddenly resentful of the time spent with me when she could be with her paints.

I just can't win.

So this morning I left her alone with the damn brushes and canvases and went over to the Cabin. Paul was there. I think he understands my frustration. He essentially told me I should go back in the field. That I shouldn't let Willa interfere so much with my work. "It's far too important," he said with unsettling intensity.

Does he know? How could he? No. No, it's impossible. Don't be paranoid.

He's probably just as fed up as I am. God knows he and Jocelyn have been at odds lately. Last night when the wind dropped, I could hear them arguing again, though I couldn't make out any words. Just raised voices. I wonder if she found out about his secret?

Thankfully, the new field/tourist season is almost upon us. Oh, how we need some new faces around here! Some fresh personalities to shake things up. We have been cooped up far too long now with each other's insecurities and resentments. So . . . maybe now that Willa's need isn't so overwhelming, I can get back to my ptarmigan. Paul is right. My work is important (more important than he knows). If Willa was sick or in a true crisis situation, obviously it would be a different matter—though I suppose one could argue that her creative difficulties are a form of crisis. I feel twitchy. Like I need to keep moving. I have to get back out there.

A sense of relief washes over me as I write these words, but it is a relief tempered by apprehension. I've sent the first batch of samples down to Edmonton. Did I collect enough for a representative sample? What if they don't find anything?

What if they do?

**9**

After a second cup of coffee (*sans* soy milk), I headed back to the tent. Jocelyn needed to do some baking for her anticipated guests, Kelt needed to make a few work-related phone calls. And as for myself . . . I needed to have a look at Selena Barry's field notes.

The plan was to hike out to Pika Camp the following day, but after seeing the cabin where Selena had been murdered, I suddenly found that I couldn't, in all conscience, flit off to the field. Not without taking a quick look at what was in the brown cardboard boxes. Obviously I wasn't about to involve myself in a murder investigation, but the fact remained that Selena Barry had left her notes to me. I could and should do whatever possible to inform the RCMP about her work. At the very least, it would help them piece together the story of her life. And besides, I didn't fancy the idea of telling the intimidating Constable Matas that I hadn't gotten around to it yet.

I ducked inside the tent. The air smelled musty after the freshness of outdoors. In the muted light, I could see the pile of boxes crouching in the middle of the space like a squat sentinel. Daring me to open their flaps. To enter the world of the dead. I shivered, feeling like I'd stepped into the mines of Moria. I took a deep breath. Clearly, I'd been reading way too much Tolkien. "Right," I told them. "Let's have a look then."

I shifted the boxes over to the bed and arranged them in a semicircle on top of the blankets. Might as well be comfortable for this. I dug out my Swiss army knife from my pack and seated myself in front of the boxes, cross-legged. Then I took another deep breath and sliced neatly through the layers of duct tape.

The envelope was sitting on top of all the papers in the first box. A plain white business envelope, unsealed, with my name and address printed neatly on the front of it. I didn't recognize the handwriting. The letter inside had been typed on plain bond paper. Cold and official-looking.

Dear Robyn,

I am entrusting you with my field notes, abstracts, and papers—everything, in fact, which constitutes the sum total of my research work with the white-tailed ptarmigan of the northern Ogilvie mountain range. As you know, I am not closely associated with a university or any other research institute. As such, I believe you are the best person to receive this information given both your personality and your past experiences. Among the papers and research notes, you will find field notebooks dated from three years ago to the present. All notations and abbreviations are fairly standard and should therefore be easy for you to decipher.

I know you will be conscientious about my findings and will be able to determine the proper course of action.

Best regards,

Selena Barry


I read the letter a second time, then a third out loud. It still didn't make any sense. My personality? My past experiences? Now I knew why Constable Matas had seemed suspicious about my lack of connection with Selena Barry. It certainly sounded like she knew me.

I chewed my lip thoughtfully. In all likelihood, Kelt had told her about me. But what past experiences could she be referring to? What exactly had Kelt said to her? I folded the letter back into its envelope and started to go through the contents of the box.

One of the first items I found was the tattered cover from a yellow Rite in the Rain field notebook, folded twice over to pocket size. I opened it up. The reverse side was filled with codes written in black grease pencil. Several columns of tiny, neat numbers. In one column, a series of four-digit numbers had been carefully recorded, each preceded by the letters WTP. They were too short to be band numbers, but WTP obviously stood for white-tailed ptarmigan. Some kind of identification number, I guessed. Beside each ID number was a transmitter frequency. Dwayne had told me Selena was radio tracking the birds. This was probably the reference card she would have clipped to the map of her study area.

I bounced the cover on my hand for a moment, considering it. There seemed to be a lot of numbers here. I did a quick count. Seventy-four. That was quite a study site. I'd have to double-check, but I didn't think ptarmigan were normally found in such high densities. I wondered how large an area she was covering. I set the cover to one side and dug deeper into the first box, hoping to find a map.

There was a thin book, which outlined all the possible color combinations for color banding. And more notebooks with bright yellow covers. There were photocopied papers about ptarmigan and tear sheets from journal articles and tattered birding cards and aerial photographs and a copy of Robert Kenward's *Manual for Wildlife Radio Tagging*, which had seen better days. I found a bag of colored plastic bands—everything from pink to blue to yellow to several shades of green—and another bag of aluminum bands, each sporting a nine-digit number and the address of The Canadian Bird Banding offices in Ottawa. All of it jumbled together with little semblance of order. But there were no maps.

I skimmed the abstracts from a few of the papers to get a feel for how she was directing her research. Most of them seemed to concentrate on social behavior. Things like territoriality, courtship, nesting, and feeding. Kelt had said she'd been studying the effects of climate change on ptarmigan, but there was nothing about that—at least, not at first glance.

I flipped through a couple of the field notebooks. Selena Barry had kept good notes. Consistently neat with detailed descriptions of habitat, vegetation types, as well as ecological conditions at the site. There was information about each bird: its band number, age, sex, wing length, whether it was gravid, injured, emaciated, or fat. Nothing unusual there. Just nothing to indicate where these birds were. And still no mention of climate change.

In the second box, I found something more promising. It looked like the very rough first draft of an academic paper. There were paragraphs crossed out and notes scrawled in the margins. It was dated a year and a half ago and, according to the handwritten abstract, dealt with the effects of climate change on winter survival rates. Quickly, I scanned through the text. From the sounds of it, the Ogilvie Mountain ptarmigan weren't doing so well. Numbers were down, winter mortality rates were rising.

I finished reading it and tapped the pages thoughtfully against my chin. I tried to keep up with the professional literature, but I didn't recall ever seeing such a paper. I wondered if Selena had submitted it for publication.

So. Now I knew for sure that she'd been studying the effects of climate change on ptarmigan, but I still didn't know where. There hadn't been a single map in the second box either. I wasn't too concerned—she'd kept such detailed notes about habitat, it was possible I could find her site without one—but it was still puzzling. Usually you'd have a whole set of them when you were in the field. After all, if you were in the middle of nowhere, the last thing you'd want to discover is that you were missing a crucial map. Maybe they were in one of the other boxes.

By the bottom of the third box, I still hadn't discovered a map. But I did find a handful of small glass vials.

I pulled these out and examined them closely. They contained bits of feathers and what looked like toenail clippings.

Strange.

I wondered why she'd collected them—and when. There were no dates on the vials. No labels of any kind. Which was odd in itself for someone who'd kept such meticulous notes.

I shook out one of the feathers onto my palm. It was brown and speckled. It certainly looked like a ptarmigan feather. But why collect feathers and toenails for a climate change study? Puzzled, I put the feather back in its vial.

What exactly had she been looking for?

"Hi Kelt!"

"Michele? What are you doing here?"

I was still in the tent—I hadn't even opened the fourth box yet—so I couldn't see Kelt's face, but I could hear the surprise in his voice. Surprise that sharpened quickly into concern. "Is everything okay at camp?" he demanded.

"It's fine." Michele sounded puzzled by the question.

"Yo, Kelt." Another voice joined in.

"Hey, Jim. How's it going?"

"Marmots love my pee, man," Jim answered somewhat cryptically. "Life is good."

Kelt laughed. "Doesn't get much better than that," he agreed. There was an awkward pause. "So . . . uh, what *are* you doing here?"

"We're here for our break," Michele replied. "You said we could come out today. We *are* overdue for it." She sounded almost, but not quite, critical.

"I said you should come out *tomorrow*," Kelt corrected her. "After I got back."

"It was today," Michele insisted in a tone of voice I wouldn't have used with *my* boss. She paused, then added sweetly. "Are we having a gendered moment here?"

A gendered moment?

"Meaning what, exactly?" Kelt's tone echoed my thoughts.

"Women are better at schedules and directions. Everybody knows that."

"Reading a schedule properly is not a gender issue," Kelt said. A distinct warning note in his voice.

Michele didn't say anything.

"Sorry man," Jim apologized. "I kinda lost track of the days. Michele told me we were to come out. I didn't even think to look at the schedule myself . . . "

"No worries," Kelt told him. "It's not the end of the world."

I'd been listening in on their conversation by the door of the tent. Now would probably be a good time to make my appearance. I pulled open the flap and stepped outside.

"Hey!" I greeted them brightly.

There were two people standing with Kelt, each laden with a hefty-looking backpack. The man, a wide-eyed undergrad type, had the build and posture of a telephone pole. His flame-colored hair was a bright bird nest on top of his lanky body. The woman was quite a bit shorter. Snowy-skinned and delicate, with curly black hair and the sort of pouty, trembling lips that seemed constantly on the verge of saying "I am helpless, please take care of me." I disliked her on sight.

"Jim, Michele, this is Robyn," Kelt introduced me. "She just got here yesterday. We were about to go on a hike."

What followed was an odd moment of role reversal. I've mentioned before that I am, in no way, shape or form, an elf. Too short, too shapely, and definitely lacking in the bone-structure department, but I've been ogled by men before. Maybe not my fair share of them, but enough to know when I'm being checked out. I was being ogled right now. Leered at right under Kelt's eyes. But it wasn't by Jim.

"You look strong," Michele said by way of greeting. She held my hand a little too long for comfort. Her dark eyes gazed into mine soulfully. The lips quivered at me.

"Uh, thanks," I replied, throwing a puzzled glance at Kelt.

"Nice big legs," she said. Admiration coloring her tone.

I didn't know what to say to that. It *sounded* like she was giving me a compliment.

"Hi," Jim rescued me by holding his hand out. "I'm Jim from Winnipeg."

I disengaged my hand from Michele's and smiled at him gratefully. "Hey, Jim from Winnipeg," I said. "Good to meet you."

He moved in closer to shake my hand. A waft of body odor preceded him. I wrinkled my nose and suppressed a cough.

"Sorry about the smell," he apologized sheepishly. "Haven't had a real bath in almost a month."

"Life in the field, eh?" I held my breath and grinned up at him. He was very tall. "I assume you have designs on the hot tub?"

He nodded vigorously. "Michele and I tossed for it. I won first dibs."

He sounded excessively pleased with himself. I laughed.

"You'd better go and make sure it's free, then," I advised him. "Sounds like Jocelyn wasn't expecting you guys till tomorrow."

All of a sudden, Jim looked worried. "That's right, isn't it? And I gotta scare up some soap too. Um, if you don't mind . . ."

"Not in the least," I told him sincerely, waving him off. "Jocelyn's in the big cabin."

"Thanks." He was already moving away. "You're still coming to Pika Camp, right?"

I frowned a little. "Of course, why wouldn't I?"

"Smack 'n Splat's at 192."

"The what?"

"Smack 'n Splat. The number of bugs you squish in a single smack."

"Ah." I said, enlightened, "Well. I'm not afraid of a few bugs."

Jim grinned. "Good. Kelt'll be happy. He's been a total hose beast, you know." he explained.

Kelt had been talking with Michele, but he overheard Jim's remark—as he was, no doubt, intended to.

"*What?*" he exclaimed in mock anger. He pretended to charge Jim, but the younger man dodged the attack nimbly.

"See ya, Robyn!" Jim waved as he disappeared around the corner of the cabin.

"Cheeky bugger," Kelt called after him.

Kelt grinned at me but his smile faded as he returned his attention to Michele. They'd exchanged words while I'd been chatting with Jim. From the look on her face, she hadn't cared much for them.

"Can you give us a minute, Robyn?" Kelt asked. "I just need to sort a few things out here."

"Take your time," I told him. "I'll pack those boxes back up while I'm waiting."

"See you, Robyn." Michele's voice was soft, almost a caress.

"Uh, right. Later," I said ducking quickly into the tent, conscious that I was retreating. And quite okay with that.

The woman unsettled me.

# 10

I didn't see Michele or Jim again until dinner. And when we all met in the common cabin for the meal, there were more surprises waiting. Dwayne Hicks was comfortably ensconced between Jim and Michele on one of the blanket-covered couches. Ed Farrell was sprawled across the other.

"Yo, Robyn!" Dwayne called out. "Good to see you made it here all right."

"With your much-appreciated help," I said, smiling in greeting. "What are you doing in these parts?"

Dwayne grinned and smacked his lips. "Came for the grub. Jocelyn's the best cook on the Dempster. Man can't survive on cinnamon bun alone, y'know."

"Men are wimps," I teased. "That's all I ever ate in university."

Dwayne laughed.

"Hey, Ed," I said, turning towards him. "Good to see you too. I thought you'd be in Vancouver by now."

"Miracles of the electronic age," he explained

with an easy shrug. "We hammered things out in a conference call, so I figured, why waste the trip? Rather be out in the field. G'day Kelt, how's it going, mate?" Ed shifted over to make room for us on the couch. "Here, take a load off."

The place was full that night. There was a large group of well-fed blond men seated around one of the tables at the far end of the room. Curious, I turned for a moment and listened to their conversation. They were speaking German. I smiled to myself. So Jocelyn's much-anticipated entomologists had arrived—early, no less. They appeared to be a jolly bunch, laughing and, judging from the empties on their table, quaffing astonishing amounts of Yukon Gold beer with equal enthusiasm. The retreat already felt different. Warmer. Happier. I hoped they'd be staying for a good long while.

The remaining smaller tables were taken up by a raucous crowd of English-speaking strangers. A road maintenance crew, Dwayne told me when I asked, here to sample Jocelyn's famous cuisine. I noticed Terry sitting with them and, though he didn't appear to be taking part in their conversation, he showed no inclination to join our group. Jocelyn was bustling around the kitchen.

"Any word on . . . you know, Selena?" Ed asked Kelt in an undertone. "Didn't want to ask Jocelyn about it."

Dwayne leaned in closer.

Kelt frowned a little and shook his head. "Not much," he told them. "You heard they're still trying to find that tourist?"

Both Ed and Dwayne nodded solemnly.

"Well, that's all I know. The rest of his group said that he'd gone backcountry up by Inuvik."

"Cripes, he could be anywhere." Ed turned to Dwayne and pulled a face. "What do you think—"

"I don't know." Dwayne cut him off with a significant glance at the kitchen. "And I don't think we should talk about it here."

Ed's eyes slid over to where Jocelyn was working. He nodded once. "Too right, mate. Apologies."

The German entomologists burst out laughing, effectively drowning out anything else Ed might have said. By the time they quieted down enough, Kelt and Dwayne were deep in a conversation about Pika Camp.

"Back in a sec," I murmured.

I went over to the kitchen counter, almost tripping over Karma in the process.

"Hey, Jocelyn, you need a hand here?" I offered.

She looked over at me and smiled. "Thanks, Robyn, but it's all under control." Her eyes were bright.

I slid onto one of the stools. Karma jumped up beside me and started rubbing against my knee. "I see your bug guys arrived early," I said, stroking the cat.

Jocelyn nodded. "They called this afternoon to see if it was okay." She smiled again happily. "It's so nice to have a full house for dinner."

"What's on the menu?"

"Bison stroganoff, homemade focaccia bread, salad, broccoli with toasted almonds . . . coffee cake for dessert. Sound good?"

"Yummy." I watched her wrap a focaccia bread in foil and put it in the oven to warm.

Jocelyn straightened up and scanned the room. "You haven't seen Paul around, have you?"

I turned and looked around. "No, I don't think I've seen him since this morning."

She blew out a frustrated breath. "Honestly, that man! He's never around when I need him."

"What do you need?"

"He's supposed to be here to put the tables together. When there's a big crowd like this, I like to have one long table. It makes it easier to serve. He *knows* that."

"Jocelyn," I said. "Take a look around. What do you see?"

Her eyes swept the room. "A lot of tables that haven't been arranged."

"And?"

She frowned. "And . . . hungry guests?"

"Hungry *field scientists* and *construction guys.*"

"Oh." Her frown grew thoughtful. "You think they'll help?"

"Threaten them with a late dinner and you can count on it."

"Really?"

"Trust me."

A few minutes later, the dining room had been arranged to Jocelyn's specifications. The road crew even helped set the table, laying out navy placemats, matching napkins and hunter green candles. All in all, it was quite elegant. Kelt and I exchanged a grin as an older man, a tough-looking character with a face the color of cooked ham, instructed one of the younger men on the correct placement of salad forks with language that would singe the ears off Miss Manners.

Once the candles had been lit and the cutlery correctly arranged, the Germans settled at one end of the long table while our little group claimed the other. The road crew took up the spaces in between. Dwayne presided over our end, with Ed, Jim, and Michele on one side and Kelt, Terry, and myself on the other. There was still no sign of Paul.

Karma jumped up onto Terry's chair just as he was pulling it out. He put his hand down to nudge her off and she hissed and took a swipe at him. Four bloody lines appeared on his hand.

"Bad Karma!" I scolded. She jumped off the chair with a disdainful flick of her tail.

Terry sat down. He hadn't said a word, hadn't even made a sound.

"Are you okay?" I asked him, peering at the deep gashes.

He dropped his eyes and twisted his mouth into a smile. "I'm fine," he said in his soft voice.

I looked at him for a moment longer.

"Karma doesn't like me much," he mumbled with a shrug. He dabbed at his bleeding hand with a napkin and looked away. His face was pale.

He obviously didn't want to make a big deal of it. Fair enough. I settled for a sympathetic smile and dropped the subject.

I looked up when the door opened, expecting to see Paul. Frank Matas was standing there instead. He was dressed in civvies—jeans and a green corduroy shirt—but his ramrod posture still screamed *cop*. Either that or *tight ass*. Maybe both. Jocelyn, however, seemed happy enough to see him and she waved him over to the empty seat beside Michele. Lucky Michele. Not.

The seat was across from Terry's and as Frank sat down, I saw Terry start as if he'd been kicked.

"Oh. Sorry," Frank said, sounding anything but.

Terry dropped his eyes and muttered something.

That was the end of it, though I caught the faintly contemptuous curl of Matas' lip as he eyed Terry. Then Michele said something to him and he turned away. Terry kept his gaze on his cutlery.

Interesting.

"So Jim," I said, raising my voice over the general noise. "I have to ask you . . . what's up with marmots loving your pee?"

Jim flushed and grinned self-consciously.

"What's this?" Ed demanded. His eyes were bright above his tangled gray beard. "You blokes pissin' on the wildlife?"

"It's a new wildlife reality show," Kelt told him without cracking a smile. "Xtreme marmots."

Ed looked startled. "What kind of research camp are you running up there, mate?"

Kelt started to laugh.

"Don't listen to him!" Jim protested. "We're not peeing *on* the marmots, we have to use urine to bait the traps."

"Crikey! And they like it?"

"They *love* it," Jim told him. "It's gross, but they love

it. We tried everything else . . . carrots, apples, peanut butter, local vegetation. Nothing else did the trick."

"And how exactly did you discover this little gem of a scientific method?" I inquired.

Jim's eyes danced. "The latrine," he replied. "They're always hanging around. You go out in the morning and sit down and before you know it, everything under you is moving."

"Well, I guess that's one way to flush 'em out," I said. Unable to resist.

Groans and laughter followed this. Michele's high-pitched giggle rose above the general noise, but when I glanced over at her, I realized she and Frank hadn't been following our conversation. They were, instead, quite involved in one of their own. She was leaning toward him, gazing up soulfully into his eyes and flashing him the trembly lips. He didn't appear to mind.

That, too, was interesting (if somewhat icky). Obviously, Michele swung both ways, but her lack of taste (in this instance, at least) was appalling. I suppressed a shudder and turned my attention gratefully back to pee and marmots.

"Marmots are real characters," Jim was saying. "The subjuveniles form into gangs and if you put your coat or your camera down, they'll run off with it, if they get half a chance." He shook his head ruefully. "Second week out, I turned around to see my four-hundred-dollar digital camera bouncing across the tundra."

"Ouch," I said.

One of the road crew, a young sun-reddened kid sitting beside Ed, had been listening in on the conversation. "Doesn't it freak you out?" he asked. "Not the animals, I mean, just bein' out there by yourself in the middle of nowhere."

I saw Jocelyn stiffen.

"Uh, noooo." Jim shook his head. Clearly puzzled by the question. "It's actually kinda nice to get away from everything. Why would I be freaked out?"

I held my breath. The kid wouldn't be insensitive enough—clued-out enough—to be referring to the murder, would he?

"Not afraid that aliens are going to abduct you?" Another crew member asked, elbowing the young kid pointedly.

The kid flushed even redder and told him to piss off.

"'Cause, y'know, Karl here's a card-carryin' member of the Yukon Extraterrestrial Association. Claims aliens have been abducting him for years—"

"I have not," the kid retorted, rolling his eyes. "I just said it was *possible* people were getting' abducted. We don't know everything that happens. Not even the government knows."

Dwayne had perked up at the word *aliens*. "And these aliens are abducting us for what, exactly?" he asked.

"Sexual experiments," the kid replied without hesitation. "There're all kinds of stories about it. From all different countries an' everything. They put men and women together an' sometimes"—he lowered his voice—"they even do it with us themselves. More an' more stories are comin' out about that." He lowered his voice even further. "Y'know . . . *breedin'* experiments."

"Cripes, mate," Ed interjected. "You're not serious?"

The kid flushed again, but stubbornly held his own. "It's on all the Web sites," he insisted. "I've read about it. They wouldn't publish that stuff if it was bullshit. It's true, man." He bobbed his head up and down like a coot.

Ed's eyes had crinkled in amusement. "Hell's bells, if so many aliens want to do the naughty with us, then we've got to be the hottest species in the galaxy, mate. Reckon they're sittin' around with a tinnie right now saying, 'Gotta get me some of that Earth poontang.'"

The entire room dissolved into gales of laughter. The German entomologists guffawed, though I wasn't sure how much of the conversation they'd understood. Even Frank Matas was chuckling, though his smile disappeared when his beeper went off. He excused himself from the table and went outside.

Ed was still teasing the kid. "Best watch yer back out there, mate. Or maybe I should say your back*side*?"

Which led to more hilarity.

Michele was the only one who seemed wholly unimpressed. She sat at the table, arms folded tightly across her chest. Her quivery lips were tightly pursed. Her gaze as she looked around the room was unamused.

Maybe she didn't approve of foul language, I speculated. Or maybe she'd been abducted by aliens and didn't appreciate people joking about it.

She caught my eye and curled her lip in disgust. "It's just so heterosexual," she said.

Puzzled, I frowned. "Excuse me?"

"It's so heterosexual. Aliens abducting people and forcing them to have sex."

I was at a loss for words. "Um . . . "

"I just find it interesting that there aren't any stories about aliens conducting same-sex experiments."

"Um," I said again.

I was rescued by Dwayne.

"How would anybody know?" he asked Michele. "These aliens probably have what you might call different equipment. Some of those abductees could've been bonking same-sex aliens an' never had a clue."

Which led the conversation on a slightly different, and quite graphic, tangent.

As I sat and listened to Dwayne and the road crew argue about alien genitalia, I gave my head a mental shake. I had to admit, I'd never given any thought to the idea of alien abduction as being a primarily heterosexual phenomenon, but . . . what a weird thing to complain about.

"I think perhaps we've heard enough about aliens and sex!" Jocelyn finally suggested. "Maybe we can try to elevate the conversation over dessert?"

Dwayne was the first to take the hint, changing the subject to the film *Aliens*, which, though perhaps not exactly polite dessert conversation, at least had the advantage of never having explored the aliens' sexual proclivities.

The road crew was a little slower to settle down, but as Jocelyn brought out the coffee pots and cups, they buttoned up and busied themselves with the cream and sugar.

"Now, I hope nobody has a soy allergy," Jocelyn said, setting a platter of coffee cake down with a flourish. "I made this with soy milk."

"*Soy milk!*" Terry burst out.

We all stopped what we were doing and stared at him. I wouldn't have believed him capable of such a tone. Or volume.

"Ye-es?" Jocelyn dragged out the word, making it a question.

"Why did you use the soy milk?" he demanded, sounding even more agitated.

Annoyance flickered across Jocelyn's face. "Because we had it," she said crisply. "And it was going to expire and I don't believe in wasting food. Now, if you don't like it, don't eat it. Honestly, you can't taste the soy in something like this," she said to the rest of us. "Not with all the cinnamon and cloves."

Terry's face was flushed. "But," he stammered, "people . . . they might be allergic to it, you know. I've heard about that. It can really be serious."

"I know," Jocelyn said, a puzzled wrinkle appearing on her forehead. "That's why I asked."

"Well, no allergies here, mate," Ed said as he reached for the plate. The road crew was right behind him, followed closely by Kelt and me and the entomologists.

"Tasty," I told Jocelyn after the first mouthful.

"Mmmmf," Kelt agreed, his voice muffled by crumbs.

Jocelyn smiled her thanks and helped herself to a piece of cake. The entomologists were already on seconds.

Terry sat watching us, his dessert plate empty in front of him. His expression was unreadable. I wondered if he was always this picky about his food. His eyes met mine for a second and he pushed himself abruptly away from the table.

"I've got some things to do," he muttered. And with that he left the room. Almost, but not quite, slamming the door.

I gave Jocelyn a quizzical look, but she just pursed her lips and shrugged.

## May 6

Some tourists and several scientists arrived yesterday, including a geologist from Australia who is new this year. He's not an attractive man, but his accent sounds so much like home I almost kissed him. I never realized how much I missed Australia, until I heard that first crikey. He seems quite nice and, from the twinkle in his eye, I doubt he would have minded being kissed. For some reason, he smells like lavender—which is definitely NOT Australian! In my experience, Australian men are far too macho to be caught dead in such a scent. Sweat and old socks are more their fragrance of choice. I find it amusing and rather endearing that he is comfortable enough with his masculinity to spritz himself with lavender.

As for the others . . . the entomologists are looking for a rare moth and seem incapable of conversing about anything else. And the biologists have come to study pikas and marmots. They come every year. Still more climate change research. We're all fairly certain what the answers will be. After all, the climate's become unpredictable, the Arctic sea ice is thinner than ever before, and the permafrost is shifting north. But we have to play the game. Provide the facts—the science—that will say, yes, climate change is happening and here is the proof. Why do we always insist on this level of proof? Do we really think that industry and governments will listen if we give them hard facts? They haven't yet. But that is the illusion we all work with. The hope, I suppose. And so, the biologists will hike into the mountains and trap their animals and take their notes and write their papers. As will I. I, too, must play the game. Must maintain the illusion that it is climate change that drives me. At least their presence means a breath of fresh air for the retreat.

## May 7

An addendum to my entry regarding the team of biologists. One of the younger ones stands out a bit from the others. She's talented and intelligent and rather beautiful. And she is oh so bisexual. I think she must have come to this recently, given her eagerness to let everybody know her proclivities. She hasn't yet realized that most people don't appreciate comments on the "tyranny" of monogamy.

When she found out Willa and I were in a same-sex relationship, her eyes began to sparkle with the burning glow of sisterhood. She has managed to come up with excuses to visit our cabin several times in the last two days. Though Willa is far lovelier than I am, Michele seems quite taken with me. Always brushing against my arm or hip whenever possible. Liane was the same way at first (I must give off a strange pheromone or something). Willa understands. And really, Michele, like Liane, can be accused of nothing save being very young. Both Willa and I have been in the space she occupies. Still, I'll be glad when they leave to set up their field camp. Michele is not a problem, but she is a nuisance.

# 11

"It's hot!" I complained, dipping my toe in the water.

Kelt was already immersed to his neck. Rising steam bathed his reddening face. "It's supposed to be hot," he said. "You know, a *hot* tub?"

I sucked in a breath as I lowered myself into the tub. The steaming water lapped at my breasts. "Ow, ow, ow," I said.

"I thought you hobbits liked hot water."

I reached out with my foot and poked him with my toe. He grinned and ran his hand slowly up my leg.

"We like comfort," I corrected him, slapping his hand down. "Scalding water is *not* comfortable."

"I could try adding more creek water," Kelt offered. "Cool it down a bit. I think I saw the hose around here somewhere." He peered over the edge of the tub.

"Nah, that's okay. I'm getting used to it." My muscles were starting to loosen with the heat. I took a deep breath and leaned back, looking up at the dark trees around us.

Kelt and I had gone on a long stroll after dinner—

mostly to work off two helpings of Jocelyn's excellent stroganoff. By the time we'd come back for our turn in the hot tub, guests and staff had retired for the night. All the tents were dark, though a couple of the cabins still had lights on in them.

Despite the lateness of the hour, it was still fairly bright out. More like early twilight than midnight. The sun had slipped behind the mountains, embroidering the edges of the jagged peaks with amber thread. The retreat was in shadows. Silent and somehow mysterious in the low light. The "In Use" sign at the foot of the path guaranteed our privacy.

I breathed in the night-cooled air. "This is nice," I sighed.

Kelt propelled himself over beside me. "Very," he agreed.

He wasn't looking at trees.

He slid his arm around my bare shoulders. "Look who's all pink and glowing now," he said.

"It's because you're stewing me," I retorted, splashing him.

We tussled a bit in the hot water, poking each other and laughing.

"Ugh!" I said, standing up after a few minutes. "It's too hot for this."

I pulled myself up onto the edge of the tub to cool off. Steam curled up from my naked body, dissipating into the chilly night air. Kelt seemed to appreciate the sight.

"You asked for the water to be this hot on purpose," I accused, catching his ill-concealed leer.

He grinned at me. Unrepentant.

"Wanna play alien abduction?" he asked, wiggling his eyebrows.

I giggled and slid back into the tub. "Just keep your anal probe to yourself, my friend."

Kelt chuckled and began nibbling at my neck, tongue flicking out to lick the droplets of sweat from my skin. I felt a surge of heat. Too much heat. I was burning up. And then the thought fell on me like an anvil. Pregnant women weren't supposed to go in hot tubs.

*Shit.*

I pushed Kelt away and stood up, flushed from hot water, arousal and—now—alarm. I hadn't been in the tub for longer than about five minutes. How long was too long? What was supposed to happen if you stayed in too long?

Kelt was staring at me in hurt surprise.

"Ugh," I said again, knowing I had to give him a plausible reason for shoving him away. One that wouldn't lead to a much longer and far more difficult conversation. "It's . . . it's too hot for that too."

"But . . ."

With an effort, I shoved my worries to one side. I hadn't been in the hot water that long. No longer than a regular bath. I was just being paranoid.

Kelt still looked a little uncertain. I bent down and kissed him lightly, letting my tongue tickle his upper lip. "Come on, why don't we go back to the mothership?" I suggested. "We can always leave the sign up and come back afterwards."

*Or not.*

It worked. Kelt pulled himself out of the tub with alacrity.

"Race ya," he said with a grin.

Hand in hand, our towels clutched around us, we scampered past the cabins, our wet feet squelching in our hiking boots. Kelt slid on a bit of mud, inadvertently mooning the Cabin. I was still laughing when I ducked into the tent ahead of him.

"Last one in is the—" I stopped dead. Appalled.

Kelt bumped into my back. "Hey, warn a guy," he said, the words trailing off as he followed my gaze.

The interior of the tent was much as we'd left it before our post-dinner walk. My gear piled haphazardly to one side, Kelt's neatly stowed in the red milk crates. The blankets were rumpled and bunched up on the bed. But beside the small table, where the boxes of Selena Barry's notes had been, there was only a ghostly rectangular outline in the canvas.

"Oh, shit," Kelt said succinctly.

I couldn't have put it better myself.

## 12

I knocked on the camper's narrow door, feeling like I was marching myself to the scaffold. Strains from Berlioz' *Symphonie Fantastique* played in my head. I tried to ignore them. A pleasant-looking woman answered my knock.

"Can I help you?" she asked.

"Yes. My name's Robyn Devara," I began. "I know it's late, but I'm looking for Inspector Chesnut."

"You've found her." She swung the door open. "Come on in."

"Thanks." I stepped up into the camper.

The RCMP's camper van looked like every other RV I'd seen. A tiny sleeping nook at one end, an even tinier kitchen area in the center, and a fold-out table with cushioned benches at the other end. There was a bag of Oreo cookies and a half-empty cup of coffee on the table. An open book lay face down beside it. Some kind of whodunit, judging by the cover. I wondered if it was any good.

"Would you like a cup of coffee?" Inspector Chesnut asked, peering at me over stylish black-framed glasses.

"No, I'm okay," I told her, then wished I'd accepted her offer. I wasn't quite sure how to break my news. "Um . . . Inspector Chesnut," I began.

She held up her hand. "Please, call me Gaylene."

I smiled my thanks. "Gaylene, I'm . . . uh, afraid I have some bad news. It looks like somebody's lifted Selena Barry's notes."

"What are you talking about?" Her tone had sharpened.

I tried not to wince. "Constable Matas brought the notes to our tent yesterday evening. I didn't have time for more than a quick look at them. I'd intended to have a longer look tomorrow. But when we went back to the tent this evening, they were gone. All the boxes, I mean."

Gaylene's expression grew darker with each word.

"Let me get something straight," she said, forming the words with icy precision. "Constable Matas brought those notes to you and then *he left them with you*?"

"Um . . . yes."

"He left them. In an unsecured tent?" Incredulity was making her voice rise.

I squirmed. "Well, technically, *I* left them in an unsecured tent, but he didn't, uh, say I shouldn't."

With a visible effort, Gaylene got herself under control. It was clear she was furious.

"Tell me," she demanded.

So I told her about Matas bringing me the notes. About signing for them and taking a quick look at them.

Then I told her about going back to the tent after our bath and finding the boxes missing.

"Was anything else taken?"

I shook my head. "I don't think so. I mean, we haven't gone through every piece of our gear or anything, but it doesn't look like anything else is missing."

"Who knew you had the notes in your tent?"

"Well, Kelt, of course." I paused trying to recall if I'd mentioned it to anybody else. "Um . . . I think maybe Michele and Jim from Pika Camp might have known. In fact, I remember mentioning it in front of them—in front of Michele, for sure. I can't remember if Jim was still there."

Gaylene was jotting notes in a small book. She was pressing down very hard with the pen. "Anyone else?"

I thought for a while longer, then threw up my hands. "I don't know," I told her honestly. "Kelt and I ate dinner with everybody this evening. All the retreat staff, the road crew, the entomologists, Dwayne and Ed. Selena was mentioned, but I can't remember if I said anything about her stuff being in my tent. I'm pretty sure I didn't. And we didn't talk about her for long. I mean, I don't think anybody really wants to talk about it anymore. Because of Jocelyn, you know? I don't think I said anything about boxes in the tent." I shut my mouth, aware I was babbling.

"I see." Gaylene scribbled a few more words. She did not look happy. "Have Dwayne and the others gone yet?"

"I think so—at least I saw the road crew leave right after dinner. I don't know if Dwayne was staying the night. He and Kelt needed to talk about some work stuff so he might have crashed here."

Gaylene pursed her lips tightly. Outside, I could hear a vehicle pull into the little parking lot.

"I'm sorry," I ventured. "I didn't know—"

"How could you?" Gaylene cut me off. She took a deep breath and gave me a tight smile. "Robyn, I'm not angry with you," she assured me. "Proper protocol wasn't followed. But that's hardly your fault."

"I still feel bad."

"Don't," she advised crisply.

A loud knock on the door startled me.

"Come in," Gaylene called.

The door opened and Constable Matas peered in.

"Frank," Gaylene greeted him in a decidedly frosty tone.

Matas's eyes darted from me to Gaylene. "What's going on?" he drawled, squeezing his broad shoulders past the narrow doorframe. "Is there a problem?"

He stepped up into the camper, towering over Gaylene, clearly enjoying the advantage of his height. Unfazed, she glared up at him, doing a mighty fine impression of a basilisk.

"Frank, Selena Barry's notes have been stolen," she said quietly.

Matas stared at her for a second. Then his eyes slid away. Suddenly, he didn't seem quite so imposing. A tic in his jaw started twitching.

Gaylene pushed herself to her feet, forcing Matas to squeeze against the tiny counter. "Thanks for reporting this so promptly," she said to me with a smile that still managed to look pissed off (though not, thank the gods, with me). "I'll let you know if we need anything else. Right now, *Constable* Matas and I have a search to conduct."

I couldn't help noticing the emphasis she put on his rank. From the look on his face, Matas had noticed too. Eager to leave the heavy atmosphere, I jumped up and bolted as politely as possible.

"How could you be such a bloody idiot?" Gaylene didn't even wait for the door to finish closing.

Frank Matas was going to get his ass reamed out.

"Are you a cadet? You *knew* it wasn't proper protocol to let those papers out of a secure place. What did you think you were doing?"

The door snicked closed, but I could still hear Gaylene's voice. Berating her junior with crisp, well-chosen phrases.

Matas, I reflected, was not going to like that much.

"How'd it go?" Kelt asked as I stepped back into the tent.

"It was okay for me," I told him. "Not so much for your buddy Frank. Inspector Chesnut was pretty pissed off that he'd left the boxes here. Improper protocol and all that."

Kelt wrinkled his nose. "Hmm. I never thought of that."

"Me either."

"There is a bit of good news, though."

I raised one eyebrow in inquiry.

"I found this in the blankets." He produced a scrap of yellow paper. "It's not mine."

Puzzled, I took it and examined it, squinting in the

dim light. It was the tattered cover from a yellow Rite in the Rain field notebook. Neatly inscribed columns of codes covered the reverse face.

"This is Selena's reference card," I told Kelt. "Look, these are frequencies and I'm pretty sure this column here is band numbers. Huh, I must have missed it when I put everything back in the boxes."

Absently, I bounced it on the palm of my hand. "I'm not sure how much good it'll do me though. I don't know where her study site was."

Kelt leaned back against the pillows. "Two valleys east of Pika Camp and one south."

I blinked and turned to look at him.

"At least, I'm pretty sure she was south of us. She sometimes stopped by Pika Camp on her way to or from her study site," he said. "I couldn't tell you exactly where she was working, but if you hike along the ridges, you could probably pick up those signals."

"Really." I mulled that over. "You know, if I could find some of her birds, maybe I could get an idea of what she was looking for." I started pacing. "I mean, if she'd only collared the hens, then she would've been looking at breeding patterns, which sort of makes sense for a climate change study. Although, if she was looking at winter survival rates, she'd have been collaring the males too. But then why collect those samples? If only I'd had a chance to look in the last box, then maybe . . ."

I stopped, catching Kelt's rueful grimace.

"I knew you'd do this," he said.

I opened my mouth, prepared to argue with him. Then I realized there was nothing accusatory in his tone.

"It's okay," he said. "Find out what she was studying. I know you won't give it a rest until you do."

"It might be relevant to the investigation," I began.

"I know."

"At least it'll help them figure out who she was."

"I know."

"And maybe she *did* find something strange and that's why her notes were lifted."

"I know."

I stopped pacing and gave him a long look. He seemed uncharacteristically accommodating.

"You're one of the few people who can fill in those blanks," he told me. "I accept that—I don't have much choice. And I agree with you. The simple fact that somebody stole her field notes . . . well, maybe there *was* something in them. Something that might shed some light on . . . things."

"I thought you didn't want me to get involved."

His black brows snapped together. "I don't! It scares the shit out of me!"

Something about his concern totally disarmed me. He really did care. Even though we'd been arguing since I got here, even though we seemed on completely different wavelengths at times, he really did care about me. With that realization, the universe seemed to unfold. It was time. Time to finally share my worries. Time to tell him we might be parents. I took a breath and opened my mouth, the words ready to leap off my tongue.

"But don't forget," he continued softly. Oblivious to both my epiphany and its accompanying agenda. "*I* found her."

Her. Selena Barry.

I felt the universe cough and fold up again. I closed my mouth and sank down beside him on the bed.

"I still see her, you know. Every time I shut my eyes."

I knew. I'd slept beside him for the last two nights.

I reached out and covered his hand with mine. "I'm sorry."

"I want to see this solved just as much as the next guy," he said after a moment. "And if you can help out … hell, who am I to get in the way?"

I leaned over and kissed him on the cheek.

Kelt shook himself and gave me a lopsided smile. "Look, we can grab a few hours' sleep and leave early. We'll be at Pika Camp by noon. Give me a day or two at camp and then, depending on what's happening there, I can take you to Selena's study site—or at least where I think her study site is."

"That'd be great."

"But if the weather's decent and things are heating up with the pikas, I may not be able to leave. Jim thinks we may be starting crunch time early—and he's got pretty good instincts."

"Fair enough. Can you point me in the direction of the site if that's the case?"

"I'll even lend you some radio equipment."

"Thanks, Kelt," I told him. "I'd like to get this figured out as quickly as possible."

"We'll leave for camp by 7:00," Kelt promised.

Rashly, as it turned out.

It was a good plan. Just bad timing. That night, Selena Barry's cabin burned to the ground.

# 13

I wasn't sure what woke me up.

I was sitting upright in bed. I could hear voices outside. Panicky-sounding voices.

"Wha—?" Kelt mumbled.

Then I heard an odd, low sort of growl. I flung off the covers. Kelt was still struggling out of sleep.

"Something's going on," I told him, pulling on my clothes. "I'm going to go check it out."

That woke him up pretty fast.

"Robyn! Wait!" He thrashed around in the blankets.

"Hurry up," I said over my shoulder. I was already fumbling with the doorknob. I had it open before Kelt managed to get out of bed.

Cautiously, I peered out into the clearing.

I had no idea what time it was. It was light out, of course, but it felt like the middle of the night. The shouts were coming from the far side of the retreat. I took a step outside and a waft of air blew the smell of smoke into my face.

*Oh shit.*

Quickly, I poked my head back inside the tent. "I think there's a fire," I told Kelt grimly. "A big one."

He yanked on his pants, grabbed a T-shirt, and rammed his feet into runners. Together, we ran towards the sounds. I could see the rosy glow of flames through the trees. The low growl set the air vibrating, punctuated by sharp, cracking retorts.

Selena Barry's cabin was essentially gone by the time we burst into the clearing. Half-clothed figures—including a pajama-clad Inspector Chesnut—had lined up in an impromptu bucket brigade. It was a sobering moment for me. We were out of the 9-1-1 emergency area. There would be no fire trucks screaming to the rescue. No paramedics in ambulances ready to help in case someone was injured. We were on our own out here. *This* was real life in the Yukon.

Kelt and I rushed to join the others. Ed and Jim were close on our heels. Ed was wearing only hiking boots, a lumberjack shirt, and a pair of boxers covered with neon green happy faces. I didn't have time to laugh.

"Forget about the cabin!" Dwayne was shouting instructions. "Soak the ground! Try to keep it from spreading!"

For those first, adrenaline-pumped minutes, I didn't even have time to think. Grab the bucket, turn, pass it to Kelt. Grab the empty one, pass it back to Ed.

We worked like a well-oiled machine. As if we'd been doing this all our lives.

Grab. Turn. Pass.

In the flame-heated air, we saturated the ground with creek water.

Grab. Turn. Pass.

Peripherally, I was aware of the German entomologists forming a second line on the other side of the fire.

Grab. Turn. Pass.

We were at it for twenty, or thirty, or forty minutes. It was impossible to gauge time. Sweat ran freely down my face and my shoulders began to throb and ache. But we seemed to be getting things under control—either that or there simply wasn't anything left to burn. Regardless, the fire wasn't spreading.

As if we all realized this at the same time, the pace slowed. I scrubbed an arm across my face and glanced around, surprised at how little was left of the cabin. I knew it had been an old building, but how long had it been burning before somebody had noticed? It was then that I noticed the two figures standing off to one side.

Jocelyn and Willa stood side by side, facing the dying fire. They weren't part of the bucket brigade. In some ways, they didn't even seem to be part of this reality.

Until that moment, I'd forgotten that there was someone else—someone still alive—who had called the old cabin home. As the last remnants of her house collapsed in on themselves, Willa watched, her head lolling slightly to one side. An expression of utter indifference had settled on her face. Jocelyn stood beside her, arms folded impassively across her chest. It could have been a trick of the lighting, but it seemed like there was a faint smile hovering around her lips.

Not surprisingly, our departure for Pika Camp was delayed the following morning. It was a cool, gray day. The clouds were low and claustrophobic and intermittent drizzle kept the air unpleasantly damp. The smoky smell of scorched wood hung over the retreat, trapped there by the heavy clouds. I could even smell it in the RCMP camper van-turned-office.

"Have a seat, Robyn," Gaylene said as I stepped through the door. She was sitting at the small table, dark circles under her eyes the only sign of the disturbed night. File folders and other papers were stacked neatly to one side.

"Thanks."

I slid onto the bench seat across from her, refusing the cup of coffee she offered me. Everything tasted like smoke this morning.

The questions she asked were routine. Had I heard or seen anything out of the ordinary last night? When did I realize there was a fire? What had I been doing between 1:00 and 2:00 a.m.?

After she ran through all the questions and I gave all the appropriate answers, Gaylene fell silent for a moment. She was tapping her pen against the table. The rapid *tick tick tick* was the only sound in the van.

"We haven't found Selena's notes, you know," she said, watching me closely. "But then, we didn't look for them in the old cabin."

I opened my mouth. Closed it. That particular possibility hadn't occurred to me.

"There's nothing left of the place," she continued. "If the papers were in there, they're gone now."

She paused and I waited.

"We're left without a clue about what Selena was studying. And, after the theft—and probable destruction—of her notes, I'm left with a distinct impression that I really need to know what she was doing up there."

"I could try to help you with that," I offered. "I had a look at her notes. A brief, superficial look, but still . . . "

Gaylene smiled at me. A genuine, friendly sort of smile that brightened her tired eyes. "I was hoping you'd say that."

"I'm not sure how much help I'll be," I warned. "I've only got a vague idea of what she was doing. I didn't even get to the last box."

"You might want to try talking to Willa," Gaylene suggested. "Maybe she has some insights into what Selena was looking for."

"I'll try," I said. Unenthusiastic. I still remembered my last encounter with Selena's partner.

"Try hard," Gaylene advised, her friendly manner suddenly coolly official.

I closed my mouth.

Gaylene put down the pen and sighed. "Look, we still have no idea why Selena was killed," she told me. "The MO doesn't suggest a random killing. Given how remote this place is, that was never much of a possibility anyway. "

"I thought you guys were looking for a tourist. Some hiker that was staying here."

"We'd like to talk to him," Gaylene agreed, poker face giving nothing away, her tone not quite doing the same.

I got the impression Inspector Chesnut didn't think much of the hiker-as-killer theory. I considered the alternatives and decided I didn't like them at all.

"Selena had only been in the Yukon for a few years, but she was well-liked in the community. Or perhaps I should say she never got anybody's back up. Which is quite a feat for an environmentalist in a mining-friendly town like Dawson City." Gaylene leaned forward. "Selena was in a happy relationship. She was quiet. From what I gather, she left others to follow their own path." She leaned back again with a sigh. "And that leaves me with very little to go on. I'm left with examining every single detail that strikes me as strange. And, Robyn, I have to say, apart from the smeared blood on the wall, as horrific as that was, Selena leaving you her work . . . "

"Was strange," I finished for her.

Gaylene nodded. "Firstly, you never met her before and yet she leaves you her field notes. Secondly, you take possession of these papers and, almost immediately, they're stolen. I might have been able to write the first off as a meaningless oddity. Meaningless in terms of our investigation, that is. One of those strange occurrences that life tosses up every now and again. But," she paused and gave me a long look. "Now we have two strange things—three, if you count the fire."

"You think she was killed because of her work?" It was the same question I'd asked Dwayne so skeptically the other day. Now it didn't seem quite so unbelievable.

Gaylene sat back and shrugged. "I don't know. But I need you to help me find out. I'm not a biologist. Neither is Frank. And you're the only one who had a good look at her papers."

"I had a *brief* look at them," I corrected her. "But everything appeared to be fairly normal. I mean, there didn't seem to be anything strange. At least . . . well, there were some samples."

"Samples?"

"Feathers and toenails."

"Why is that strange? I thought biologists were always collecting bits of things."

"We are. We do. When it's necessary for your study." I paused, frowning. "I just don't know why Selena would've collected them. She was studying climate change. You don't need samples like that for a climate change study. It doesn't make sense."

"Well, then we're back at square one," Gaylene said. "Unless Willa can help. Obviously, we've already interviewed her, but you're the scientist. Would you talk to her? You'll probably ask questions we couldn't even think of. At this point, anything you can find out would be helpful."

"I'll speak to her," I promised. "I could also visit Selena's study site. I talked to Kelt about it last night. Apparently it's not too far from Pika Camp. He says I could probably hike it in a day."

"Thanks," Gaylene told me, her smile reinforcing the words. "But do me a favor? Be careful out there. I don't want any more trouble."

"I will," I promised, thinking uncomfortably about what the missing hiker might have done and where he might be now.

"Here." Gaylene held out a business card. "I know you've just got a radio at the camp, but there's a satellite phone here. If I'm not here, call me when you know something." She started straightening the papers on her desk. A clear dismissal.

I nodded and stuffed the card in my coat pocket. "Um, there's one other thing," I said.

She paused and looked at me over the rim of her glasses.

"Whoever stole the notes missed something."

Gaylene's gaze sharpened. "They missed something? Why did you wait so long to tell me this?" she demanded. The cool RCMP inspector was back again.

"Because it's not much," I hastened to explain. I fumbled in my pocket for the folded yellow card. "It's just a list of frequencies. It was one of the first things I found. I just set it to one side and I guess it got lost on the bed when I put everything back. Kelt found it in the blankets last night."

Gaylene took the card and examined the neat rows of numbers carefully.

"Frequencies for what?" she asked, a little friendlier now.

"Radio tags," I replied. "Selena was tracking the birds. See, this column has all the band numbers for each bird and these other numbers are the frequencies for each collar."

Gaylene stared at the card for a few more seconds then handed it back to me. "What do you think you'll find out from this?"

"Apart from where the birds are?" I shrugged. "I don't know. That's why I didn't come to you last night with it. All I can do is try to find her site and have a look around. Pika Camp's got a radio and antenna I can borrow. I figure I can get there in the next couple of days."

"Fine," Gaylene agreed. "Let me know if you find anything strange—even if it doesn't seem to be relevant."

"I will," I promised.

# 14

So now I had the go-ahead from the RCMP as well as from Kelt. I *had* been looking forward to spending time with Kelt. To learning first-hand about pikas and marmots and alpine ecosystems. But the pikas, it appeared, were going to have to wait. I was on a mission for ptarmigan.

I kept my promise to Gaylene and tried to talk to Willa. I'd found her sitting on the steps in front of the Moose cabin, staring off into the distance.

It was a nice enough view. The creek burbling in the foreground, mountains rising up into the clouds beyond. But Willa's eyes weren't focused on the scenery and she seemed somehow removed. Like she wasn't quite part of the functioning world. I wondered if she was taking sedatives.

Medicated or not, she couldn't—or wouldn't—tell me much about Selena's work, except that she'd done too much of it.

"Driven. Obsessed." The words were clipped, the shrug that accompanied them was bitter. "Whatever you want to call it. The last few months, she *lived* for those damn birds."

"What was so important about them?" I asked quietly.

Willa lifted her shoulders again. Indifferent. "Search me. It's not like the climate's changing *that* quickly. To listen to Selena, you'd think they were going to go extinct overnight." Her voice sounded thin and reedy now. Stretched. "Drab little brown things. I never understood why she came halfway around the world to study them."

"Halfway around the world?"

Willa gazed into the distance, her odd, metallic eyes reflecting the grayness of the day. I waited several heartbeats. Willa continued to stare at nothing. I was beginning to feel like I was having a conversation with someone from another dimension.

"What?" she asked finally, bringing her attention back to me.

I'd almost forgotten my question.

"Uh, where did Selena come from?"

"Australia."

"And she came here for ptarmigan?" It *did* seem a long way to travel.

"Well, she sure didn't come here for me," Willa snapped.

I closed my mouth.

Realizing she'd been rude, Willa relented a bit. "She came to Canada to study ptarmigan in an alpine environment," she explained. "She always talked about them being indicators of climate change. Like canaries in the mines or some damn thing."

"That makes sense," I ventured when Willa fell silent again. "I mean, they're living on the edge up here. Any change in their environment is bound to have a noticeable impact."

But Willa wasn't listening. "She always said it was a bonus to find me here too," she said pensively. "Her soulmate." She barked a laugh that had little to do with amusement. "You know, I found a love poem to her. A *love poem*, for chrissake! I've never written a poem in my life. So much for *soulmates*." The word was pure acid in her mouth.

"Um, why wasn't she associated with any universities?" I asked, trying to steer the conversation back to less personal topics. "I mean . . . well, it just seems a bit odd. Where was she getting her funding?"

Willa shrugged. It seemed to be a popular gesture with her. "She had some kind of falling out with one of the universities. It totally turned her off academia."

"But where did she get her money from?" I pressed.

Willa went back to staring out the window. "I don't know," she sighed. Her voice had gone soft and whispery again. "Some environmental organization. She had money from her divorce too."

Divorce?

I hadn't realized that Selena had been married. I was curious, but I knew enough not to touch it. Certainly not with Willa, anyhow.

Willa was not what I'd describe as forthcoming

when it came to Selena's work, but what I had first taken for obstructionism was now beginning to appear as simple ignorance. It seemed she really hadn't known much about the professional aspect of her partner. I had, I suspected, gotten all I was going to get from her.

But just as I rose and started to say goodby, Willa suddenly snapped back to the here and now.

"Look, I'm sorry about the other day," she said, her voice gaining strength and clarity. "In the Cabin."

"Oh. Um . . . don't worry about it," I told her. "You were under a lot of stress."

She shook her head vigorously, blond hair fanning out. "That's no excuse. I jumped all over you and I feel bad. You were . . . very nice about it."

"It's okay," told her sincerely. "Really."

She leapt to her feet, startling me.

"Hang on a minute," she said. "I've got something I'd like you to have."

"That's not necessary," I protested.

But she wasn't paying attention. She'd flung open the door of the cabin and disappeared into the darkness inside. I stood on the step and fidgeted. I didn't want anything from Willa.

When she came out, she had a book tucked under her arm. It was one of those large coffee-table tomes. At least a couple of inches thick. The glossy dust jacket was a photograph of a raven against a purply-blue sky. I glanced at the title. *Birds of the Yukon Territory*. It was a lovely book. It looked expensive.

"This was Selena's," Willa said as she tried to pass it to me. "She left it in the truck, so it didn't burn in the fire. I want you to have it."

I shoved my hands in my pockets and shook my head. Troubled. "I can't accept this. Honestly, there are no hard feelings here."

"Please." Mercury eyes pleaded with me. "I don't want it. I don't even want to *look* at it. It's all about the birds up here. Their biology and life history and . . . I don't know, that kind of thing. You're a bird person. What else am I going to do with it? I gave it to her last Christmas. It cost a small fortune, I'd rather not throw it out, but"—she paused and her face spasmed—"I don't even want to look at it," she repeated.

She seemed so desperate. Reluctantly my hands came out of my pockets and reached out to accept her gift. "I don't think I—" I began.

"I want you to have it."

"If you change your mind—"

"I won't." Willa shook her head decisively and put her hands behind her back, making it impossible for me to give it back.

"Thank you," I said, not really meaning it.

I turned and made my way slowly back to the tent I shared with Kelt. The book felt like it weighed a thousand pounds.

# 15

It was after midday by the time we waded across Willow Creek and headed west into the mountains. It wasn't, I mused sloshing through the icy water, exactly the trip I'd been anticipating.

I'd forgotten to check my e-mail before we left and the prospect of being unplugged for several weeks was making me cranky. I am not, however, obsessed. In fact, there were any number of things that could be contributing to my foul mood. For one thing, we'd ended up leaving much later in the day than we'd planned (so no stopping to gawk at the scenery if we wanted to make it to Pika Camp by dinner). For another thing, I was having serious second thoughts about Willa's "gift" (I'd left the book back in the tent, but part of me was hoping it would disappear just as mysteriously as Selena's notebooks had). And lastly, most importantly, I still hadn't told Kelt I might be pregnant.

The longer I waited, the harder it was getting to tell him. On one hand I felt like I was going to explode if I didn't say something soon. On the other hand, the longer

I waited, the scarier the whole prospect seemed. I just couldn't predict his reaction—I couldn't even guess at it. And now, just when I'd counted on having the time for a lengthy, personal-type discussion, I found that Kelt and I were not hiking alone.

After what had happened the night before, it didn't surprise me that everybody who could leave Willow Creek did. The ship wasn't sinking, but the rodents knew a bad bet when they saw it. Not that I blamed them.

Dwayne had been one of the first to desert that morning, just after the German entomologists who had quietly packed up all their gear and headed out a full two days early. I think Jim and Michele wanted to come back to Pika Camp with us, but Kelt had taken one look at Jocelyn's face and pulled them aside.

"Look, you're pretty tired," he said to them. "We've been working like dogs for a couple of months now. Trust me. You need this break. Just hole up in your tents for a few days. Read trashy novels. Go into Dawson for some fish and chips at Sourdough Joe's. Stay out of everybody's way and you'll be fine. We're heading into pika crunch time. I'm gonna need you rested, okay?"

Neither Jim nor Michele was terribly happy, but when we left the retreat later that afternoon, they weren't with us. Ed, however, was.

"Mind if I join you for a spell?" he'd asked as we were stuffing the last supplies in our backpacks.

"I didn't know you were prospecting out our way," Kelt said in some surprise.

"Not exactly your way," Ed told him. "You're more *on* the way, if you know what I mean."

"On the way to the Lost Valley of Blue Beryls?" I asked.

"Too right, mate." Ed grinned toothily and wiggled his eyebrows. "Actually, there's a nice-looking water-course I've a mind to follow. I can hook up with it half-way to Pika Camp."

Personally I'd much rather have had Kelt to myself for a while (privacy in a field camp being in short sup-ply), and I had half-thought to use the hike to ease into the topic of children. But Kelt agreed to Ed's request with such a ready smile that I couldn't very well refuse it without seeming snuffy. The universe, I reflected sourly, appeared to be taking its own sweet time to unfold.

I was more than a little miffed but my nose didn't stay out of joint for very long. Not when I was hiking through country like this. Willow Creek flowed north of the Blackstone Uplands, still within the Ogilvie Mountain range, but skirting an area known as Beringia. There was lots of vegetation in the lower valleys here. Black spruce, muskeg, and tussock tundra, mostly. Quaking aspen and white spruce bordered the creeks and rivers. There was permafrost up here too, underlying the entire region. The poor drainage and harsh conditions caused trees to tilt or topple drunkenly. The so-called Drunken Forest was further south off the Klondike Highway, but up here in Beringia, all the trees looked like they were three leaves to the wind.

Tussock tundra proved a bit of a bugger to walk on. Sort of like hiking on a giant trampoline.

"Mossercize," I remarked to Kelt with a crooked grin as I sank up to my calves in sproingy plants.

I felt a little guilty tromping on the stuff. Knowing I was crushing plants that, despite their small stature, might be a hundred years old. But then I noticed how quickly they sprang back. Returning to their former position with a jaunty bounce. Concealing all traces of my footprints. A single person walking across the tundra wasn't a problem, but I suspected the bounce-back effect would weaken in direct proportion to the number of curious footsteps. All of a sudden, I was glad that Willow Creek—and, indeed, much of the Yukon—was so inaccessible by southern standards.

Higher up, the slopes of the Ogilvie Mountains were bare of anything except the greenish-gray mosses and lichens that, according to Kelt, feed vast herds of caribou in the winter. The colors up here were so very northern, all pearly blues and grays and lavenders, delicately gilded with gold and silver. One would never mistake this for a southern climate. And yet, despite the muted palette, the landscape somehow possessed an extraordinary clarity.

Because the high mountains on the Pacific coast block any moist air that might blow into the region, Beringia had never been glaciated during the last Ice Age. It had simply been too dry. As a result, it had been a refuge for many endemic and rare species, some of which had survived, others of which had not. The land I was traveling across had felt the footsteps of giant elk and heard the trumpetings of wooly mammoth.

I felt my spirits lifting with each step away from the smoke-saturated retreat (even Ed's lavender-scented self had smelled slightly charred that morning). I breathed deeply from the diaphragm. The universe will unfold as it should, I chanted softly to myself. The wind was up and the air was sharp, cool and clean in my lungs. Already I was in danger of losing my soul to this place.

"Odd business last night," Ed said into the silence. "Wonder who torched the place."

So much for soaring spirits.

Kelt swung around to stare at him. "Torched?"

"'Course," Ed nodded. "Cripes, she went up like a firecracker. I'm no expert, but I'm no mug, either. I reckon that wasn't an accident, mate. Fair dinkum."

"You don't think Jocelyn—" I blurted out thoughtlessly, then stopped.

Both Kelt and Ed turned to look at me. Surprised.

I colored under their gaze.

"I don't think Jocelyn what?" Ed asked.

I tried to wave it off. "Nothing. It was nothing."

They kept looking at me.

"It was just . . . it was what she said to us yesterday," I said to Kelt. "When she was showing us around."

Kelt's eyebrows drew together in a thick black line. Like my brother, he was pretty good at the unibrow thing. And probably for similar reasons.

Ed's eyes were bright with interest. "I wasn't there, mate," he reminded me.

"She said something about wishing the place would burn to the ground. The old cabin, I mean," I explained reluctantly. Wishing now I'd kept my mouth shut. This smacked of gossip and I knew all too well how Kelt felt about loose tongues. "She didn't think Willa—or anybody else—would be able to go back there."

Ed stroked his tangled beard. "I'd say that's a good point."

"Of *course* it's a good point," Kelt interrupted, his frown deepening. "Who would *want* to go back there after something like that? But it doesn't mean she took a match to the place."

Ed and I were silent.

"That retreat is her life," Kelt said after a moment. "And if Dwayne hadn't woken up and seen the fire, who knows how much of it might have burned. Shit, the whole place could have gone up. People could have been hurt. Or killed! Come on, I can't see Jocelyn doing that."

Ed dropped his eyes to avoid Kelt's glare.

"Can you?" Kelt insisted.

"No. No, 'course not, mate." Ed shook his head. But he did it very slowly.

After Ed left us in search of his beryls, I caught hell for even suggesting such a thing. Anticipation didn't make the lecture any easier to take.

"How could you, Robyn?" Kelt rapped out as soon as Ed was out of earshot.

At least I hoped he was out of earshot. Somehow Kelt managed to sound angry and disappointed and disgusted all at once.

"I didn't mean anything by it," I snapped back, my hackles raised by his tone.

"That's not what it sounded like to me. Or to Ed! Did you see the look on his face? He's already convinced Jocelyn did it."

"You're reading too much into it," I told him, trying to quash my own feelings of guilt. "Ed was just surprised. And I wasn't gossiping!"

"I didn't say you were."

I made a rude noise. "Even you have to admit, it's a

bit of a coincidence," I said, trying to maintain a reasonable tone. "Jocelyn wishes the old cabin would burn and, *pfffft*, there it goes the very same night."

"That doesn't mean you should have said anything about it. Shit, we don't even know for sure it was arson."

"Hell of a coincidence if it wasn't."

Kelt snapped his mouth shut and started walking again.

"I just don't think you should have said anything," he muttered. "At least not to Ed. You could have waited until we were alone."

"It slipped out," I told his rigid back. "I mean, the arson thing sounds plausible now, but I hadn't really thought it through until Ed mentioned it. I didn't *mean* to say anything about Jocelyn."

Kelt heaved a sigh. His shoulders came down a fraction. "I know," he said. "I just hope nothing comes of it."

"What's going to come of it?" I argued. Knowing I should just let it go. "So Jocelyn said she wished the place would burn to the ground. So what? Gods, I've said things like that myself over the years. Hell, last year I was wishing that stupid Drumheller report would fry to a crisp."

One side of Kelt's mouth twitched up in a half smile. "I remember."

"There you go," I said with a flourish. "People say stuff like that all the time. I could kill so and so. I'd like to torch the place. It doesn't mean that they'd do it—or that anybody would think they were serious about it."

His smile had died before it was born. "I still don't think you should have given anybody any ideas," Kelt said repressively before turning to continue up the path.

I was really starting to get annoyed now.

"It wasn't like I stood up at a town meeting," I retorted hotly. "Now there are three of us who know what she said. Four, if you count Jocelyn. Big whoop. *I'm* not going to say anything. *You're* not going to say anything. *Jocelyn's* not going to say anything. And I highly doubt whether Ed's the type to gossip around the water cooler."

"Let's hope not," Kelt said over his shoulder. His tone indicated the conversation was over.

I thought he was being unfair (the words *sanctimonious jerk* were leaping to mind). I really hadn't said anything intentionally, but I knew that was as much of a concession as I was likely to get. I heaved a quiet sigh into the chilly wind.

No, this definitely was not the trip I had been anticipating.

**16**

We didn't see a pika until we were hiking up the final valley before the field camp. Too bad. It might have helped to improve Kelt's mood. I know it would've improved the hike, which had involved far too many uncomfortable silences to be entirely enjoyable. Needless to say, the subject of children did not come up.

But Kelt seemed to lighten once we'd spotted the pika, and his shoulders visibly relaxed once we'd reached the camp. As we shucked our backpacks, he offered me the first genuine smile I'd seen all afternoon.

"Welcome to Pika Camp, Robyn," he said, dropping a quick kiss on my lips.

I would have preferred a somewhat longer snog. One of those I'm-sorry-I-was-mad-at-you-honey kinds of kisses. Or even an it-was-all-my-fault-please-forgive-me sort of smooch. Or (even better) an I-love-you-forever-I-want-to-make-babies-with-you peck. But Kelt seemed more interested in showing off his field camp. So I followed him around, snogless, and made the appropriate noises.

Pika Camp was your basic alpine field camp. Colorful dome-shaped tents hunkered down in a dry creek bed for protection from the wind. The project was well funded, so the camp also boasted three white Weatherhaven shelters, which served as storage, dining hall, and lab, respectively (though the lab had clearly overflowed into the dining tent—at least, I hoped the evil-smelling buckets were a lab experiment and not dinner).

The tents had all been set up on plywood platforms to protect the tundra. And the entire camp was encircled by a thin electrified wire to protect the inhabitants from bears.

"Where do you get the power from?" I asked Kelt.

He gestured toward one of the Weatherhavens. "There's a solar panel and a wind generator just behind the lab. The panel's a bit on the finicky side, but we get enough to power the fence and charge the walkie-talkies. First rule of Pika Camp. Always take a walkie-talkie with you when you're going out."

"How far away are we from the study sites?"

"Not that far," Kelt told me. "We're smack in the middle of the valley, so we're no more than fifteen or twenty minutes away from most of the sites."

"Handy."

"Just smart. You don't want to spend all your time getting to and from your study area. Plus, if something goes wrong, you're not waiting hours for help to arrive. We've got to be careful up here. There's no med evac. Nothing formal, anyways."

I shielded my eyes from the sun and turned around slowly so I could get a sense of the whole valley. It was bare of any significantly sized vegetation, though there were stunted willows lining the rocky creek beds. One creek still had flowing water—probably the reason Pika Camp had been set up in this particular valley. I saw movement and squinted. A ptarmigan was foraging among the willows.

The slopes were covered in talus, which was ideal pika habitat, and many of the rocks were covered in grayish-rust lichen, which was ideal pika camouflage. There were plenty of grasses and sedges and the like for fine pika dining and the narrow, but still flowing, stream for when they got thirsty. In other words, everything the modern pika could desire.

The air was achingly cold, the wind chilling it even further. I was glad for my parka. "So which way is Selena's site?" I asked.

"Up in that direction," Kelt told me, pointing to the northeast. "Sometimes she'd swing by on her way out. She always followed the creek bed when she left. Up through that pass."

"Any idea how far?"

Kelt shook his head. "Not really, but she said it was far enough away so that we didn't interfere with each other, but close enough to call for help if something went wrong."

"Like a bear encounter?"

"Or a broken leg or even a bad gas flare-up on the stove. Everybody at Pika Camp has advanced first aid training, you know. And there are always at least two people here."

"Selena camped alone, didn't she?"

Kelt nodded. "Yeah. Bare bones only. No Weather-havens or generators. Just a backpack and a tent."

I turned and looked again at the electric fence surrounding Pika Camp.

"Brave," I said.

Kelt shrugged. "I'd call it a little overconfident."

"Oh?"

"There *are* a lot of bears up here—grizzlies mostly—and no tall trees to sling up your food and garbage. Selena always said she wasn't afraid of bears. That she figured she was in their home and as long as she respected that she'd be okay."

"There's something to be said for that."

"And more to be said for having an electric fence around your camp, especially when you're storing several weeks' worth of food."

"True enough," I conceded, glad that I'd be sleeping within its perimeter at night. "You know, this is a great setup you've got, Kelt. No wonder you love it up here."

He seemed pleased. "I was hoping you'd like it," he admitted. "I hate being away from you for so long, but if I have to do it, I can't think of a better place to be. I'm glad you could come and see it."

And for that I forgave him. Both for my snogless state and for his snarky comments earlier.

I might not have been so quick to reconcile if I'd met the rest of his research team right away. They came striding into camp just before dinner (which, thankfully, was a hearty soup and not the contents of the buckets) and I immediately began feeling the same way Frodo must have felt in Rivendell. A short, plump hobbit surrounded by taller, much more attractive elves.

Stavros was a Greek foreign student who looked like he'd leapt off one of those ancient vases (if Greek vase painters had known about parkas). His Mediterranean good looks were marred only by a cold-reddened nose—a fact that faded to insignificance when he flashed a handsome, friendly smile.

"Nice to meet you, Robyn." He smiled down at me, taking my hand in both of his. "A great pleasure."

I smiled back, a little flustered.

But if Stavros made me feel like a hobbit, Rachel made me feel positively dwarfish. She was tall with short, ruffly, blond hair and a professional dancer's grace. Huge smile. Lush lips. Great skin.

Funny Kelt hadn't mentioned a significant portion of his field team was made up of elves.

"Hey," Rachel drawled, giving me a quick wink. "Good to have you on board. Maybe now Kelt'll cut us some slack."

"Huh," I said, slanting a glance over to Kelt. "Jim mentioned he'd been a bit of a . . . what was the word he used?"—I snapped my fingers—"a hose beast. Could it be that power has gone to his head?"

Rachel rolled her eyes dramatically. "Girlfriend, you have *no* idea."

I grinned, liking her in spite of her astonishing good looks. "Perhaps I should have a small talk with him," I said, feigning deep thought.

"Talk nothing! Try some one-on-one time in the ol' sleeping bag," she said with a suggestive wiggle. "That'll fix his apple cart."

Rachel was certainly an earthy sort of elf.

I stroked my chin. "You know, that's a really excellent thought. I wonder if it would help."

"Can't hurt. Hell, it worked for Stav here," she threw Stavros a smoldering look.

"I never was a hose beast," he protested.

She reached out and patted his cheek in delight. "And deluded too! You poor poop."

Grinning, I glanced over at Kelt. He seemed surprised by their behavior, which meant that either the relationship was new or that Kelt was just your basic clued-out kinda guy.

Stavros slid his arm around Rachel. "And now if only we can find someone for Michele, then all the apple carts will be fixed."

Kelt's shoulders slumped perceptibly. "What's Michele been doing now?" he asked.

Rachel gave an inelegant snort.

Beside her Stavros wrinkled his nose. When he spoke, it was with some reluctance. "You know, Kelt, all the gender stuff, it was annoying, yes?" He paused for Kelt to agree. "She would not shut up about it. The alphabet being invented by men and all that. But whatever. We are all having quirks, you know?" He paused again.

Kelt nodded.

"But now it is different," Stavros continued. "Now she is coming on to me. The hand touching, bumping against me, the big eye looks. Like a cat in heat. I am not interested. I *told* her I am not interested. I have Rachel. But Michele is not taking no for an answer. I am just happy that Rachel is not jealous."

"Not my style, twinkie," she agreed amiably.

"I would not say anything normally," Stavros said. "I know it is not your problem. And I am sorry, Robyn, for talking about this in front of you."

Wordlessly, I waved off his apology.

"We are all adults and professionals," he said, "but I tell you, it's really getting on my nerves."

Kelt was silent for a moment. Then he blew out his breath in a long sigh.

"You know it's the reason Trina left early," Rachel said.

"What!" Kelt's green eyes were startled.

Rachel's expression was eloquent. "You didn't know? Honestly, the woman is worse than a marmot in mating season, Kelt. She pretty much made her way through the retreat before we got here."

"I *thought* there was something going on with Selena."

Rachel made a face. "And Terry and a couple of those American geologists and that Swedish woman who was here for a few days. God, she even did that tight-ass cop when she arrived in Dawson. Didn't she tell you about it?"

"Michele actually *slept* with Frank Matas?" I wrinkled my nose.

Rachel shrugged and gave me a sour smile. "It's one way of avoiding a speeding ticket."

Kelt rubbed his forehead and muttered a swear word. "Why haven't I heard any of this? I thought Trina . . . I thought she'd just finished gathering her data . . . "

Rachel and Stavros regarded him silently for a moment.

"Don't worry," Stavros reassured him. "I am not going to leave because of Michele. There is too much to do still. I would just like to do it without . . . that."

"She's hit on everybody here, you know," Rachel told Kelt.

"She hasn't hit on me!" Kelt said. A bit defensively.

Rachel shrugged. "Of course not, you're running the joint. Look, I'm just telling it like it is, boss. She's bad news in a field camp. Jim's just as uncomfortable with it as we are. Maybe it wouldn't be a problem if she had someone in her sleeping bag, but the way things are now . . ."

"I think it is more than sex," Stavros mused. "You know what she's like. Very helpless with cooking. When was the last time she took her full turn in the kitchen? And all last week, she was always needing help with her plants. And then her tent blew over and 'oh, Stavros, I can't put it back up by myself.' It's very strange. She says she is a feminist, but it is like she is wanting someone to take care of her."

"We're a field camp," Kelt said, frowning. "Not a bloody daycare."

Rachel and Stavros went silent again. Not needing to say anything more.

Kelt scrubbed at his face again. "Okay. Thanks, guys. I appreciate your honesty. I'll have a talk with her."

# 17

Kelt and I did manage to get some one-on-one time in the sleeping bag at night (and it did seem to alleviate certain apple-cart-type problems), but the majority of the next two days was spent trapping pikas.

Long, long days.

It was crunch time in the world of pika biology, the time of year when pikas start accumulating piles of local vegetation to see them through the winter. They forage from daybreak to well into the evening, scurrying back to their boulders periodically with their haul. They spread these cuttings out to dry in the sun, creating haypiles, which, when dry, are then stored deep in the pika's rocky den. Late-night snacks for the long winter months.

You'd think these haypiles would make pikas easy to trap. Bait the trap with a nice fat haypile and, presto, you have yourself a pika. Ha. Pikas are cute, but they're paranoid little buggers, always worried that another, less scrupulous, pika is going to come along and screw with their haypile. Not to say that they don't have cause for worry. Pikas seem to like stealing just as much as they enjoy foraging. But it makes them a bugger to trap.

"They're the least trappable of all the mammals," Kelt informed me late on the second day.

It was almost 9:00 p.m. and we'd only successfully trapped two pikas, despite starting out at 8:00 that morning.

"Now he tells me," I sighed as I watched what I'd hoped would be pika number three skip past my carefully collected haypile and beat a hasty retreat to the rocks. "Gods, give me a nice bird anytime!"

"A bird? Birds peck."

"So?"

"So, those chickadees I helped you band last summer kept going for my cuticles. Little bastards drew *blood*. Pikas don't make you bleed."

"Bitch, bitch, bitch. At least you had a bird in hand. That's probably worth way more than a bunch of pikas in talus." I gestured toward the rocks. Several sets of dark shining eyes peered out suspiciously at us.

I wasn't really that frustrated. The work was hard, yes, but it was fun. The setting was gorgeous, the air cleaner than anything you find down south. The bugs were a bitch (the Smack 'n Splat currently stood at 257), but spending serious face time with Kelt more than made up for it. We hadn't had a fight for two days and it felt good.

"Maybe we should call it a day," Kelt said, looking at his watch.

"I am a bit tired," I admitted.

"Hopefully not *too* tired," he said significantly.

Yup. Things between us were starting to feel normal again. Like we belonged together again. It felt good. I didn't even miss my e-mail.

I knew I should be bringing up more serious subjects. It wasn't like it was going to get any easier. But I just couldn't bring myself to do it. Cowardly? No . . . well, maybe. A bit. But our relationship had taken a few hits lately and I didn't want to screw up our present accord. It felt too good. Too tentative. Still. I couldn't put it off forever. Tomorrow night, I promised myself as we hiked back to Pika Camp. I'd talk to Kelt about it tomorrow night after I got back.

Despite the obvious attractions of trapping pikas and spending time with Kelt, I'd already decided to try to find Selena's lost study site the next day. I'd told Gaylene I'd look for it, and my conscience had been muttering ever since.

The next morning, I packed three sandwiches (climbing mountains is hungry work), filled two large water bottles and prepared to do some exploring. Kelt wasn't coming along (too many pika-type things to do), but he insisted I take along a walkie-talkie. I suspected Selena's site was out of range, but I thought about the murder suspect who may or may not have gone up to Inuvik and didn't argue with him. I set out with a radio slung across my shoulders, a handheld antenna in my backpack and the walkie-talkie clipped to my belt.

It was another lovely day. Small clusters of clouds cast marching shadows on the slopes, and there was just enough of a breeze to keep my brow cool and the swarms of blood-sucking invertebrates down. It took me four hours, one and a half sandwiches, a golden eagle sighting, a grizzly sighting (thankfully on a far slope), and a few false starts. But I finally found Selena Barry's study site.

At first glance, the place looked a lot like Kelt's study site. Same lichen-covered rocks. Same talus slopes and sedge meadows and tussock fields. Same stunted, prostrate willows lining the same small, rocky, creek beds. Pretty much all the valleys up here looked like that. But the other valleys didn't give off beeping signals when I swooped the antenna back and forth.

I'd like to think it was my outstanding scientific method that pinpointed the site. Or perhaps my feminine intuition. But the ptarmigan waddling across my path with what looked like a camera slung around its neck was a dead giveaway. And when I spotted five of them clustered together on a rock—all looking like a group of Japanese tourists in Banff—I knew I was in the right place. Selena had tagged them with Holohill necklace transmitters. I set up the radio and antenna, dug out the yellow reference card, and prepared to get down to business.

White-tailed ptarmigan are the least-often encountered of the three ptarmigan species—mostly because they tend to hang out in the highest, most desolate reaches of alpine tundra. They're the smallest of the ptarmigan too, well adapted for their high-elevation lifestyle. And they're generally rather tame (no doubt due to the fact that they are least-often encountered). In the summer, they basically look like rocks with feet, though the white tail is a key field mark in summer and winter. Their feet are feathered, they've got a red comb above the eye, and their high-pitched cackling call can be a bit freaky-sounding if you're not expecting it (other grouses tend more toward a deeper croaking sort of song).

White-tailed ptarmigan are described in my bird book as localized, but fairly common. After several hours I was beginning to have my doubts about the description. Signal bounce can be a problem in mountainous terrain, so I'd taken several bearings from different places to triangulate the signals I was picking up. But out of seventy-four birds, I had found only seventeen. Not even enough for a decent sample size. I might've put the missing ptarmigan down to winter kill or predation—after all, I had no idea how long ago Selena had used this reference card—but all the birds I'd found sported band numbers from the first column on the card. Nature simply wasn't that neat and tidy. It wouldn't pick off birds in order of their band numbers on a reference card. That was just weird. One of those strange occurrences Inspector Chesnut disliked so much.

Couldn't say I was much enamored with it myself.

Maybe the second column of numbers was from a previous year. No. That didn't make any sense. If anything, the first column should have been from an earlier time. Another location, then? I shrugged inwardly. There'd been no mention of different sites in her notes. There could've been something about it in the fourth box—the one I hadn't had a chance to open. But if that were the case, you'd think somebody would have mentioned multiple sites. So, what was left? An equipment problem? Possible. Maybe she'd gotten a bad batch of transmitters.

I tramped up and down the valley until 8:00 p.m.,

trying to find the rest of the birds. I even hiked into two of the adjacent valleys. No luck. I was tired and discouraged. It wasn't like I was trying to capture the birds—that would probably take several weeks. All I wanted to do was find out if they were still transmitting. Still alive and well.

My stomach grumbled and I remembered that the third sandwich had not lasted past mid-afternoon. My right leg, injured several years ago, had started to ache from all the unaccustomed climbing. It was time to head back to Pika Camp to regroup and refuel.

It was close to 10:00 when the walkie-talkie I was carrying sputtered to life.

"Robyn! Are you there? Robyn!"

I fumbled it off my belt and pressed talk. "Present and accounted for, Kelt. What's up?"

"*What's up?* What's up is that you've been gone all day and most of the evening! *Where have you been?* You didn't even check in."

The walkie-talkie may have been on the old and crackly side, but Kelt's anger was coming through crisp and clear. I was tired, my feet were hot and sore, my leg hurt and my stomach was growling. I didn't need this shit.

"I tried," I snapped back. "But I was out of range, wasn't I."

There was a pause, then the walkie-talkie sputtered again. "—*could* have come back a little sooner."

I hitched the radio higher on my shoulder and took a deep breath, trying not to blow up. I could be a bit of a bag when my blood sugar plummeted and I didn't want to chomp Kelt's head off. I knew he was angry only because he'd been worried. "Time got away from me," I said, calm and reasoned.

"What, you don't have a watch?"

"I have a watch." I gritted my teeth. "But with all this extended daylight, it's a little hard to keep track. I haven't been up here for months getting used to it, you know."

There was a much longer pause. "Did you find the study site?" he asked. Less frantic now.

"Yeah," I was too tired to go into it right now. "Look, can we talk about this later? Seriously, I'm only about twenty minutes away. I can even see the Weatherhavens from here."

I squinted at the camp down in the valley and, on cue, a tiny figure came around the side of the shelter and waved.

"I see you." The figure waved again.

"Good." I waved back. "Then maybe you could throw some supper on the stove for me. I'm starving."

The rest of the conversation took place in our tent later that night.

"That was a little harsh earlier," I said carefully. Trying not to start a fight. "It wasn't my fault the site was out of range. You could have *guessed* that it would have been out of range."

"I was worried."

"And that gives you the right to bitch at me?"

He didn't answer me. "Why were you gone so long?" he asked instead.

"Hello? I was trying to find the site. Your directions weren't exactly precise, you know."

"If you were having that much trouble, you should have come back. You could have gone out again tomorrow."

"I wasn't having trouble," I argued. "I found the damn site. I even found some of the birds. I stayed because I was trying to find the rest of them."

"You can't do that kind of thing up here, Robyn. Not unless you're prepared. We can get serious snow anytime of the year. Hell, we had a blizzard two weeks ago! You didn't have a tent or a sleeping bag or anything."

"So now you're telling me I'm *incompetent*?" My voice started to rise.

"No! Just inexperienced—"

"I've done alpine work before, Kelt, I'm hardly a novice." I tried not to spit out the words.

"It's different up here," Kelt insisted. "Harsher. The weather can change like that." He snapped his fingers.

"Then I would have hunkered down until it blew over."

"And what if it lasted for days?"

He had a point, but I was far too irritated to concede it. "Give me some credit for self-sufficiency here. I've been working in the field since long before I met you."

"Fine." Kelt bit off the word. "Excuse me for being worried about you."

There was an icy silence.

"Next time I'll take a tent," I promised.

He didn't say anything.

"Look, you just need to give me some space," I said, trying to soften the atmosphere. "Trust that I know what I'm doing."

"Fine," Kelt said again.

It was a small tent, but I got my space. There was no one-on-one in the sleeping bag that night. There wasn't even a goodnight kiss. Just an argument about keeping the tent tidy (he was; I, apparently, was not).

Kelt fell asleep right away—I don't *think* he was faking it—but it took me a lot longer to settle down. To settle my mind down. All Kelt and I seemed to have done since I arrived was argue. Mostly about stupid stuff (I mean, who cares if a few shirts get tossed around the tent?). I knew he was stressed—he'd told me that himself—but I was beginning to have a bad feeling about the whole thing.

## May 8

Pika Camp left this morning and how I envy them! Willa has crashed again. The paints, it seems, have failed her. Along with inspiration, creativity, and everybody who ever loved her—including me. She's so jealous of my time. Resentful of the hours I spend in work when she cannot. And somehow, she fails to see that I might feel the same when our positions are reversed. When she gets like this, there is no such thing as privacy in my life. No action, no thought that does not, in her mind, rightfully belong to her. I love Willa, but these episodes are becoming more difficult, her tantrums more immature. I want to be partner, not parent. Willa has Jocelyn for that—however unhealthy I find that particular relationship.

I need to get back out in the field, but how can I leave Willa like this? A rhetorical question. Obviously, I can't. And so I am stuck here. Babysitting. Scribbling furtive thoughts whenever she is distracted. I feel like a teenager, hiding these pages in my bird book, but I know it's the one place Willa will never look. Her hated rival. A much-needed oasis of privacy for me.

I'm afraid the males will have started calling and I won't be there to hear them. Afraid I won't be in time to collar the females. If I don't collar them, how am I supposed to find their nests? How am I supposed to determine their breeding success? How will I get the proof I need? Am I supposed to wait another year?

I, too, am feeling resentful—and not a little guilty.

## May 16

Finally got away late last week. Willa still teetered on the edge of depression, but I think Paul must have had a word with her. I saw them deep in conversation on Wednesday and, on Thursday morning, Willa practically pushed me out the door. She managed to paste a smile on her lips, but her eyes were bitterly cold. I pretended not to see them. I had to. Time is getting away from me.

It's a good thing I got out when I did. Breeding seems to be occurring earlier than last year. Climate change? Probably. I must remember to check my dates. The males were calling by the time I arrived. I worked like a fiend and managed to collar 23 females over the next several days—a personal record.

Stopped at Pika Camp on my way home. What a difference funding makes! Half of me envies their camp, but the other half of me prefers my own arrangements, the feeling that I'm part of the world I'm studying.

I found Kelt immersed in paperwork. The price you pay for generous funding. He offered to make me some tea. So good to talk shop with another biologist, I'm glad he'll be coming back next year. He's recently found the love of his life, an ornithologist back in Calgary. A bit of a character, judging from the stories he told me about her. He's so obviously smitten with her, I was almost jealous. Given the past few weeks with Willa, I can't help but envy him the relative simplicity of his relationship with Robyn.

Such a calm, relaxing afternoon. I didn't want to go back to the retreat. Back to Willa's overwhelming need and Jocelyn's quiet condemnation. It was getting late and a cold, sleety drizzle had started. I'd just decided to stay the night when Michele came back to camp.

Her face lit up like a sun when she saw me, and I stopped her from hugging me only by turning away at the last moment. Even Kelt seemed uncomfortable with her behavior. In her own way Michele is as needy as Willa. I left, obviously. Tired, chilled, and irritated, I slogged home to yet another fight with Willa.

## May 21

I find it ironic that in the midst of all this endless northern wilderness, of these wide, wide spaces, I can feel so trapped.

I am trapped by my work. Trapped by my home life. I am suffocating under the expectations and needs and demands of those who people both my worlds. Willa is painting again, thank god, but she is still haranguing me about working too much. As if I had a choice right now. There are still females needing to be collared. If I can't track them, I can't find their nests. So how am I supposed to determine their reproductive success? How am I supposed to prove what I suspect?

And now, Jocelyn is pressuring me to (of all things) take more of a part in the community. To socialize and interact. What's next, a goddamn Tupperware party? "You're working so hard, Selena.

Too hard," she says in her most concerned voice. God, I wish Paul hadn't gotten himself fixed, Jocelyn could really use a baby. Maybe then she'd leave the rest of us alone. She keeps telling me how tired and stressed I look and how badly I need some down time. Even Paul agreed with her on that one, though at least he offered to help instead of criticize. I just need some space! I can't even find quiet at home. Willa's work, once confined to her studio, has invaded every corner of our house like a colony of mindless bacteriophages. The noise—physical and psychic—is becoming unbearable.

And so I retreat again to the mountains. Breathe air that nobody else has exhaled. See sights that no other eyes observe. Listen to nothing but the wind.

But lately, it is not enough. Voices from the past are whispering to me. I hear their small, angry mutterings even over the sigh of the wind. Why haven't I kept my promise, they demand. I tell them that I'm trying to. It isn't easy in this day of global warming and extinction and environmental disasters. But the voices care nothing for this. They know as well as I do, there is no such thing as try.

Even out here I am trapped. The present and the past.

## May 22

Willa has gone down to Edmonton. Some gallery opening. I'm not sure why she thought it necessary to spend the money, but I didn't want to ask. We so badly need a break from each other's expectations and disappointments. Perhaps she recognizes it as well and this is why she has gone.

I spent the evening playing cards with Jocelyn, Terry, and Ed.

Aussies against Canucks. Aussies won. Three cheers for the home team. That's me, socializing and interacting in the community.

All the while worrying, worrying about my ptarmigan.

## May 26

The males are quieting now, and the females should be starting to nest, though I haven't discovered any as yet. I can't decide if I hope the birds' breeding success is being compromised or not. A terrible thing to say, but if breeding is affected, then my case grows stronger.

With Willa gone, I no longer have to hide where I'm going. I can spend the day in the field and still get back to Willow Creek in time for a late dinner. A very late dinner usually, but Jocelyn has been leaving me out a plate of food with no questions asked. So unlike her. Perhaps she's finally decided to leave me alone? More likely it's because Willa is not here "needing" protection. Still, it's nice not to have to explain myself all the time—and even nicer to have dinner waiting after a long, hard day of work. Jocelyn's heart really is in the right place. I should try to be more tolerant.

Sometimes I think it would be easier if I could tell Willa about Regent. Tell her why my ptarmigan are so important. I've come close a few times, so close I could actually taste the words. But I always swallow them at the last minute. Coward!

Guilty as charged.

I know what will happen if people find out I'm working at Regent. The whole story—the history of the place—will be revealed. Connections will be made. How can they not be? At the length, truth will out. I'm too afraid of Willa's reaction. Afraid of what she will think of me. Forgiveness? For some sins, there is no such thing. I can't tell Willa about the Regent because then I'd have to tell her why. And then she would know about the children.

# 18

We were eating breakfast the next morning when Michele and Jim arrived back at Pika Camp. They were two days and several hours early. And it was clear from their expressions that something had happened.

Kelt looked up in alarm. "What's wrong?" he demanded.

Michele and Jim exchanged a look.

"It's too damn weird back there," Jim started to explain.

"Selena Barry was pregnant." Michele interrupted him.

"*What?*"

"It's true." Jim was nodding solemnly. "The forensic report came in. The cops are going nuts. Jocelyn's freaking out. I guess Willa Groot totally wigged. I suppose we should have radioed you but"—he shrugged uncomfortably—"we just had to bail, you know?"

"Holy shit." Kelt took a deep breath as the ramifications began to percolate.

"But," Stavros frowned. "Wasn't she . . . I mean . . . her partner was a woman."

"There's always in vitro," Rachel said.

"I don't think so." Jim shook his head. "Or if it was, it was news to Willa."

"Oh," Rachel screwed up her face. "Ouch."

"Yeah, well, it gets worse," Jim said grimly. "They also found that guy—Lance whatever-his-name-is. You know, the one who went backcountry. And now they're saying he's just a plain old tourist. He didn't have anything to do with what happened to Selena."

Shock was evident on all the faces around the table.

Stavros frowned. "But . . . then, who do they think is responsible?"

"I dunno. Somebody from the retreat. Or from the camps. Take your pick."

I started chewing my lip. Was it my imagination, or was everyone suddenly avoiding each other's eyes?

"Just as well you came back, then," Kelt told Michele and Jim. "Until they get this thing solved, I think we should stick close to camp. We're coming into crunch time anyhow, so it's not like there's nothing to do." He picked up his coffee cup and drained it in one absent-minded swallow. "Stav, you were due for a break this week—"

"I am happy to be staying here," Stavros waved it off.

"I'm good too," said Rachel when Kelt looked at her.

"Fair enough." Kelt turned back to the other two. "And what about you guys? You okay?" He was facing Jim, but his eyes slid toward Michele who seemed uncharacteristically silent.

"I'm not a guy," she told Kelt flatly.

Sympathy warred with irritation on his face. "Sorry," he apologized, sympathy winning. "How are you *two* doing?"

"Fine," she answered, her voice still flat.

Kelt looked at her for a long moment, then let it go.

"I'm okay," Jim said in the awkward silence that followed. "I just felt weird, you know? I mean, it's nice to have a hot bath and sleep in a real bed and everything, but frankly, it's a little nerve-wracking to think that you might be talking to somebody who might have . . . you know." He swallowed audibly. "I'd just rather be here working."

"And I'd rather have you here working," Kelt assured him, taking the cue. "We're having a hell of a time trapping the little beggars. I think they're getting even more paranoid."

Much like ourselves, I thought privately.

"I've been eight days trying to get that one with the torn ear," Stavros said. "I thought I had him yesterday but . . . " he shrugged.

"Well, let's get out there," Jim said, clearly eager to get back in the saddle. "How're the traps holding up? Did you manage to get that spring fixed—?"

"Well, *I'd* really like some breakfast," Michele interrupted. "There wasn't time before we left the retreat, you know. Stav, is there any toast left?"

It was a natural enough question, given that we were just finishing breakfast, but it was the *way* she said it. All trembly lips. The voice a soft caress. Helpless and intimate at the same time.

I glanced at Stavros. His jaw had tightened. He didn't look at Michele.

"I don't know," he grunted.

There was an awkward silence. "There's a bit of bread left," Rachel said finally. Her eyes were bright with either irritation or amusement. I couldn't tell which. I did, however, catch the are-you-getting-this look she shot Kelt.

"Is there coffee too?" Michele tried the big eyes on Rachel.

Rachel shrugged. As unimpressed as Stavros was. "Not sure, Michele. I guess you'll have to check the pot."

Michele stared at her.

Stavros stood up abruptly. "Well, me, I'm ready to get to work."

"Right behind you, twinkie," Rachel said.

"Count me in," Jim told them. "Just let me dump my stuff first."

Kelt and I pushed our plates back and got to our feet as well. I took care to avoid Michele's eyes as we cleared the dishes off the table.

"Look, why don't you grab some breakfast and meet us out there," Kelt told Michele kindly. "We're on the south slope today."

In the general rush out the door, I managed to pull Kelt aside.

"Listen, I'm going back to Selena's site," I told him quietly.

He drew in a breath to protest.

"I won't be as late as I was yesterday," I promised before he could say anything. "And I'll take the walkie-talkie *and* that little red pup tent. I just . . . I need to find those ptarmigan."

Green eyes searched my face closely. I knew he wasn't happy about it. But my words last night about needing space clearly still smarted. "Be careful out there," he said finally.

"Always." I reached up and touched his cheek gently. A gesture of appeasement.

His expression softened and he offered me a gentle smile.

I felt like a cad.

Oh, it was true that I needed to find the missing ptarmigan. True that I needed to figure out what was going on with them. But it wasn't the real reason I wanted to leave Pika Camp. The truth of the matter was that the news of Selena Barry's pregnancy had hit home in a way her death had not. I seriously needed some time alone to think.

**19**

The universe still hadn't unfolded as it should (in some ways the sucker seemed to be unraveling rather than unfolding). I hadn't even broached the subject of children with Kelt. Chickenheartedness? Probably. But he and I were still arguing, still fighting about stupid stuff. And I guess part of me kept hoping I was wrong. That I was just late. The stress. The travel. A crappy diet. The excitement of seeing Kelt again after so long. But I couldn't hide from it forever. There was more than a distinct possibility that I was pregnant and I needed to tell him.

Gods, what would he say?

We were still in the honeymoon phase of our relationship (though lately it was starting to feel like the pre-divorce phase). Still getting to know each other. What we wanted from life. From one another. I didn't even know if he *wanted* kids. We hadn't gotten that far yet. Maybe if he hadn't gone back to school, or gone out in the field for so long. Or been so preoccupied with the change in his career. Maybe then we might have discussed it.

Or not. I was honest enough to admit that I had a tendency to avoid the harder questions in life. Those major life decisions that seemed to require copious amounts of deep thought and inner exploration. I'd always given them the slip whenever I could. Distracting myself with work or play. And now they'd jumped up to bite me rather forcefully on the bum.

Did *I* want children?

I stopped and sank down onto the ground to think about it.

Having children had always seemed like a foreign concept to me. Something other people did. I'd thought about it—like most women in their thirties do—but when you don't have a partner, it's sort of a moot point. Well, now I had a partner and the point might be far from moot.

In a lot of ways, it was a terrifying thought. A small person. Always around. Utterly dependent on you. Was I ready for that? Gods, even the thought of it was unnerving.

I took a deep breath and blew it out slowly. A gust of wind tugged at my hair.

There was a tumble of rocks a few feet to my left. As I watched, a pika poked its head out cautiously. There was a small clump of vegetation spread out on one of the rocks. Its haypile, I realized belatedly, drying in the sun. The pika's nose twitched, sniffing the air to catch my scent. To see if I posed a threat to its stash. If things were different, I might have smiled at its suspicion, chuckled at its twitching nose. But they weren't and I didn't.

Did I want children?

It might be fun to show a little person a pika. To

teach a child about birds and plants and squishy things that live in the mud. But what about the other stuff? The sleep deprivation. All those late-night feedings. The diapers. The work. I'd have to take a year off. And the responsibility of it! A small child looking to me for direction. *Me!* What the hell did *I* know about anything?

Did I want children?

Maybe.

Maybe not.

The pika twitched its nose again and meeped at me before disappearing into the shadowed rocks. I tried and failed to summon a smile.

It occurred to me to wonder if Selena Barry had asked herself the same questions. Had wrestled with the same issues.

Most gay people I knew had come to terms with the fact that their orientation generally precluded having children—though, as Rachel had pointed out, it didn't have to be the case. It was possible Selena had been raped, but then, why did nobody know about it? The Willow Creek community was too small to keep a secret like that. Had Selena intended to get pregnant then? Jim said it had been a surprise to Willa, which didn't necessarily mean that Selena hadn't planned the whole thing, just that the two women hadn't had the healthiest of relationships. Well, Selena's affair had already proven that.

Obviously her affair had been with a man. If that was the case, then who had it been? And had he known about her pregnancy? It was an unpleasant thought, which led to other, even less pleasant, thoughts.

Had Selena's killer known about her pregnancy?

I stood abruptly, feeling suddenly nauseated. I needed to keep moving. To distance myself from such thoughts. At this point, it was all pure speculation anyhow. The best thing I could do right now was to find Selena's missing ptarmigan. To see if her work had had anything to do with her murder. And right now, it was a hell of lot easier to concentrate on that than on anybody's pregnancy.

# 20

"So over half the birds are missing?" Rachel asked.

I shrugged. "I found seven more today. That puts me at twenty-four. Out of seventy-four."

Jim was setting the table for dinner. "A mass winter die-off?" he suggested.

It was chilly that night in the Weatherhaven. Cold enough that we'd all kept our parkas on. Stavros was heating up some soup on the gas stove. It smelled spicy and hot. My mouth was watering. I seemed to be hungry all the time lately.

"I don't know." I shook my head. "I don't think so. I mean, yeah, some of 'em won't have made it. But look"— I pulled out the yellow card and showed it around the table—"this was Selena's reference card. All the ptarmigan I found at her site are here in this first column of numbers. None from the second column."

"That's weird," Rachel frowned.

"Tell me about it."

"Maybe the tags from the second column are defunct," Kelt said.

"Or maybe she never actually got around to tagging those ones."

Stavros brought the pot of soup to the table and starting slopping it into the bowls. "Maybe she made a mistake with the frequencies," he said. "She could have written them not correctly."

"I don't think so," I said, doubt coloring my tone. "I saw her notes. She was pretty careful."

"Are you going out again?" Kelt asked casually.

I turned to him and shrugged. "Probably. It's weird. And you know how much I hate weird."

His expression was closed.

"You could come with," I offered. "Maybe with two of us, we'll have more luck."

Kelt shook his head, though his eyes softened. "I can't. Sorry. Not at crunch time."

His green eyes smiled at me in apology. He seemed to be making a special effort. Ever since our fight the other night. Ever since we'd found out about Selena Barry's pregnancy.

I should tell him, I tried to convince myself. He was a sensitive sort of guy. He wasn't likely to go Cro-Magnon on me. And if he *was* going to be a dad, I'd have to bring it up sooner or later. I could tell him tonight. After we went to bed.

It was a scary thought. I wished I knew if Kelt even *liked* children. He didn't have any nieces or nephews, and none of our friends had kids. I tried to recall any comments he'd made about kids, about children we'd seen at the bookstore or in the park. But I couldn't think of a single instance when he'd even mentioned them.

Maybe that was a sign. Maybe he never talked about children because he didn't like children. Maybe—

"I really admire your tenacity, Robyn," Michele interrupted my thoughts.

I glanced at her. "It's the least I can do," I said shortly. "I told the RCMP I'd see what I could find."

"Still. It's great."

I gave her a small smile and reached across the table for the bannock.

"You have such nice nails," she remarked, gazing at my hand.

"Uh, thanks," I muttered, wishing she'd leave me alone.

"I haven't been able to have long nails for ages." She held her own hands up as if to prove her point. "Because I've been dating women."

I blinked. Could I have heard correctly? The sudden silence told me I had. Talk about too much information. I wasn't the only one to think so. I caught Rachel covering her ears and mouthing "happy place" to Stavros.

"Yours are lovely," Michele purred at me.

I glanced over at Kelt. He was eating his soup with unnatural concentration. I wondered if he realized Michele was hitting on me. If he did, he was obviously leaving me to deal with it.

*Like he'd leave me to deal with parenthood?*

I grimaced and caught a sympathetic look from Rachel. She winked at me, then launched into a lengthy anecdote that had nothing to do with fingernails or sex. I turned my attention back to my dinner, grateful for the intervention.

I could see now what Kelt had meant about Michele. And why he'd said I would have to experience her myself to understand (though I doubt it had occurred to him she might put the moves on me). Field camps were, by nature, earthy sorts of places when it came to conversation and humor. It was part of the fun of them, after all. Part of spending your days watching everything have sex except yourself.

But Michele seemed to go just a little too far. To take the conversation just past the comfort zone. And hitting on the boss's girlfriend under his (admittedly unperceptive) nose was hardly appropriate (or intelligent). Combined with her stridently vocal views on sexual politics and her all-consuming need to be cared for, it made her a difficult personality. No wonder Kelt was thinking of sending her back.

Despite this, it was Michele who provided the only really helpful suggestion in the case of the missing ptarmigan.

"Why don't you go up in the plane?" she said after dinner as we were washing up. "Selena got Dwayne to take her up. Maybe she was having the same kind of trouble."

Surprised, I turned toward her. "You know, that's a really good idea."

Michele preened under my gaze.

"Dwayne did tell me he'd taken her up, although—" I paused and tapped my bottom lip in thought. "I think he said it was an equipment malfunction."

"So?"

"So I'm using Pika Camp's equipment. Not Selena's. I shouldn't be having the same problem."

"Unless it's a problem with the transmitters."

"True."

"Radio phone's in the lab," Rachel told me. "Just call the retreat and get Jocelyn to pass the message along. Of course, you'll have to hike back out to meet Dwayne. The airstrip's back a few kilometers down the Dempster."

"Thanks." I smiled and turned to Kelt. "You won't mind if I take off for a bit?"

Judging from his expression, he minded quite a bit. There was an awkward pause. Rachel and Michele turned to look at him.

"No," he told me insincerely, "just . . ."

"I'll be careful," I promised.

I could tell he wanted to say more, but then Rachel started talking about something else and the moment passed.

Another thought occurred to me. "Hey, they have Internet access at the retreat, right?"

Rachel nodded. "They do. Why? You going to check your e-mail?"

"I see someone's been telling stories." I made a face at Kelt. "No, I thought I might do some searching. Find out what, if anything, Selena published in the last few years."

"I guess even if she wasn't part of academia, she must have published *something*."

"My thought exactly."

"The computers are screwed up," Michele said too loudly, trying to be a part of our conversation.

I raised one eyebrow in inquiry.

"It's true," Kelt told me. "Some virus buggered everything up. Even my laptop."

"*Nobody's* got a functioning computer?"

"Paul *said* he'd fix them," Michele sneered, her tone indicating the small likelihood of that.

She was probably right, but she didn't have to be such a skanky hose beast about it.

"He's actually pretty good with computers," Kelt said mildly, ignoring the implied criticism. "I don't know if he's gotten around to it yet, but you might want to ask him about it when you go to meet Dwayne."

**21**

"Hey Jack, it's me."

"Turd! I've been worried about you. How . . . are things?"

I shrugged, as if he could see me through the phone. "I dunno."

There was a silence. I stared around the empty cabin. The sun was streaming cheerfully through the windows, casting yellow carpet squares of light and warmth on the wooden floor. I regarded them morosely and picked at a loose thread on my shirt, very far from feeling cheerful myself.

"What do you mean you don't know? Is Kelt pissed off?"

"He might be." I paused again. "If I'd, y' know, actually . . . told him."

"Robyn!"

"I tried," I said, a little too defensively. When my brother called me by my proper name, I knew he was seriously ticked. "I really tried," I said again. "We just keep fighting. I don't know, Jack. We've been arguing

ever since I got here and it's not getting any better. I'm
. . . I'm thinking of not telling him." The words came
out in a rush. I bit my lip apprehensively, waiting for his
response.

It was a few seconds coming.

"You're thinking of not telling him." His tone was
flat. Unimpressed.

"I don't know if we're right for each other."

"Why?"

"Because we keep fighting! It's always stupid stuff.
Stuff that doesn't matter, but we can't seem to get past
it."

"So? You've been apart for months now, it's natural
to have a period of re-adjustment."

"But—"

"And you're both under stress. He's trying to run a
field camp in the middle of a murder investigation, and
you think you're pregnant. Life is hardly happy and normal at the moment, Turd."

I sighed, my shoulders drooping. "I know."

"Look, I can't even imagine how hard it is having
something like this eating at you, but you've really got to
share it with him. Do you honestly think you're not right
for each other?"

I didn't say anything.

"Or are you just using that as an excuse so you don't
have to tell him?"

I opened my mouth. Shut it again.

"Do you love him?"

I didn't answer right away. Then, "Yes," I said so
softly, I didn't think he'd hear me.

But he did. Or he guessed. "Then hang in there," he

said. "And quit being so wimpy. I think you guys really work, you know—and I think you'll get through this. But, Turd, you gotta tell him. You owe it to him—and you owe it to yourself not to go through this alone. Okay?"

I nodded. "Okay."

"Promise?"

"I promise." I inhaled a shaky breath. "Hey, how's my cat?" I asked in a lighter tone. His long-suffering sigh coaxed a grin out of me in spite of myself.

"*That cat*," he pronounced.

Uh oh.

"What did he do?"

"*That cat* damn near emasculated me the other day."

"He didn't! How?"

"Never mind. Let's just say he has a hate on for anything male."

"He loves Kelt."

"All the more reason for you two to kiss and make up, then," Jack shot back. "Because if you decide to wait around for *that cat* to approve of another man, you're going to end up a lonely old woman with *fifty* Guidos."

**22**

I hooked up with Dwayne on the dirt airstrip that runs alongside the Dempster in the Blackstone Uplands. He was leaning easily against the wheel of his plane, gnawing on the end of a bloated, disgusting-looking cigar. He grinned when he saw me.

"How're ya doin', sweetheart?"

"Hey, Dwayne. I'm coping. How's it going with you?"

"On a bit of schedule, honey, gotta pack it in."

"Okay, this is me packin'," I said, tossing my switchbox and the headphones into the plane.

There were brackets on the fixed struts of the aircraft. Together, Dwayne and I mounted the two H antennas, centering one on each strut. We used duct tape to attach the coaxial cables along the outside of the wing and in through the plane's small windows.

"Buggers'll vibrate right off otherwise," Dwayne explained around his cigar as he tore off a generous length of tape. The cigar, I was happy to note, was not lit.

Once we'd rigged it all up, I clambered up into the cockpit and plugged the antenna into my switchbox. Then I fitted the headphones over my ears. They were huge things straight out of the 1970s. But some of the beeps were so quiet, you needed that kind of silence— especially on a plane. Twiddling with the knobs, I tested first the left antenna, then the right.

"We're good to go," I told Dwayne. "And hey, before I forget, I really appreciate this."

"No problemo." He grinned and fired up the engine. "You wouldn't have gotten far on foot."

The cigar was now resting in a Styrofoam cup by his seat. It looked soggy.

"You're wantin' to fly low, right?" he shouted over the whine of the propellers. "Over the study site?"

"That's Plan A," I shouted back. "If we can't hear anything, we'll move to Plan B."

"What's the range on that thing?" he asked, gesturing towards the radio.

"Up to fifty klicks. If we can avoid any interference from the mountains."

He nodded and flipped a few more switches. "We'll take her in along the ridges," he shouted. "That oughtta help with signal bounce. All set?"

I checked my seat belt and gave him the thumbs up. The plane's engines kicked into high gear and we started speeding down the runway.

I watched out the window, my stomach clenching as the ground fell away, and tried not to think about morning sickness. I hated flying. I *always* felt queasy in a plane. It didn't mean anything.

The lichens and mosses blurred with distance into

the mother of all Astroturf. The only shadows on the landscape came from rocky outcroppings or from the mountains themselves. We circled once, then headed northeast towards Selena's study site.

I wasn't an easy flier and it showed in my body language, which (in true action movie fashion) was screaming *let's get the hell outta here.*

Dwayne threw me a sympathetic look. "How many drops is this for you, Lieutenant?" he asked.

Fortunately, I'd seen *Aliens* a few times. I recognized the line, and knew the response. "Thirty-eight," I answered. Paused. "Simulated."

Dwayne's grin split his face in two. He laughed and slapped his knee, delighted to have found a fellow nerd.

I smiled back at him a little uneasily, then turned my attention to the equipment, trying to distract myself with work. I had the yellow notebook cover with the frequency numbers clipped to a map of the area. I tuned the radio to a frequency I knew I'd picked up before. We should be close enough to . . . yes. The radio started beeping immediately. A nice strong beep. WTP007 was present and accounted for. I checked another frequency just to make sure. I waited a few moments, then the radio beeped again.

"And two points for WTP012," I muttered under my breath. No problem picking up the birds I'd seen at the study site. "Now, let's see where the others are hiding."

I ran my finger down the column until I came to the missing frequency numbers. I tuned the radio to the first frequency and waited.

Nothing.

It was possible the birds had gone beyond their usual

territory. Or that we weren't facing the right direction. Or that we were getting interference from the mountains.

Dwayne tapped my knee to get my attention. "We'll be right over the site in another minute or so," he told me.

I nodded and waited.

Still nothing.

I tried the second and third and fourth frequencies. The radio stayed silent. We flew low over the terrain. The only sound I could hear was the muffled whine of the engines. I could see when we passed over the tents and Weatherhaven shelters of Pika Camp. A small figure in a red parka waved at the plane. I waved back but we'd already passed overhead. And then, with a gut-churning dip, we flew down into the valley.

We were at the study site but the radio stayed stubbornly silent. I held my breath. Listening. Not so much as a pulse. It looked like we'd be going to Plan B.

For the next forty minutes, we conducted a systematic transect-based search, flying along ridges and dipping down into valleys. I had the switchbox set to both antennas. If either one beeped, I'd hear it. So far, there was zip.

*beep*

A tiny little pulse. So faint, I almost missed it. I touched Dwayne's arm to get his attention. Had I imagined it?

*beep beep*

No. There was definitely something there. I fiddled with the knobs, listening to each antenna individually, trying to pinpoint the sound. I couldn't tell if I was reading signal bounce or not.

*beep beep beep BEEP beep BEEP BEEP*

"Go that way," I ordered Dwayne, pointing to the northwest. "It's stronger over there."

"Affirmative." He snapped off a salute. "Uh, you know we're nowhere near the study site, right?"

I lifted the headphones away from my ears. "What?"

Dwayne repeated his words.

"Yeah, I know. But the signal's strong that way."

The plane dipped down on the left and started to turn. The beeping grew stronger. Steadier. I stared out the window.

"What kind of range are we lookin' at?" he asked. "How far will one of these ptarmigan go?"

"Not far," I answered. "Maybe seven hectares. Tops."

"I hate to rain on your parade, man, but we're way past seven hectares from the study site."

"I know." I shrugged. "Maybe it's the Ferdinand Magellan of ptarmigan."

"See if you can find another one."

"I'm on it," I told him, already tuning the radio to the next frequency listed in the book.

BEEP BEEP BEEP

I tried another.

BEEP BEEP BEEP

And another.

BEEP BEEP BEEP

What the hell was going on here? How could so many birds have migrated so far?

BEEP BEEP BEEP

I held the headphones up to Dwayne's ear.

"Stop yer grinnin' and drop yer linen," he hooted. "It's like a goddamn town meeting."

But I was too puzzled for *Alien*isms right now. "What's over there?" I asked.

Dwayne shrugged. "Just the Regent."

"The what?"

"The Regent gold mine. Operated for almost twenty years before the price of gold plummeted and the owners pissed off. Used to be over a hundred workers living out this way."

"Does anyone still live there?"

Maybe the birds had been trapped.

Before Dwayne shook his head, I realized that explanation didn't make sense. These birds were still alive. Selena's tags had all been equipped with a mortality mode. If a ptarmigan didn't move for a set period of time, then its radio tag would jump from forty beeps a minute to over one hundred. It meant either the necklace tag had come off, or the bird was dead. But these beeps weren't that fast. These radios weren't in mortality mode.

"Nah, place's been closed for over ten years now," Dwayne was saying.

But I wasn't listening.

"Son of a bitch," I swore in belated understanding.

Dwayne threw me a questioning look.

I let the switchbox fall in my lap. I knew where all the missing ptarmigan were now. And I knew why I hadn't been able to find them before. The birds hadn't moved to another area. Their transmitters weren't damaged or defective.

Selena Barry had had a second study site.

## June 1

I knew it! The results just came in from my samples. Extremely high levels of arsenic. No time for a longer entry, I've got the results and I've got photos. I'm heading down to Whitehorse to meet with Drew Trimble. As the Yukon's so-called environment minister, he has to listen now.

## June 3

T.S. Eliot once asked, "Where is the wisdom that is lost in knowledge? Where is the knowledge that is lost in information?" We are so "informed" now that the information itself has become meaningless. An end unto itself. Information without real knowledge behind it and definitely without anything resembling wisdom.

I went down to Whitehorse yesterday and met with Trimble. It was not the trip I had been anticipating. A waste of time, in fact. The government doesn't want to hear about knowledge. They are too eager to cash in on the mineral riches of the land. To see the same prosperity the Northwest Territories are enjoying in the wake of their diamond rush. They don't want to hear about abandoned mine sites so toxic they're poisoning the very soul of Canada. Too depressing. Bad publicity. And so, my research will be labeled "information" and will be neatly filed away in a separate cabinet from knowledge and wisdom. Maybe if I collected more data. If I had more proof the mine is still killing. Maybe.

But next time, I won't take it to Drew Trimble.

I suppose I can't blame him for being weak. Up here, resource extraction is celebrated, even venerated. It's all part of the Territory's proud history. The romance of the gold rush continues today, carefully orchestrated by those with an eye for tourist dollars. And now those same eyes are sparkling with diamond lust.

It shouldn't surprise me that environmental concerns are low on the list of priorities. Regent is just one of many, many such sites. Worse than most, of course, but still one of far too many. Not even the environmental groups can whip up much interest in it. There are too many other abandoned sites, much less remote, that require action. And, as Trimble informed me so succinctly, there is little money to clean up any of them.

I've thought of going to the media, but I can't chance it. There are too many questions I wouldn't want to answer. Besides, they probably wouldn't care either—for much the same reasons that everybody else has.

How should we live? I keep thinking about that question. The answer is, I don't think we know how to live anymore—certainly not on a species level. Or on a personal level. Look at me, I can't even fix a past mistake.

## June 5

Out again today. Not sure why, but I have to do something, even if nobody listens. A strange thing . . . I ran into Ed just a few kilometers outside the northeast boundary. The wind was up so I didn't hear him and he was dressed in fatigues so I didn't see him right away either. Nearly scared me out of my skin when I did see him. I think the feeling was mutual. He had an ax and a sack full of claiming posts—at least, that's what I think they were. White squared-off posts with metal tags attached to the tops. What else could they have been? I'm not sure what he thinks he's found, but he was definitely unhappy to see me. Probably thinks I'll stake a few claims myself.

As if I care about that.

**23**

We flew over the old mine site on our way to the ptarmigan.

"They left all the buildings?" I asked, my nose pressed to the window.

Dwayne nodded and leaned closer to me. "Offices. Roaster complex. Stacks. Living quarters. Tailings processing plant over to the left." He pointed each one out as we flew over them. "Company said it was too expensive to move," he shouted in my ear. "The buildings are designed to be portable, but I guess it was cheaper just to let 'em sit and rust."

The mine site was bleak. A barely healed scar on the land. The buildings, even when new, must have had little to recommend them in terms of esthetics. Boxy prefab structures with flat tops and few windows. Originally painted in 1970s harvest gold, now speckled with brown-red splotches like ptarmigan in the summer. The rust ran down the walls, staining the ground with dirty reddish runoff. There had clearly been no attempt at remediation. Most of the site had been scraped clear of any greenery, though I could make out some scrubby brown vegetation slowly filling in the gravel roads that led to the unfilled pits. The trees were all dead, the rocks tinged reddish-brown. From up here, the whole site looked like it had been burned.

I wrinkled my nose and swore softly.

"One of the great sights of the Yukon," Dwayne agreed sourly. "Tailings pond is over that way." He dipped the plane so I could get a better look.

With a surprised yelp, I grabbed at the door handle and swallowed hard to keep my stomach where it belonged. I shot Dwayne a dirty look, but he hadn't noticed my discomfort. When I was sure I wasn't going to ruin the upholstery, I peered cautiously out the window to where Dwaync had pointed.

The water in the pond was brown and thick-looking, shot through with swirling strands of a darker, shinier substance. Rocks along the pond's edges were encrusted with an unwholesome-looking yellowish-white precipitate. Nasty.

At my request, Dwayne brought us down a little lower. No evidence of birdlife on this water. I examined the pond carefully and muttered under my breath. The water was obviously contaminated, but there wasn't even so much as a screen over it to keep out the wildlife.

Criminal.

The environmental consultant in me itched to get down there and start evaluating the site. To start planning the remediation and reclamation. The tailings pond was an immediate problem, that was clear. But just how bad was the water? And was it already leaking into the water table? And what about . . . I gave myself a mental shake. This wasn't why I was here. Not this time. Right now, I needed to concentrate on ptarmigan. I resettled the switchbox on my lap and started fiddling with the knobs.

In total, we found thirty-two of the thirty-seven missing birds. All of them in or around the far northwest corner of the mine site. If we'd had more time, we could have landed and gotten visual confirmation of the ptarmigan. Not that I needed it. The birds were there. Their signals were loud and clear and not in mortality mode. But what I *did* need were a few explanations. First up was why nobody had mentioned to me that Selena had had two study sites.

"You didn't know about this second site?" I asked Dwayne as we winged our way back to the Dempster Highway's airstrip.

Dwayne was shaking his head. "Not a clue," he told me, shouting over the sound of the engines. "The day I took her up, we stuck pretty close to that first place. The one over by Pika Camp. She hadn't been getting a signal from the ground. Turned out she was just having problems with her equipment. She felt bad hauling me out for that. I didn't mind, though."

"And she never mentioned this place—what did you call it? The Regent Mine?"

"Not to me."

I was quiet for a while. Content to let the whine of the engines fill the silence. Dwayne didn't say anything, either. In the distance, I could see my red SUV waiting beside the landing strip.

Dwayne landed us more smoothly than I believed possible. I'd had bumpier bus rides. We unloaded my gear and stripped the tape and coaxial cables from the wings. Not saying much. Just what was necessary to get the job done.

I was thinking hard about Selena Barry and her work. All her most recent notes, all her papers indicated an interest in climate change. So why had she set up a second study site? It wasn't that far away from her first site. For all intents and purposes, it had the same kind of terrain. Why would she be conducting two climate change studies in two such similar environments? She wouldn't. Which meant there was something else going on. Something nobody seemed to know about.

"What can you tell me about this gold mine?" I asked finally.

Dwayne shrugged. The cigar was back in his mouth. Its appearance hadn't improved any. "What do you want to know?"

"Everything."

"Everything, eh?" He grinned and moved his cigar over to the side of his mouth. "Well, let's see . . . it was a hard rock mine," he began. "Not placer mining like they do down around Dawson."

"What's the difference?"

"Placer mining, you just wash the gold out of the river or the sediments. Hard rock gold, you gotta blast your rock, then extract the gold either by leaching it out with cyanide or by roasting it."

"That sounds . . . environmentally unfriendly."

"Doesn't have to be—at least not too unfriendly."

"Why do I sense a 'but'?"

Dwayne shifted the cigar again. It made a disgustingly squishy sound. "Yeah." He drawled out the word.

"Yeah. There's a 'but.'" He leaned against his plane and crossed his arms over his chest. "'Course, you probably saw that for yourself when we flew over it."

"Mmm," I agreed, the sight still fresh in my mind.

"Thing is, folks up here were pretty happy when Della James decided to open up the Regent Mine. It was going to be *so* good for the people of the Yukon. More jobs. More money coming into the territory. All the usual promises. And, to be fair, Regent employed a lot of people when it was operating. Even flew for them myself a coupla years."

"So what happened?"

"The usual story, I guess. Price of gold fell, and suddenly, there was all this talk about how the mine was no longer 'economically viable.' Della James took off. The company went bankrupt and the whole place was abandoned."

"Abandoned as in shut down?"

Dwayne snorted and chomped down on his cigar. "Abandoned as in everything left there to rot. You saw for yourself. It's not just buildings down there, Robyn. There's equipment and furniture—even records and stuff. All just sittin' there. You know, most of the equipment still has gas in the tanks."

"Unreal."

"All too real. When a place like Regent shuts down, there're things that should be done. Stuff that should be cleared out. Taken apart. Decommissioned. You don't just up and walk away from it all—unless you're Della James, I guess. And then, of course, there's all the waste."

"Waste? As in . . ."

"As in the toxic shit left over from the roasting process," Dwayne said.

"What, they walked away from that too?"

His bark of laughter was bitter. "Welcome to the North, my friend. We've got more abandoned mine sites up here than you can shake a stick at. Was a time not too long ago when as soon as a mine was all finished up, company would declare bankruptcy and the land and all its problems would revert to the Crown. Report came out a coupla years back estimating that cleanup costs for mines just in the Yukon, the Territories, and Nunavut'll cost taxpayers somewhere along the line of half a *billion* dollars. And no guarantees that a complete cleanup is even possible." Dwayne smiled bitterly at the look on my face. "It only looks pristine up here, I'm afraid."

"I had no idea it was so bad," I admitted. "But . . . didn't Regent have to pay some kind of financial security?"

"Yeah. Two hundred thousand bucks. Big deal. It'll take ten times that much to even *start* to clean the place up."

I digested that for a moment.

Dwayne scratched his head and looked out over the landscape. "Regent *did* get fined just before everything went belly up. One point six million. They got caught allowing cyanide and arsenic to leak from the site, but they filed for receivership and never paid a cent."

"They *allowed* the stuff to leak out?"

Dwayne nodded. "Della never wanted to deal with it. Not properly, anyhow." His mustache twitched angrily. "Man, she was Queen Bitch of the Universe, that one. Most she ever did was pick a few of the old mine shafts and had all the drums dumped into it. That'd be right before she buggered off."

"I see."

"Arsenic trioxide," Dwayne told me before I could ask. "Rocks out here're full of arsenopyrite. Naturally occurring, from what I understand. Problem is, when you take the gold out, you're left with a whole whack of arsenic trioxide dust." He shook his head and gazed off into the distance.

"How much is down there? In the mine shafts, I mean."

"Lots. Enough to poison every living creature on the planet if it ever got into the water table. Way I understand it, the site's so polluted, they don't even know *how* to clean it up."

The real world's version of a Balrog.

I shook my head slowly. "You know, I heard there were problems with abandoned mine sites—big ones— but I honestly had no idea things were this bad."

"Scarier than any Terminator," Dwayne agreed.

"So why would Selena have chosen the old Regent mine as a study site?" I muttered to myself, already knowing the answer.

"Well, if I had to make a guess, I'd say she was wondering about the arsenic."

All of a sudden, I remembered the vials I'd found in Selena's things. The toenails and bits of feather. Didn't arsenic accumulate in hair and nails?

"You know, Dwayne," I said. "I think you may be right."

Dwayne had proved to be a fount of information about the history of the site, but he didn't know much about its present-day status. Namely who was looking to clean the place up. Somebody must have commissioned Selena's study. Why else would she have been working there?

It wasn't unusual for a researcher to have more than one project on the go, but everybody seemed to know all about Selena's first study and nothing about her second. And why hadn't there been any documentation about Regent in her papers? It was possible the information had been in the fourth, unopened box, but still. Why did everybody—including her partner—know only about her work with ptarmigan and climate change?

Dwayne merely shrugged when I asked him. "Talk to Jocelyn," he suggested. "I haven't heard anything, but she's more plugged in than I am. Seems to me INAC assumed responsibility for the site years ago, but I could be wrong about that."

INAC. Indian and Northern Affairs Canada. If Dwayne was right, then that meant a government job. Which made my questions even more pertinent.

As I drove back to Willow Creek, my head felt hot and full. What with worrying about my personal life, I hadn't slept well the night before and now I had all these unanswered questions about Selena and the Regent mine buzzing around. A headache throbbed to life behind my eyes.

Jocelyn wasn't in the Cabin when I arrived, but I could smell a freshly brewed pot of coffee perking on the stove. At any other time, I would have appreciated the warm aroma. Now it just made my stomach queasy. I fought off a wave of nausea, and tried to convince myself it was headache-induced. It couldn't be morning sickness. Not this soon.

I took a deep breath and rolled my shoulders back. The retreat seemed quiet and deserted, but the coffee hadn't perked itself. Somebody had to be around. I stepped back outside to see if I could find anybody.

I did, but it wasn't the person I'd been hoping for.

"Robyn! A word please."

I started and looked over my shoulder. Frank Matas was bulldozing his way toward me.

There's something about a fully uniformed police officer marching purposefully toward you that makes you want to run. It's not that I make a habit of breaking the law, it's just that grim-faced, purposeful police officers—especially ones like Frank Matas—are rarely looking to wish you a pleasant day. I tried to suppress the urge to break into a sprint. He probably just wanted an update on Selena's work. To find out what, if anything, I'd found.And besides, the guy could probably run me down in a second.

I turned toward him.

"Constable Matas," I said in greeting.

"Afternoon," he replied curtly. "Have you had any luck yet with the Barry work?"

"I'm afraid not," I told him apologetically. "I'm chasing something down right now, but it could be nothing."

"We're a little pressed for time," Matas said. Edgily. "This *is* a murder investigation."

I tried not to bristle. "I'm aware of that."

"Are you? It seems to be taking you an awfully long time to figure out what the woman was studying. It's biology. How hard could it be? Even if the notes were lost."

The implication rankled.

"The notes were *stolen*," I said struggling to keep the anger out of my voice. "Not lost. And without those notebooks for direction, figuring out where and what she was studying and why she thought *I'd* be interested really hasn't been all that easy." I could feel myself getting angrier. What gave him the right to get pissy with me anyway? "I know she was looking at basic things like reproductive success and winter survival rates. Somehow, I don't think that has anything to do with why someone took a knife to her."

It was a small lie, but his manner didn't exactly invite confidences. If Inspector Chesnut had asked me, I would have told her about Regent—even though, at this point, I was just guessing what Selena had been doing out there. With Matas, I wanted to be sure before I said anything. I could just imagine his scorn if my suspicions proved baseless.

"Maybe you should try talking to the Groot woman. Maybe she can help you." His tone was nasty.

"Selena's partner?"

"If you want to call her that."

I searched his face closely. "You don't like that, do you?" I said, surprised. "Their lifestyle. You didn't agree with it."

His eyes grew flinty. "It's not my business if two consenting adults want to engage in deviant behavior."

Deviant behavior?

"They're gay."

"They're dykes."

"That's not deviant."

"Did you talk to Willa Groot?" he asked, ignoring my comment.

"Of course I did." The headache was making me scornful. "Inspector Chesnut suggested it *days* ago."

Matas' expression hardened.

"Excuse me for duplicating instructions," he snarled. "I was just trying to help." And with that, he spun on his heel and strode off.

I stood and watched him march away, already regretting my snarkiness. I had the unpleasant feeling that sometime, somehow, Constable Matas was going to make me pay for it.

# 24

I finally found Jocelyn sitting on a rock by the edge of the creek. She was watching an American dipper—probably the same one I'd seen a few days before—in its perpetual quest for food. Up to its neck in icy water, it probed the creek bed for tasty morsels, maneuvering through the fast-flowing stream with its wings. At times its head was completely under water.

I was beginning to know the feeling.

Jocelyn looked up before I could say anything.

"Robyn! When did you . . . oooh, you don't look very well." Her tone darkened from surprise to concern. She jumped to her feet. "Are you sick?"

"It's nothing," I lied. "I'm sorry, I didn't mean to disturb you." I scrubbed at my forehead. "I've got a bitch of a headache. And I just had a run-in with Frank Matas. It's nothing serious."

She dealt with the more immediate problem first. "Migraine?"

I nodded, then wished I hadn't. "I think so."

"Come with me," she ordered. "I've got some pills that'll do the trick."

I followed her down the path towards the Bear cabin.

"I got them from an English woman who stayed with us last year," Jocelyn said over her shoulder. "You can only get them in Britain, but they'll take the edge right off. I think they're magic."

"That'd be nice," I whispered, my eyes starting to cross from the pain.

She escorted me into the cool, dark cabin and sat me down in a large, overstuffed chair. There were shelves of books on every wall, but it hurt too much to try to focus on them, so I sat there and closed my eyes.

"I get migraines every month," Jocelyn told me. "I have since I was a teenager. They're horrible things. Do you get tunnel vision? I do sometimes but not always, thank god . . ."

I let her monologue wash over me.

"Here."

I opened my eyes. Jocelyn was standing in front of me, holding out a glass of water and two large, fluorescent pink pills.

"Colors not found in nature," I said accepting them with a weak smile.

"Maybe not, but they work like a hot damn," Jocelyn said. "And speaking of hot—or I suppose, cold—let me get you a damp cloth for your head."

I started to put the pills in my mouth when it occurred to me to wonder if they were safe for pregnant women to take. *Shit!* Weren't there drugs you were supposed to avoid if you were pregnant?

I palmed the pills, tucking them into my shirt pocket, and drained the glass of water just as Jocelyn came back with the cloth.

"Thanks," I told her as I pressed the cool cloth against my aching temples.

"You'll be feeling better in no time," she promised as she dropped gracefully into the chair across from me.

We sat quietly for a time. Karma sauntered over and jumped up on Jocelyn's lap. Her purr was a soothing rumble in the silence.

"I really appreciate this," I murmured.

"No problem. You're looking green around the edges."

I had my eyes closed, but I could hear the comforting smile in her voice.

She was quiet for a while longer, then, "Did Frank give you a hard time?" she asked sympathetically. "Or was it just the migraine?"

"A bit of both, I think," I grimaced and cracked my eyes open to look at her. "What the hell is that guy's problem, anyway?"

Jocelyn stroked Karma a few times before answering. "He's not a bad man, Robyn. Really he's not." Her tone was troubled. "He comes up here every so often to hunt and fish or just to have dinner. And he keeps to himself for the most part, so I can't say I know him all that well.  It's just . . . well, he's got some nasty demons."

My silence was eloquent.

"His daughter ran away a couple of years ago," Jocelyn explained after a moment.

"He's *married*?" I blurted, trying to imagine what

kind of woman would say "I do" to Frank Matas. I winced as my head protested the abrupt movement.

"Not anymore," Jocelyn told me. "Connie left a year before Liane did. It was pretty ugly."

I waited.

"Frank's daughter was a lovely girl—despite the friction at home. Attractive. Bright. When she left, it twisted him in a way that Connie's leaving never did. He's not a bad man," she said again, sounding like she was trying to convince herself of it. "But he's got some awfully old-fashioned ideas about gender roles."

And gender issues, I added to myself, remembering his comments about Selena and Willa.

"That's why his daughter left?" I asked instead.

Jocelyn nodded. "He got very protective after Connie left. Too protective, really. Frank decided he'd been too lenient with his wife—a very old-fashioned idea, I know—and he was going to make damn sure he didn't make the same mistake with his daughter. I've never been a parent, but even I could see he was being too heavy-handed. You can't control teenagers like that." Jocelyn paused, pursing her lips into a thin red line. Her eyes weren't seeing me anymore.

"And so Liane ran off. Nobody blamed her—my god, most of us wished that we'd intervened, you know? It was months before Frank tracked her down. She'd ended up in Vancouver. On the streets. By the time Frank found her, she was turning tricks for a living."

I sucked in my breath sharply. An unwilling rush of sympathy for Frank Matas washed over me. "What happened then?"

Jocelyn scratched Karma under the chin and shrugged. "He tried to get her off the street and away from that life. She came home for a while, but it didn't last. We even had her staying here with us for a couple of months, but . . . " Jocelyn lifted her shoulders again—"for a lot of people, the Yukon is a place to start over. For Liane, I think maybe it was the place she had to leave so she could start over. Frank hasn't heard from her in over a year now, neither has anybody else. He doesn't talk about it."

"That's a sad story," I mumbled after a moment.

"It is. There's a lot of that up here. I've learned not to be too judgmental—even with people like Frank. You just never know what kind of baggage somebody might be hauling around."

I sat watching Jocelyn stroke Karma. Thinking about Frank Matas and his lost daughter.

It was Jocelyn who eventually broke the silence that had fallen over us. "Were you looking for me?" she asked. "Or just in search of migraine medicine?"

I'd almost forgotten about the mine site. Briefly I described what Dwayne and I had found.

"Selena had a study site at *Regent*?"

"Sure seems that way."

Jocelyn's eyebrows were scrunched together in a puzzled frown. "That's the first I've heard about it."

"Have you heard about anybody cleaning the place up? Maybe doing some preliminary work?"

Jocelyn was shaking her head. "Not a peep."

"Well, *somebody* must have commissioned Selena's study. Who owns the site now?"

"INAC, I believe. Unless they've sold it to another mining interest. Sometimes that happens. The new company will assume responsibility for the clean-up in exchange for various incentives."

"Ye-es," I dragged the word out. "But in my experience that sort of thing usually doesn't happen when the site's as contaminated as this one seems to be." I put the damp cloth over my eyes again. I was finding it difficult to think coherently. If only I could take Jocelyn's pink pills. "I wonder if Terry's heard anything," I mused aloud. "He's always going into Dawson City, isn't he?"

"*You can't ask Terry!*" Jocelyn's vehemence was shocking.

I dropped the cloth and blinked owlishly at her.

Her cheeks reddened. "I didn't mean to raise my voice," she apologized. "It's just . . . you can't ask *Terry*. Not about the Regent Mine."

"Why not?"

"Another very sad story," Jocelyn said with a quiet sigh. "The saddest." She fell silent then.

I waited. The silence dragged on. Just as I was starting to wonder if she was going to say anything more, she started to speak.

"I never tell people about it." She shook her head slightly. "It's an old story now, but it's not mine, and it's not my place to share it. But . . . well, I can't have you asking Terry about Regent. I really can't."

She paused. When she started to speak again I could hear the reluctance in her voice. "You see, Terry's wife—ex-wife now—used to work as a secretary at the mine. This was back in the late 1970s, just before the price of gold fell and the company left. They—the company, that is—had already been filling drums with arsenic trioxide. There was a huge cache of them over by the roaster complex. They just hadn't dumped them in the pits yet."

Jocelyn's eyes were dark as she stared into the past. "It was winter. We'd had lots of snow that year, which isn't always the case up here. Anyway, Terry and the kids had come to pick up their mum. They were two boys, just young kids—the oldest wasn't even five yet." She stopped and took a deep breath. "To make a long story short, Terry left them playing outside while he went in to find Susan. The boys found the huge pile of drums and started playing around them. Climbing on them. Sliding off them. And they ate some of the snow. The arsenic was already starting to leach out."

"Oh shit," I blurted. Aghast. "Were they okay?"

"Robyn, they both died."

## June 6

I should have known better than to drink on an empty stomach.

Last night I was angry and depressed after my meeting with Trimble. Scared too. Finally realizing the very real possibility that there will be no atonement for me. No way to make reparation for past sins. How could I live with that? I cried for a while, tried to find something to distract me. Nothing worked. I couldn't think straight. I felt like I was going to crawl out of my skin if I didn't tell someone!

I found myself heading to the Cabin. I don't know who I thought I was going to talk to. Willa was gone, Jocelyn and Paul had gone out, and even if they hadn't, I'd never confide in Jocelyn. Maybe I was looking for Paul. He's always been sympathetic to me. Maybe I was hoping he'd stayed behind when Jocelyn had gone out. But instead of Paul, I found Terry sitting in front of the woodstove.

Terry and I have never had much to do with each other, but there's always been something about him. A quietness of spirit, a centeredness that I, for one, do not possess. I don't really know how to explain it. I know that others here like to talk to him. I've seen him in Dawson, sitting at the corner table in Sourdough Joe's. Always with someone different. Always listening quietly while they poured their hearts out to him. Our very own Father Confessor. When I found him alone in the Cabin last night, it seemed like fate.

He could tell I was upset, but he didn't ask me what was wrong. Not right away. He offered me some wine. I had a few glasses. And then came the gentle question in his soft, whispery voice. Before I could change my mind, the whole ugly, poisonous story began to hemorrhage. Spewing out of my soul. Raw. Untreated.

Twenty-one years later.

God, how did the time go so quickly? Twenty-one years ago I was a wide-eyed grad student eager to experience the world beyond Australia. Full of smug confidence and trying not to think too much about the fact that my new summer job as part of the Regent Mine Task Force was basically a crappy research position. Reviewing the current practices for arsenic disposal throughout North America and reporting to Dr. Bruce Dyer, the Administrator of Environmental Health. Strange that I can still remember the wording of the job ad. I still remember being more excited by the salary too—at last, I'd be able to start paying down some of my student debt, the job itself was secondary. I can't believe I was so self-absorbed.

You could argue that it wasn't my fault. That Bruce was to blame for failing to act swiftly enough. Or that the owners of Regent were at fault for dumping the stuff there in the first place. For cutting costs so much that safety procedures were compromised. You could argue all these things, but I know—I feel—differently. It was me who couldn't make Bruce see the urgency of the situation. I'd gone out there, I'd seen the leaking drums, but I failed to goad him into action. And two boys paid the price.

I should have tried harder. I know that. I should have shown him photos or taken samples or maybe even booked him a plane ticket so he could go out there and see for himself. I don't know. I should have thought of a way. I should have made him listen to me.

I told Terry . . . and I saw the revulsion in his eyes. Revulsion, shock, anger, and I don't know what else. Any quietness of spirit he'd possessed had fled, eradicated by my story. He left without a word. I sat alone in the shadowed dining room and shook like a leaf as the weight of what I'd confided came crashing down. After all these years, it's finally come out—and the reaction was exactly what I'd anticipated.

Thank god I never told Willa. Bad enough that Terry now knows. I finished the bottle of wine. I'm drunk and depressed and I can't sleep for thinking about the past.

## June 7

Not drunk anymore, but still depressed. Still lost in the past.

Running back to Australia after the children died was a horrible idea, I can see that now. Ditto for rushing into that ill-conceived marriage. Poor Murray. A macho asshole to be sure, but he didn't deserve the baggage I brought. I'm sure a therapist would say I did it on purpose to punish myself. Or that I felt I didn't deserve anything better. Who knows? I'm just sorry it took me five years to figure out I'd made a terrible mistake.

All through the divorce, the bullshit with my family, the change in career, Regent has never been far from my mind—especially after I found myself back here in Canada. It kept haunting me—are you still there, Selena? Do you still remember?—tangling the threads of my life. It brought me Willa. How else could I have fallen in love with someone from the Yukon? I'd fully intended to work in northern British Columbia, to study climate change on the ptarmigan there. But then there was that night in Calgary when Willa told me about Willow Creek, about where she lived. "There are ptarmigan all over the place," she said. "You could just as easily do your research there." I pretended surprise, but felt none. Processed the words and their meaning, but heard in the depths of my being the gibbering beginnings of silent, demented laughter. I always knew Regent would bring me back some day.

And now, what we did twenty years ago to solve the problem has done nothing but create new ones. Does that make me doubly guilty? I feel it does. After all, I had doubts twenty years ago, and I said nothing. Questioned nobody. Unwilling to rock the boat.

Does Bruce hear voices in the wind, I wonder? Does Della James? Or the plant manager or the safety inspector whose names escape me now? Do they ever lie awake and think about the past?

Jeff and Kyle Starr. I still whisper their names to myself in the dark hours of night. It's important to remember the names of those you kill. Will there be other names to remember? God, I hope not. Only time will tell.

## June 14

Pika Camp has come back to Willow Creek for a few days. Too much snow in the higher elevations. They all seem so very hopeful to me. So very young. With the burning enthusiasm for saving the planet that so many people their age share. Hope for the future. It's not that I am less eager to do my bit, but my enthusiasm has been tempered by seeing so many setbacks over the years. By seeing how work done with the very best intentions can still lead down the path to fiery damnation. I feel old and jaded beside them all.

Willa is back from Edmonton. The gallery owner wants her to do a show so she is happily occupied in her studio room. Fine with me. I'm not fit company, though you would never know it from Michele's behavior. She follows me around like a chick follows its mother. She is lost in much the same way Liane was lost. But this time, I don't have the energy or the inclination to help. I've had a headache for two days now.

I need to talk to Terry. To ask him not to say anything to anybody. But he is avoiding me. I don't think he's told anybody—at least, I can't detect a change in the way they treat me. Why, why did I tell him? What made me think, even briefly, that his reaction—that anyone's reaction—could be anything else?

**June 17**

What is the point of continuing my work if nobody will listen? The snow has finally melted and Pika Camp left this morning. Eager to return to the field. I could hear them getting ready. Their energy was exhausting. I'm so tired lately. All I seem to want to do is sleep. If only these headaches would let up. Think I'll stay home today.

**June 21**

Forced myself to go out for a few days. I felt better for it—more positive—until I came back for another fight with Willa. She told me I looked like hell. She thinks I'm working too hard, that I'm obsessed with the ptarmigan. She just doesn't understand. Field biology is not like art, you can't just work when the mood strikes you or when the Muse inspires you. Sometimes, you have to work twelve-hour days if you're to collect the data you need. Sometimes it means being out there for days or weeks on end. Already, I've been back to the retreat more times than all the members of Pika Camp put together. But that, apparently, is not good enough for Willa.

The problem is, Willa has nothing but time—time for work, time for play, time for tantrums, time to do just about anything she wants—whereas I feel like time is running out. I have to believe that I can make a difference. I have to collect this data. And I have to do it now. I find myself tallying up my years with a fixated attention that could rival that of King Midas. Constantly counting how many years are behind me now and wondering how many lie ahead.

I feel better when I'm in the field. Living in my own little tent in the middle of wilderness. Life doesn't seem so overwhelming up there. So very, very short. Up there, it still feels like I have a chance to set things right. I wish I could make Willa understand. I wish she would at least try to understand.

Saw Ed again the other day. Still skulking about in his army wear. I don't think he saw me. Here at the retreat, however, Terry is actively avoiding me. Quite a feat in such a small place. At least he hasn't told anyone about my connection to Regent. Small miracle. I am thankful for it.

**25**

In spite of my headache, I couldn't let things rest—not with Jocelyn's horrifying revelation about Terry's children so fresh in my mind. Who had known about Selena's research? If INAC had assumed responsibility for Regent (which was the most likely scenario), then they would have to be involved in its cleanup. I started with the government listings.

Four phone calls, and three transfers later, I still didn't know. About all I discovered was the INAC guy I needed to talk to was on vacation until the end of the summer. Defeated and too nauseated to do anything else, I waved off Jocelyn's offer of supper, stumbled back to my tent and fell into bed.

By the next morning, I still didn't have any answers about Selena Barry or the Regent Mine, but my brain must have been working the problem overnight. I woke up pain-free, refreshed, and knowing exactly what to do. Specifically who to ask.

Kaye Woodrow. My boss, manager of Woodrow Consultants and keeper of sundry information such as which projects Woodrow was working on and (more importantly) bidding for. If Regent was to be cleaned up, there would have been a Request for Proposals put out. And if there had been any kind of RFP floating around, then Kaye would know about it.

I threw off the blankets and swung my feet off the bed. The morning light in the tent was soft. I glanced over at the little travel clock on the milk crate. Hmm. The *very early* morning light, I realized. It was, in fact, much too early to call Kaye (damn midnight sun kept screwing me up). My sense of purpose was deflated for an instant, until I remembered that Kaye checked her e-mail almost as religiously as I did. I could fire off an e-mail to her, have a quick breakfast and then move on to Phase 2.

Not only had I woken up knowing I needed to talk to Kaye, but I'd also realized that I needed to go into the land of Mordor itself. To the northeast corner of the old mine site. Phase 2 involved catching myself a Regent ptarmigan.

Selena's equipment had probably gone up in flames with her home, but Willow Creek was billed as an Adventure and Wilderness Retreat, which meant there was a good chance they'd have a gill net or two lying around. If I could net one of the birds that Selena had tagged, I could take samples of feathers and toenails and send them down to the toxicology lab in Edmonton. Right now, I was working with suspicions and educated guesses. I needed more. I needed to know for sure if

Selena had been studying contamination rather than climate change. If so, that could have been the reason she was killed. In my experience, people could get pretty worked up about poisoned environments. They were less likely to get murderously enraged over climate change.

The tox lab usually took anywhere from a few weeks to a few months to run tests, but one of the technicians had a bit of a crush on me and I thought I might be able to get him to fast-track my samples without mentioning why I needed the results so quickly. It was worth a shot—after all, it wasn't like I'd be asking him to run a whole season's worth of samples.

I pulled some clothes on and headed over to the Cabin in search of Kelt's laptop. The place was quiet. Everybody still a-snooze in their beds. I found the computer on a shelf by the woodstove. I lifted it down and tiptoed it over to the kitchen counter. It had a wireless modem. I could even check my own e-mail. It had been days since I'd been plugged in. Megan was still in Southeast Asia. She'd probably sent a message or two.

But the laptop was slow to boot up and once it was ready, the cursor was alternately sluggish and jumpy.

Oh. Right.

I chewed my lip and regarded the screen resentfully. I'd forgotten about the virus.

I tried a few things. Ran the antivirus program. And when that didn't work, I checked the status of the updates, unsurprised to find they weren't up to date. But my heart wasn't in it. I wanted to be *doing* something, not futzing around on a computer.

"Good morning."

The soft greeting startled me. I jumped and spun around, suddenly hyperaware of my solitude. Paul was standing in the doorway, his wild hair backlit by the sun.

"Oh! Hey, Paul." There was a slight tremble in my voice. "Jeez, you scared me. I didn't think anyone was up yet."

"I've been up for a while," he said. "For some strange reason, I do my best writing early in the morning. I'm sorry, I didn't mean to startle you."

"Must be my guilty conscience," I told him jokingly. The smile died on my lips as soon as the words left them. Somebody up here had an all-too-obvious conscience problem. I studied Paul out of the corner of my eye.

"How's your head?" he asked.

"Oh," I waved the question off. "It's fine now. All I needed was some sleep."

"And a couple of Jocelyn's magic pink pills."

I stretched my lips into a smile. The pills were still at the bottom of my shirt pocket. "Right."

There was a brief silence that felt awkward to me. Not sure how it felt to him. I decided to change the subject.

"Um, Paul, I was wondering if you guys have any fishing nets lying around."

"Fishing nets?" Confused, he glanced around as if in search of a nearby ocean that had somehow eluded him.

"Not the big maritime nets," I assured him. "One of the handheld nets. I need to catch a ptarmigan. A whitefish gill net would probably do the trick."

"A gill net?"

Hmm. Clearly Paul had little to do with the "adventure" side of the retreat.

"Would Terry know about those kinds of things?" I asked.

The relief on Paul's face was comical. "Yes," he said eagerly. "You should ask Terry about it when he gets up. He knows way more about it than I do. He should be up soon."

Soon, in this case, meant about five minutes. And as soon as I asked Terry my question, he knew exactly what I was talking about.

"Oh sure," he answered in his whisper-soft voice. "We've got several of them in the shed."

"Would it be okay if I borrowed one for the day?"

"I don't see why not," he told my shoes. "Did you want it now?"

"That'd be nice."

I waved goodby to Paul, who was trying to find the bag of coffee beans.

"First cupboard on your left," I called out. Then I followed Terry outside to the gray weathered, wooden shed that stood behind the Cabin. Terry swung open the door and disappeared into the gloom. I hesitated for a moment.

Selena's killer was not the hiking tourist. He was probably someone from the retreat. I glanced behind me. Saw Paul watching from the Cabin's window. I gave him a tight smile and followed Terry into the shed.

It looked like the inside of a mad prospector's cabin. Nets and fishing rods leaned against the walls, snow-shoes and ropes hung from hooks in the ceiling beams.

There were kayak paddles and canoe paddles and gold-washing pans and other unidentifiable items all stacked haphazardly wherever there was room.

"Here you go," Terry said, passing me the long-handled net. "Did you need a rod too?"

"Oh, I'm not fishing," I told him. "I need it to catch a ptarmigan. Although if you've got a spare dust mask lying around, that would be helpful."

It had just occurred to me that there were probably heavy metals in the dust around Regent. If the wind was up, I sure didn't want to be breathing it. All of a sudden I remembered where I was going to be when I was breathing this dust and why I shouldn't say anything to Terry about it. I held my breath, waiting for the question. It never came.

"I see," Terry said quietly. He rummaged around for a moment, then came up with a box of white dust masks.

"Uh, thanks," I stammered, accepting one of them. Still afraid he'd ask me where I was going. "I'll, um, have these things back by the end of the day."

Suddenly full of nervous energy, I turned around to leave and accidentally grazed my knuckles against the door frame.

"Ow! Shit!"

I held my finger up. A splinter stuck up out of the skin. A big bastard of a one too. I *hated* splinters.

Before I could think about it and totally give myself the willies, I grabbed the piece of wood and, gritting my teeth, I yanked it out. Blood gushed up like a mini geyser.

It was the small sound that alerted me. A sort of

mewling gurgle. I looked up. Terry's normally pale face had whitened to chalk. He was staring at my bloody finger. Transfixed.

"Whoa, there," I said to him, dropping the gill net and hiding my hand behind my back. "Hey, are you okay?"

He blinked and gulped.

"Come on out into the sun," I urged. "Do you need to sit down?"

He swallowed again. Convulsively.

"I'm okay," he told me. "Just . . . keep your hand behind your back . . . if you don't mind."

"Consider it glued there," I assured him.

He suppressed a shudder and offered my shoulder a weak smile. "Ridiculous, isn't it?" he said after a moment. His soft voice sounding embarrassed. "A grown man swooning at the sight of a little blood."

"Aaahh," I waved it off, careful to use my uninjured hand, "my brother's over six feet tall and he did a faceplant the first and only time he tried to donate blood. The nurse at the clinic still asks how he is every time I go in."

I watched Terry watch his feet.

"Maybe you should go grab a coffee or something," I suggested gently.

For a split second, Terry's eyes met mine. "You're really very kind, you know," he murmured. Then, excusing himself, he strode off toward the Cabin. A little unsteadily, I noted as I bent to retrieve the gill net.

I shrugged to myself. We all get a little weirded out by something.

## June ?

I am losing the minutiae of my life.

Small details are escaping me. Not quickly or decisively, but slowly, quietly. Like a sigh on the verge of sleep. Leaving only a void behind.

At first, I thought it was normal. One of those unpleasant consequences of middle age and too much work. A forgotten task here. A misremembered fact there. So I started making lists. But the lists grew. Kept growing in length and number until they became an ocean. Wave upon wave of torn scraps of paper overwhelming my desk, spilling over into the rest of my life. Willa noticed. Of course. "You're working too much," she told me (for the millionth time). "Always out trudging around. Taking notes. Watching your precious ptarmigan. They're not going anywhere."

She does not understand. How many times do I have to tell myself that? I don't think she'll ever understand.

I took a few days off last week. Willa insisted. We drove down to Whitehorse for the weekend. Saw a few movies. Ate at restaurants. Drank coffee in the coffee shops. And for the first time in a long while, I could see more on the horizon than mountains and tundra. It was rejuvenating—Willa had been right about that—but on the last evening, we went out for Mexican food at a place called Santos. Or was it Sanchez? The name escapes me now. The food was excellent, but when I remarked on how funny it was to have a Mexican restaurant in the Yukon, Willa gave me an odd look before agreeing that it seemed strange. That's how I knew we'd eaten there before.

I'm sitting here tonight and I can't remember my first record album, or the day I got braces, or the first book I read that made a difference. Memories of my teenage years and even parts of my undergraduate life are just . . . gone. I remember why my marriage ended, but not how. I remember meeting Willa but not asking her out. And I can't remember if I did laundry yesterday or two weeks ago, or if I bought canned tomatoes the last time I did groceries. Or if I brushed my teeth today. Small details. Nothing earth-shattering, but important all the same.

Sometimes it bothers me that I don't remember them. Other times it doesn't. I feel . . . I don't know, like I'm watching my life from behind a membrane. Transparent, yet impermeable. Nobody seems to realize I'm not really there. Or that I don't remember things. For the most part, I've been able to hide it. Make excuses. Laugh it off. But it's getting harder. I think Paul knows. Yesterday I caught him watching me. His eyes were strange.

If only my head would stop aching.

## June 29?

Dwayne was at the retreat today. I called him Ed. And when I bumped into Jocelyn at lunch, I could have sworn she was Sharon. I haven't seen Shazza since I left Australia. Seven years ago. I've been having trouble focusing my eyes and now they're playing tricks on me.

All last night I kept hearing knocks at the door, but when I got up to see who it was, there was nothing but trees rustling in the wind. I didn't get much sleep. My dreams are troubled with faces from the past. So many faces.

## July 1

Liane wrote again last night. She's found someone. Someone promising. I hope it works out. For her sake and mine. I really don't have the energy to play mentor any more. Too many of my own problems.

Have decided to go back to my control site to check for chicks. Probably too early, but with the unusually warm weather, you never know. And the data is just as important as the numbers from Regent. I need it to prove my case. I'm writing everything down, every last bit of information. I have to. I just can't seem to keep it in my head anymore. Still crushingly tired, but I think I can at least make Pika Camp today. I'll stay overnight and continue to my site tomorrow. I just have to get out and breathe.

The headache is still there and I've got a rash on my feet.

## July 5

I was feeling better. Clearer. More positive. Until I realized I'd forgotten my damn camp stove. How did I become so forgetful?

Stopped to rest at Pika Camp on the way out. Ed was visiting too. Taking a break from his work. Telling Stavros all about how he'd been prospecting in the southern valleys. Funny, that's not where I've seen him—at least I don't think so. Can't quite remember. I didn't say anything though.

Kelt was telling stories about his girlfriend again. Strong woman. I'd like to meet her someday. I could learn from her. My headache was gone by morning—I knew the air would do me good—and I headed to my valley. Sun shining. Not a cloud in the sky. Arctic lupine in full bloom. I felt hopeful and eager to see if any chicks have hatched yet.

There were a few. Fuzzy, speckled little things crouched down in the vegetation. Rocks with feet. I stayed a few days despite the lack of stove. Found several broods.

Yesterday I saw a rare sight. A pair of Lapland longspurs on their breeding grounds. The male soars up into the sky beginning his song only at the moment he starts to drift back down. The melody floated across the tundra. Unutterably beautiful. I cried for an hour. Wishing I could just stay in the mountains forever.

Came back this morning. The weather has turned cold and wet in the higher elevations. I hope the chicks will survive it. They can't thermoregulate until they're ten days old. Harsh reality.

## July 8

Willa's mad at me again. Not sure why. The headaches are back too. Stress? Must go to Regent. Check on the chicks there, but am feeling far too ill to go anywhere.

I burned the frying pan this morning. Forgot I'd turned it on. I must pay more attention to what I'm doing.

# 26

If Terry got weirded out by the sight of blood, I felt the same way about blatant disregard for our natural world. Except I didn't get woozy or weak-kneed, I got mad. And right now, I was fuming.

The Regent Mine site had not improved on closer viewing. Quite the opposite. Up close you could see the rust weeping from the aluminum-sided buildings. The brittle, orange-needled spruce trees. Up close you could see the total absence of anything fresh and green and growing. Up close you could smell the tailings pond and see the small, sad skeletons of birds not careful enough to avoid the polluted water. I thought they might have been ptarmigan.

The mine was about ten kilometers off the Dempster. It had been fenced off with chain link, now blotched with rust like everything else in sight. I'd left my vehicle parked in front of the massive gate. At one time, years ago, the gate had been chained shut, but the chains had long since rusted away. The broken links lay on the ground and the gate hung at an angle. A bit of crouching, a wriggle or two and I had accessed the site.

I had intended on going directly to the northeast corner. Straight to where the drums of arsenic had been dumped. Go in, catch a ptarmigan or two, clip a couple of toenails, get out. That was the plan. But once I slid past the rusting gate, I'd been overcome with a morbid curiosity to see the rest of the site. Dwayne had been fairly down on the place, but I'd seen some pretty toxic sites in my time. How bad could it be?

The answer was, pretty damn bad.

Broken, rusting equipment lay everywhere, surrounded at times by orange plastic fencing now crumpled and tangled. Storage tanks, eaten away by corrosion, spilled their contents onto the ground. I couldn't even guess at what had been in them, except that whatever it was had effectively killed any nearby vegetation. There were a few dead trees, pale and stunted. I knew I was letting my imagination run away with me, but they seemed twisted as if in agony. If I had any doubts the place was polluted, they were fast winging off into the distance. A site like this would take centuries to revegetate.

I'd been in the business long enough to know the soil wouldn't be acutely toxic. I didn't, for example, have to wear full protective gear. Arsenic and cyanide were slow-acting poisons unless, as was the case with Terry's children, massive quantities were ingested. Nevertheless, though the wind was quiet for the time being, I was glad for the dust mask tucked carefully away in my pocket.

And if I had any doubts that the birdlife in the area was still being poisoned, I only had to take one look at the northeast corner of the site to realize the worst of my fears were not only real, but probably understated.

The pit was at the end of a gravel road a good hour's hike from the main facility. Brown, scrubby weeds were slowly restaking their claim on the land, breaking the packed gravel in large chunks. The road just ended. There were no signs or marks to indicate what was buried there, but the cement bulkhead was a bit of a giveaway. They were often used as plugs to seal off underground chambers and stopes. I counted seven bulkheads. That was just what I could see from where I was standing, there could have been more. But the number of pits wasn't what I found so disturbing. Dwayne had said there was enough arsenic trioxide here to poison everybody on the planet. I'd been prepared for quantity. What I hadn't prepared for was the state of the vegetation.

The trees here had not shriveled or rusted like the ones closer to the stack. This corner of the site had been far enough away—and probably downwind—from the poisonous fumes sent up the smokestack over the decades. The trees weren't stellar examples of their species, but at least they were the right color. But color didn't concern me at the moment. What set my heart pounding was the way they leaned and tilted.

I cursed long and imaginatively.

There was only one thing that could cause an effect like this. That could result in another Drunken Forest. The permafrost around the storage pits was melting.

**July 11**

Paul was watching me again today he thinks I haven't noticed but I've seen him watching out of the corner of his eyes. I've seen him disappear around a cabin when I've looked up or melt away into the trees without a sound.

What does he want why does he keep watching me with those eyes?

The spiders were back too.

I swear I could see them moving dozens bulbous black bodies skittering across the logs. Jumped out of bed when I saw them banged my shins against the bed frame and the spiders. Stopped.

Knots just knots in the wood.

I wish they'd stop doing that I'll have nasty bruises on my legs now.

**27**

By definition, permafrost is soil or rock that remains frozen for two or more years. It's covered by an active layer (basically ground that thaws in summer and freezes in winter) and can take centuries to accumulate. Permafrost is not, however, as permanent as its name implies.

In fact, it can be pretty finicky, when it comes right down to it. Physiography, air temperatures, and the insulating effects of snow all affect the growth (or degradation) of permafrost. If the overlying tundra—the active layer—is removed or severely damaged, the permafrost underneath will melt. When the Dempster Highway was built, several yards of gravel were piled on top of the tundra to avoid thawing the permafrost below. A road built directly on top of the tundra would have quickly subsided and sunk as the permafrost underneath it melted from the weight of the traffic.

Mining activities had much the same effect. The disturbances associated with excavation and drilling often cause permafrost to degrade. Twenty years ago, the generally accepted thought was that any permafrost that had melted would rapidly re-establish itself once mining activities in the area had ceased. But back then, nobody factored climate change into the equation.

Climate change can warm permafrost, though the effects are considerably greater when the climate changes enough to affect snow accumulation. No snow equals no insulation. It was bad for pikas and ptarmigan. It was worse for permafrost. I was now staring at a textbook example of this.

I swore again under my breath.

Cement bulkheads aside, the one thing at Regent that had any chance of keeping the arsenic "safely" encased was the permafrost. If the permafrost was thawing, then it was a good bet the drums were rusting and probably leaking. And, judging from the angles of some of these trees, the ice had been melting for quite some time. Which meant the drums could have been leaking for quite some time.

There was no longer any doubt in my mind about what Selena had been doing here—and what she suspected. But why the big secret? Even if nobody else had noticed the tilting trees, the general condition of the Regent Mine was hardly unknown—especially up here in the North. Why hadn't she told anybody about her work here?

I spent the afternoon a attempting to net a couple of the white-tailed ptarmigan I'd spied lurking around the easternmost bulkhead. Trying the whole time to come up with a reason for her secrecy. Eventually I caught one of the birds. A first-year breeder, judging from the pigmentation of the primaries. It had also been banded and tagged.

One of Selena's. Lucky me.

I tucked the bird's head under my left arm and carefully took samples of feathers and nails before releasing it, ruffled with indignation, back into the willows. I dropped the samples in an empty envelope, labeled it, and zipped it into my jacket pocket. When the wind came up, I secured the white dust mask over my nose and mouth and continued working. The whole time, trying and failing to think of a single reason why Selena Barry had kept this to herself.

It took me the rest of the day to catch and sample the other ptarmigan. Little beggars were almost as paranoid as Kelt's pikas. Still, I was lucky to net two birds. According to her field notes, Selena had had many a day when she hadn't caught any.

I'd been at it for a good four or five hours. Honor was satisfied—at least for today. If I wanted more samples, I could come back tomorrow. Right now my back hurt from hunching over shrubs, my feet were sore from clambering over rock and stumbling over tussock tundra, my stomach had clenched up from hunger, and I was starting to get crabby. Definitely time to go. I turned and headed back to my SUV.

I hadn't thought to bring a snack with me. And because I was driving a rental, I didn't even have a piece of gum or a stray Werther's stashed in the glove compartment. Which made me even grumpier when I remembered. Gods, I was hungry.

*A pregnant woman should really take better care of herself.*

Like a biting insect, the thought pricked my consciousness. I squashed it fiercely.

I was passing by the roaster complex, on my way back to the front gate. The sun had long since disappeared behind storm clouds. The sky looked bruised. Unwholesome. Wind wheezed through dried grasses. A constant low-level rasp. I shivered and checked to make sure my dust mask was still securely in place.

The rusting structure appeared even more lonely and forlorn than it had earlier. A sickly beige box of a building. Input and output pipes going nowhere. Delivering nothing. I tried to imagine what the place had looked like when it was booming. Loaders, trucks, and other equipment rumbling in the silence. Belching black breath into the crisp air. Hundreds of workers milling around the site, busily carrying out their tasks.

*Bang!*

I almost jumped out of my skin at the sound.

*Whoa. Good imagination, Robyn.*

Then there was another sound. A sort of hollow, muffled clang. Like a metal door slamming shut.

I hadn't imagined that.

I spun around and scanned the scene. The place seemed as empty as before. But the prickly feeling on the back of my neck told me otherwise.

Someone was here.

I knew what Kelt would say. I knew it was stupid. But still, my feet walked me over to the roaster and my hand reached out for the nearest door.

Some instinct, some shred of self-preservation, made me hesitate. I suddenly realized there wasn't a soul who knew where I was. With the Dempster ten kilometers behind me, there wasn't even a tourist or trucker around to notice my SUV parked by the gate. And Selena Barry's killer was still out there. Somewhere. Thoroughly spooked, I withdrew my hand and listened hard.

Nothing but the breathy whistling of the wind.

*Gods, it's isolated out here.*

Maybe I was imagining things.

No. There had definitely been two strange sounds.

Maybe some piece of equipment was loose and banging in the wind.

Possibly.

But then why had one of the noises sounded like a door slamming shut? Why did I have the distinct feeling that somebody was watching me?

*Maybe because the wind is playing tricks on your ears. Maybe because you have an overactive imagination.*

Again, possibly.

There was only one way to find out. Before I could change my mind, I reached out to the rusting doorknob and gave it a yank.

It was locked tight.

Or rusted tight. I wasn't sure which. Annoyed, more at myself than anything else, I circled the roaster complex, looking for another way in. I found a couple more doors. All locked as securely as the first one I'd tried.

What had I expected? The place had been abandoned for years. There was no reason for anyone to be lurking around. I took a deep, shaky breath and blew it out in a sigh that was part relief, part frustration. I must've been imagining things after all. I *hated* freaking myself out like that. It was hell on the nerves.

I retraced my steps to the front gate, the hairs on the back of my neck still convinced that someone was watching me. I ignored them, though it took a certain amount of effort to refrain from looking over my shoulder.

*Damn imagination.*

I ripped my jeans wriggling back under the gate.

*Damn gate.*

And got rust stains all over my jacket when I stumbled against it.

*Damn rust.*

And because I was looking down, examining the tear in my pants, I saw the boot prints in the dust.

Large boot prints circling all around my vehicle.

## July 14

Stomach flu. Can't keep anything down. Willa is solicitous and loving feels like it did when we first met. God, feel lousy. Going back to bed. Willa keeps trying to chicken broth me back to health. Despise the stuff wish she'd remember that.

## July 16

Starting to feel better but I can't stand the taste of soy milk anymore. Strange. Hope it doesn't last. Being lactose-intolerant limits my options enough. Thought I had the energy to write, but I don't. Going back to bed.

## July 19

I've recovered from the flu but it feels like everything is going wrong. I had a big fight with Willa two days ago. About nothing, really. Her art supplies littering the house. How much time I spend in the field. How she never cleans up in the kitchen. Small, stupid things. Bitter, hurtful words. I'm sure she is just worried about her upcoming show. Not sure what my excuse is.

And after all that I lost the ptarmigan at my control site—or at least I couldn't find them yesterday with my radio. Not a peep. I panicked. Without stopping to think, I had Dwayne take me up in his plane.

Stupid.

It was a problem with my equipment—which I should have realized, had I been thinking at all clearly. One does not lose a whole flock of ptarmigan overnight. Dwayne was full of kind understanding, but I felt like an imbecile.

I've got a painful rash on my feet. My hair is dry and dull. And my fingernails are brittle and splitting down to the quick. If I didn't know that Regent wasn't acutely toxic, I might worry about poisoning. But I'm careful when I'm on-site and I've only been working there steadily for the past couple of months. It must be stress. It can really do terrible things to one's body. One more thing to worry about.

## July 21

Willa has gone to Edmonton for her show. She asked me again to come. Demanded that I come. But I couldn't summon the energy.

I'm just so damn tired lately. Trying to eat properly, but it's hard. Feel like I'm living on cereal. At least I can stomach soy milk again. Willa was angry that I wouldn't come, of course. And hurt. But she left and I stayed. It isn't like she's never had a show before. Why can't she be a little more understanding? Jocelyn's reaction was about what I expected.

Dragged myself out to Regent today. Not sure why. Validation maybe. No energy to do any meaningful work, though. Saw Ed again. So much for his claims of prospecting further south (or did I just imagine that? I can't remember now.).

I should have stayed in the field. Jocelyn kept giving me filthy looks all evening. If her lips were any tighter, they'd disappear entirely.

## July 23?

What is the color of death? The raw, red pain of suffering? Or the soft, mossy gray of nothingness? Perhaps it is a new color altogether. A shade and hue not found in any other thing.

The headaches are back. The rash has spread to my hands. I'm wondering if something else is wrong. Something beyond stress. A kind of imbalance in my body. There is something sapping my energy, closing my world in on itself. I feel on the verge of passing out most of the time. Having trouble focusing my eyes and my hands are shaking. I wake up in the morning even more exhausted than when I went to bed. I must be sick. I should go down to Whitehorse and have it checked out.

What if it's something serious? Cancer? I never thought of that, did I? Never factored in such a thing.

I need to make plans.

**July ?**

Quiet here. Still feel like utter shit. Willa called today. She's staying in Edmonton for an additional week. Said she was having trouble getting a cheap flight back, but I think she's angry. The show opened well.

Thinking about sending my notes on Regent to Kelt's girlfriend. Robyn. An ideal solution? Wouldn't have to tell her why. The data alone . . . pique her interest? She'll read them and go out and see. Explanation enough. No need to get into old history. An ideal solution.

# 28

"Hey Kaye."

"Robyn! How're you doing? Are you enjoying the Yukon?"

"It's great." I gazed out the Cabin's window at a small flock of redpolls fluttering around the feeder. The sun was just at the right angle to light up their bright red caps. "It's everything you promised it would be."

"And Kelt? He's well? Things are good between you?"

I crossed my fingers and assured her that Kelt and my relationship with him were both hale and hearty. We chatted a little longer about the birdlife in the Yukon (Kaye had become an amateur birder in the last couple of years) before I broached the subject I really wanted to talk about.

"Kaye, I was wondering . . . have there been any RFPS floating around for the Regent Mine? It was a hard rock gold mine just off the Dempster. Closed down about ten or so years ago . . . "

"Twelve, actually."

I closed my mouth. Opened it again. "You know it, then."

"I do now. An RFP was issued two weeks ago. I've had Ti-Marc digging around for background information. The place is a right mess."

"It is," I agreed.

"Oh? You've been?" Kaye sounded surprised.

"Uh, just flew over it," I lied quickly.

"So you phoned me on an expensive satellite phone because you were curious if we're going to submit a proposal?"

The thought hadn't occurred to me, but I grasped at it.

"I did wonder," I told her.

"And, of course, your interest is purely selfless. Has absolutely nothing to do with the fact that Kelt will be working in the same area."

I grinned. "It never even crossed my mind," I said innocently.

Her snort was eloquent. "Rest easy," she told me. "Ben and I have been discussing it, and we've decided to submit a bid."

It was good (if unlooked for) news. I'd pretty much cleaned out my bank account coming up here this year. Kelt's preoccupation with pikas wouldn't be so bad if we could both be working in the Yukon for the next several years. We'd be working in different areas, of course, but we'd have a better chance of seeing each other than if we relied on my meager bank account. Of course, all this was moot if Woodrow didn't get the contract. Ours was a competitive business.

And all this was moot if I was pregnant.

I tried to bury the thought. If I *were* pregnant, the next several years would be more about bottles and diapers than pikas and ptarmigan. I'd have to take maternity leave. And what about fieldwork afterwards? Both Kelt and I couldn't be in the field at the same time. How would we work that? My stomach twisted and I cut off that train of thought before I got totally panicked.

I managed to stay on the phone a little longer with Kaye, keeping the conversation light and chatty. It took effort. A lot of effort.

I rang off with a sigh of relief. Even though it was for her own good, I felt bad lying to Kaye about my interest in Regent. And the whole pregnancy issue was really starting to feel like an anvil on my shoulders.

I was accumulating secrets. Me! I'd never had a skeleton in my closet (except for the odd specimen). Never felt the need to tell lies. And here I was lying to my boss and lying by omission to my partner. I didn't like it one bit, but with Kaye so overprotective and my relationship with Kelt so shaky, I liked the alternative even less. I sighed again.

Quite apart from all this personal upheaval, Kaye's news about the RFP had only deepened the mystery of Selena Barry's work. The request had been issued two weeks ago, which meant that Selena had started her study well beforehand—maybe even years beforehand. Why?

"A copper for 'em, mate."

I nearly jumped out of my skin. I spun around and saw Ed leaning casually in the doorway. "Gods, Ed!" I gasped. "Warn a guy."

Ed uncrossed his arms and straightened up. "Sorry, Robyn," he apologized. "Wasn't trying to sneak around."

I managed a shaky smile. My nerves had taken a few too many hits today. "No, I know. I'm sorry, I was miles away. And speaking of miles away, I thought you were out prospecting. The Lost Valley of Blue Beryls, if I recall correctly."

"Ah," Ed shrugged. "Had a run of bad luck with my equipment and came back early. Bit of a pisser, really, but"—he bent down and retrieved something by his feet—"there *are* compensations." He was holding a six-pack of Yukon Gold beer. His eyes were twinkly. "Care to join me for a tinnie? I'm not much on drinkin' with flies."

"Sounds great! I—uh, on second thought, I'll just have coffee."

Ed gave me a strange look.

"Empty stomach," I lied (another lie!). "If I drink, it'll go right to my head."

While I made coffee, Ed regaled me with tales of past prospecting successes.

"Do you think Jocelyn would mind if I ate one of these muffins?" I asked when he paused to open another beer. "I'm starving."

"I'm sure it'd be fine." Ed watched as I chose a muffin and tried not to wolf it down. "Been working hard out there, have you?"

"Lots of yakka," I mumbled around the muffin. "But I found Selena's second study site."

"Come again."

I swallowed, then repeated myself.

Ed stroked his bristled chin thoughtfully. "Crikey. A *second* site?"

My mouth full with more muffin, I nodded.

"She wasn't out by Pika Camp?"

"She was," I told him. "But she also had a second site that nobody seems to have known about."

"That's odd."

I shrugged and popped the last bit of muffin in my mouth.

"Whereabouts was it?"

"By an abandoned gold mine. I found a bunch of tagged ptarmigan out there—even managed to catch a couple of 'em for sampling." I didn't mention the footprints around my car that I'd also found.

"Sampling?"

"Feathers and toenails," I explained. "To test for toxins."

"Toxins?" Ed belched quietly into his beard. "That really much of a problem up here?" He seemed doubtful.

"Oh yes, my friend." I pulled a face. "Think about it. Old hard rock mine. Arsenic-bearing rock. Leaking barrels. Melting permafrost. Yeah, I'd say it was a problem."

He took another slug of his beer. "What are you going to do, then?" he asked.

I wrapped my hands around my coffee mug and chewed my lower lip. "Not sure," I said finally. "I'll probably have to go out and sample a few more birds. Just to be sure. But, let's face it, nobody's hired me to do a study of the site. There's only so much I *can* do—apart from letting the cops know about it, of course. I *am*

266

wondering why Selena was out there in the first place. And who hired her for the job."

Ed finished his beer and shrugged. "Regent's been closed for years," he said. "Didn't think anybody was interested in it."

I grunted my agreement, then it struck me. "How did you know her site was by the Regent Mine?" I asked casually. "I don't think I mentioned the name."

Ed slanted me an odd look. "I'm a geologist, mate. I know about all the mining activities out here, past *and* present."

"Oh," I said, squirming a bit in embarrassment. "Right."

"Speaking of activities . . . what are you doing chasing ptarmigan? I thought you were helping Kelt with his little pikas."

It was an innocent question, but something about his voice triggered my internal alarm. I suddenly remembered that the last time I'd seen him, Kelt and I had been arguing. Ed was leaning toward me now, his eyes bright with speculation—and an all-too-obvious appreciation.

This was the last thing I needed.

"I *was* helping," I told him. "For a few days. But the RCMP asked me to look into Selena's work so I came out for a bit. I'll be going back to Pika Camp as soon as I'm finished."

Ed leaned back again. "Ah." He sounded a bit disappointed, but he took another sip of his beer and offered me a good-natured smile.

Just then the doorknob rattled. Ed and I looked up as Paul and his wild hair wafted into the room.

"Ed! You're back early."

Was it my imagination, or did Paul sound odd? I listened as Ed complained about torn backpacks and defective GPS units. If Paul was unhappy to see him, Ed didn't seem to be picking up on it. I was probably just paranoid.

"Is there any coffee left?" Paul asked hopefully after commiserating with Ed over his equipment problems. He had already politely declined Ed's offer of a beer. As Paul stirred several heaping spoonfuls of sugar into his mug, I told him about going out to Regent.

"Jocelyn told me you'd found some of Selena's birds out there," he said. "So, she had two studies going, did she?"

"Looks that way."

"Well." Paul tested his coffee and added more sugar. "Someone was bound to have a look around Regent one of these days. Did you know that for the first five years the mine was operating, there were no pollution control devices?" he asked.

I blinked, more surprised by his demeanor than the information. His soft, slow voice had become clearer. Stronger. He didn't sound like a dream-drenched elf anymore. He sounded like a Web site.

"I did not know that," I admitted.

"It's true. Over 7000 kilograms of arsenic trioxide dust went up that stack."

I wrinkled my nose.

"In order to extract gold from the rock, Regent used a process that produced arsenic-rich gases as a byproduct. And all that gas—well, most of it anyway—was captured in the form of arsenic trioxide dust—ATD."

"Nasty stuff, that," Ed remarked. "Sixty percent pure arsenic, if I'm not mistaken."

"Yikes," I said, glad again that I'd thought to bring a dust mask.

"Yikes is right," Paul agreed. "There weren't many people who lived around here back then, but there were some. And when they started complaining about the emissions, Regent installed a baghouse dust collector. That was in the late 1970s."

"That must've helped," Ed said.

"It did—a little. But even with the collector, there was still several hundred kilograms of ATD sent up the stack each day."

I nodded in belated understanding. "No wonder the place is a moonscape."

Ed belched his agreement and cracked open another beer—his third now. The fizzing gurgle as it hit the glass was cheerfully inviting. I topped up my coffee before I could be tempted.

"You know, for all the so-called studies they conducted," Paul said once I'd settled back down with my mug, "not one even *predicted* significant impacts on the vegetation—or the wildlife. And who knows what's happening with the barrels they 'stored' underground."

"Nothing good," I told him frankly. "Not from what I saw. Not with the permafrost melting around them."

"The permafrost's melting?" Paul's eyes widened. "That's bad news," he admitted. "I thought the permafrost was supposed to re-establish itself around the storage vaults. You know, seal in the arsenic trioxide. That's what the CPHA study said would happen."

"CPHA?"

"The Canadian Public Health Association."

"They did a study on Regent? When?"

Paul leaned back in his chair, cradling his coffee mug in his hands. "Back in the late '70s. Fellow by the name of Bruce Dyer was heading it up. Regent was storing the dust in drums. There were hundreds of them, all piled to one side of the site. There was, as the company put it, some concern in the community about arsenic poisoning. *Some* concern."

Ed snorted into his beer.

"Yeah," Paul agreed. "Anyhow, the task force conducted the study, but they weren't too quick about making any recommendations—not until it was too late."

"Terry's kids," I guessed.

"Terry's got kids?" Ed asked.

Paul was looking at me strangely. "Um . . . no, not any more," he told Ed. "They were killed in 1979 after they ate poisoned snow out at the mine."

"*Hell's bells!*"

"Yeah. The company got the drums underground pretty fast after that."

"Not fast enough, mate."

"No," Paul said. "There were never any charges laid, and the deaths were ruled accidental. Very few people know about it now. Most of the workers moved away when the mine closed. Obviously Terry doesn't talk about it."

Ed shook his head slowly. "Cripes, I'm amazed he's still standing."

"I think there were a lot of years when he wasn't," Paul said. "He's a stronger man than me. I can't imagine how you'd even begin to cope with something like that—I don't *want* to imagine it. How did *you* know about it?" This last was directed to me. Paul's attitude had changed again. He seemed tense now. Distrustful.

"Jocelyn told me."

Paul was shocked.

"She wanted to make sure I didn't ask Terry about the Regent Mine," I explained. "After I found out Selena was working there. Why is that so surprising?"

Paul blinked a few times. "It's just . . . she's very protective of Terry. She's *never* talked about this with anyone. I don't even think she ever told Willa. Frankly, I'm . . . I'm a little surprised she told you."

I squirmed, remembering that Jocelyn had, in fact, mentioned that she never spoke about the subject. *Shit.* Me and my big mouth. I was suddenly, profoundly, glad that Kelt hadn't been around to hear me let it slip.

"I'm sorry," I told Paul. "I shouldn't have said anything. I promise I won't mention it again." There was an awkward silence, then, "So . . . um, the task force actually recommended the drums be stored underground?" I asked.

Paul seemed as eager to change the subject as I was. "In stopes where permafrost was evident," he agreed, nodding. "I guess back then, it was the most acceptable means of dealing with the waste. Safe and—perhaps more to the point—permanent. But if what you say about the permafrost is true . . ." he trailed off, lost in unpleasant thoughts.

"And you said the report came out in the late '70s?"

"It was published in 1981."

"Hmm. We know a lot more now."

"And none of it good," Paul sighed.

"No."

We were quiet for a moment, then, "How do you know so much about all this?" Ed asked. His eyes were guarded, almost wary. "I mean, crikey, you sound like a bloody expert on the place."

"Oh." Paul lifted his shoulder, suddenly shy. "I'm . . . I'm kind of working on a cycle of poems about it," he said. "I've done a lot of research. I've talked to people who worked at the mine. Last summer, I even tracked down Bruce Dyer in Vancouver." He paused for a moment before continuing. "Jocelyn gets annoyed with me sometimes. She thinks I'm obsessed." He shrugged. "It's hard not to be. It's sort of like when you see an accident. You want to look away, but you can't."

"Horrified fascination," I said.

"Exactly!" Paul looked down at his empty coffee mug, hiding his expression from me. "You know, we all knew Regent was a time bomb, I just . . . I never thought it would go off during my lifetime."

"My boss said INAC's put out a request for proposals to clean it up," I told him, wanting to offer a ray of hope, however small.

But Paul was less than reassured by the news. I couldn't blame him. Offhand, I couldn't think of a feasible way to even begin cleaning up a site like Regent—and I was *in* the business.

"Well, I guess I'd better finish those poems," Paul said, lifting his head. His voice was steady with determination. "If there's finally going to be some action over there, people are going to need to be informed. And as Ed said, I'm a bloody expert on the place."

**July 25**

The weather has been terrible. Cold and very wet. Feeling better, but still tired. I think I might be getting a cold too. I started taking massive amounts of vitamin C. Not sure if it's helping or not. At worst, I'll just have expensive pee.

Terry and Paul have gone down to Vancouver for two weeks, and Jocelyn is much occupied with three elderly couples from France. The French are less than thrilled with the weather and seem to want to take it out on Jocelyn. They tax even her boundless maternal instincts (no small feat). When they're not complaining, however, they bicker constantly among themselves. Hard, clipped words pinched out in harder tones. There's been quite enough of that around here lately. I have retreated to my own little cabin for the duration of their stay.

Ed showed up at my door last night. The weather, it seems, drove him back to the retreat and the quarreling guests drove him out of the Cabin. I took pity on him and shared my spaghetti. An entertaining dinner guest. Funny. I never fully realized how unique humor is to each culture until now. That distinctive Aussie humor. How I've missed it!

This morning the cabin smells like lavender.

**July 28**

It's a relief to have Terry away. To have respite from eyes that refuse to see me. Ed and I have taken to hanging out here at home until the weather clears or the French tourists leave. Playing Trivial Pursuit and eating cookies. Jocelyn disapproves. Apparently I shouldn't be having so much fun while Willa's away.

It seems I was right about Ed staking claims out by Regent. I asked him point blank tonight and he admitted it. Most reluctantly! Prospecting, he informed me, was a profession much beset with suspicion, misdirection, and outright deceit. He told me of prospectors who 'mistakenly' leave false maps lying around in bars. Or who carefully put out that they're looking for gold when in reality, they're looking for diamonds. Or who stake only a few claims at a time so as not to trigger a claiming rush in a promising area. No wonder Ed wears army fatigues in the field. It seems an altogether strange way to make a living.

It was a night for sharing secrets—or half secrets, to be precise. In turn, Ed wanted to know what I was doing out by Regent. I told him only that I suspected the ptarmigan were being poisoned and that I was keeping it quiet until I knew for certain. He seemed surprised but agreed secrecy was probably for the best. As he put it, I'd have to be off my scone to stir up the possum for what might turn out to be nothing.

I must admit I downplayed the situation. What is happening at Regent is NOT "nothing." But I didn't want to get into further explanations (my experience with Terry was a hard lesson in the dangers of unexpurgated confidences), so I agreed with Ed and changed the subject.

I never asked Ed what he'd found, or thought he'd found, out there. He seemed to appreciate it. But after his colorful description of the prospecting world, I did assure him with right hand held high that his secret was safe with me and I swore most solemnly in my best Girl Guide manner to remove all mention of him from my field notes. We both burst out laughing then. As if the sharing of secrets had precipitated a lightening of our spirits. It really wasn't that funny, but we laughed until our eyes were swimming in tears and our sides were sore. A welcome release of tensions.

It's been a long, long time since I laughed so much. Why don't I laugh anymore?

**29**

Dinner that evening was a disaster. Willa was no longer taking her meals in her cabin, but she might as well have been for all the interest she took in both food and company. She sat at the table pinch-faced and silent, mechanically forking her food into her mouth, refusing to meet anyone's eyes. That didn't surprise me. But Jocelyn and Terry were both sober and uncommunicative as well. And Paul spent the meal with his head bent over his plate, thoughts concealed by his mass of tangled hair. Although nobody mentioned Selena, her uneasy ghost sat at the table with us. Fear and mistrust weighed heavily on the room. Even the candles Jocelyn had lit sputtered and jumped as if aware their cheery flames were out of place and unappreciated. There was no sign of Ed. Or of the RCMP officers. The only person who seemed totally oblivious to the atmosphere was Michele, who had, for some reason I still wasn't clear on, come out again from Pika Camp.

As if I didn't have enough stress in my life.

"... and when I asked for a coffee to go, he said, 'This is Paris, you have a café or you go,'" Michele tittered and looked at me expectantly.

I stared back blankly. No clue as to what she'd been talking about.

"Get it? 'You have a café or you go,'" she repeated with just a hint of irritation. She was still leaning toward me. Still flashing her trembly lips and smiling at me adoringly. She'd been doing it all through dinner. But now a tiny frown was starting to wrinkle her brow.

"I liked France," Jocelyn remarked with a shrug. "I didn't find the waiters rude at all. To tell you the truth, I was a little disappointed. I'd heard so much about them."

I chuckled and Michele looked annoyed.

"So, Robyn," she smoldered at me, "how long will we have the pleasure of your company?"

The word *pleasure* seemed to linger on her tongue. I glanced at her and she licked her lips ever so slightly.

Man, this chick was just not getting it. I was beginning to wonder if we *were* the hottest species in the galaxy. I hadn't had this many people hitting on me since ... come to think of it, I'd *never* had this many people hitting on me. Was I giving off some weirdass pheromone? At least Ed had backed off. And speaking of Ed, why wasn't he at dinner?

"Where did Ed get to?" I asked Jocelyn.

Michele pouted at me and I realized belatedly that I hadn't answered her question.

"I've no idea," Jocelyn was saying. "I thought he'd be here for dinner. He said he was hungry, but"—she shrugged—"he can always have a plate of leftovers when he gets back."

She stood up and started clearing the table. "Do you want to give me a hand, Willa?"

Willa had been staring dully into space. She gazed at Jocelyn without recognition for a second, then blinked. Back on planet Earth again. "Um, yeah. Sure."

"You need another pair of hands?" I offered.

Jocelyn gave me a small smile, but shook her head. "You're a *paying* guest," she reminded me. "And besides, Willa and I can manage. Here, hon, you clear the food and I'll get the plates."

Under the general noise of scuffling feet and chairs being pushed back, I turned to Michele. "Can I talk to you outside?" I asked quietly.

Her sulky expression suddenly cleared and her eyes shone. She nodded eagerly.

I didn't waste any time. As soon as we got outside, I crossed my arms over my chest and turned toward her.

"I'm not interested," I said without preamble.

"What do you—"

"You know what I mean," I said. "You've been hitting on me since I first met you. I'm not interested."

"Robyn, don't be trapped by the tyranny of monogamy."

*The tyranny of monogamy?*

"That's what it is, you know." She bent towards me earnestly.

I leaned away, unwilling to take a step back. To give her any ground. "And yet," I said, "strangely, I don't feel either trapped or tyrannized."

"That's because you're a victim—"

"Don't be an ass," I interrupted. "I'm no victim. I'm perfectly happy with my sexual orientation—and with my partner—"

"It doesn't seem that way to me."

I gave her a steady look. "You know, my relationship with Kelt is none of your damn business," I told her coldly. "Back off. I'm not interested in you or your uninformed theories. You have something to say about pikas or fieldwork? Fine. Anything else and, quite frankly, I'm not interested in hearing it."

I started to turn away.

"Fine!" she screeched. "Be that way! I'm used to prejudice."

I spun around so quickly Michele took an involuntary step backwards.

"Prejudice!" I exploded. "This isn't about *persecution*, Michele."

I took a deep breath and tried to lower my voice to a more normal level. I really should have taken this further away from the Cabin. Everybody inside was probably listening. Too late now.

"I don't give a rat's ass which sex gets you off," I told her. "I really don't. What I *do* care about is the fact that you keep hitting on me when I've made it quite clear I'm not interested. And it has nothing to do with you being a woman. And it has nothing to do with you being bisexual. If you were a heterosexual male, I'd be saying exactly the same thing."

"Sure you would," she sneered.

I shook my head and threw up my hands. I might as well be talking to a ptarmigan.

She reached out and grabbed at my arm. "Robyn—"

I shook her hand off. "Leave me alone, Michele. I'd really rather not go to Kelt with this."

She dropped her hand and stared at me. Her lips trembled (big surprise).

I sighed inwardly, my anger draining away. There was nothing I could say that she was going to understand. In a way, I felt sorry for her.

"Goodnight, Michele." I took a few backwards steps, watching to make sure she wasn't following me, then I turned on to the path heading back to my tent.

Michele may be a good scientist, but, gods, the woman was clueless when it came to just about everything else. I mean, what the hell did she think she was doing—

Stepping around the corner of the Cabin, I nearly smacked face-first into Frank Matas. I rocked back on my heels.

"Constable!" I blurted.

He barely registered my presence. He was staring past me. In that unguarded moment, his face registered shock, anger, and a deep, deep revulsion. I took an involuntary step backwards and glanced over my shoulder. Michele had already started to move away.

When I looked back at Matas again, he had his face under control. Cold, rigid, professional.

"Having trouble?" he asked. His tone deceptively mild, but the slight flicker in his left eye betrayed him.

"Nothing I can't handle," I told him. Still trying to figure out what had shocked him so much. His eyes had wandered back to Michele's receding figure. The flicker was still evident. Quickly I reviewed my conversation with her. It had been brief and to the point. There had been nothing shocking about it—unless, of course, you didn't know about Michele's orientation. I paused to consider that.

Could it be that Frank Matas had failed to clue in to the fact that Michele was bisexual? That would explain the revulsion. The man was a total homophobe. And wasn't there some talk that Michele had had a fling with him? Yes, Rachel had mentioned something about Michele sleeping her way out of a traffic ticket. That would explain the shock.

Well, I'd already had an earful of Matas' prejudices. I wasn't about to waste anymore of my life hearing them again. "Excuse me," I said pointedly.

He transferred his gaze to me.

"I'd like to get by," I said.

"Of course." He stepped to one side with exaggerated politeness.

I brushed by him and continued to my tent. I could feel his eyes on my back the whole time.

## July 29

Oh god. How could I have been so stupid?

Is it because sex with a man is easier than sex with another woman? Requiring less effort, less involvement? Or is it just because Ed sounds like a distant memory of home? These past few months, I've felt so removed from everything. Distant and cold. Lonely. Dead. But last night, for a brief time, I truly felt present. Alive in the here and now. And I was utterly seduced by it.

To be perfectly honest, I was seduced by him too. By his gentleness, that incongruous smell of lavender, and by that damn accent. He was a tender, surprising lover—he even wrote me a poem. Left it on my pillow this morning. A man with hidden depths. So very different from Murray, who was about as deep as a bird bath.

Still, how could I have been so stupid? I love my Willa. We've been going through some difficult times, I know, but she is both best friend and soulmate. How could I even think of jeopardizing that with a one-night stand? I refused Liane. Refused Michele— and she practically threw herself at me. So why couldn't I say no to him?

Why did Willa have to stay in Edmonton?

## July 30

I told Ed last night. Just as his hands were about to slide around me in greeting.

It was a mistake, I said. A moment of weakness. Not to be repeated. I was prepared to be firm. Had prepared for it all that afternoon. I expected him to be angry, but somehow I never expected him to be hurt. He didn't say a word, just looked at me, his gaze cutting through me like an Xacto blade. Then he turned and walked away. I wanted to call him back to explain. To apologize. But he kept walking and I stayed silent. I barely know this man. Why do I feel his hurt so intensely?

The weather cleared overnight and Jocelyn tells me Ed went back out early this morning. Even before the sun was up.

Is there anything I can do right in this life?

## August 1

Paul was looking at me strangely today. As if he knows. Jocelyn was quiet and unfriendly. More than usual? I can't tell. Does it show?

Stupid, stupid, stupid.

If only I could take back that night.

**30**

Of course, by the following morning, I was regretting my words. Well . . . maybe not my *words*, but I was regretting the harshness of their delivery. Michele had Issues with a capital I. Problems that had little to do with her sexual orientation (I hadn't been lying about my utter indifference to that aspect of her) and more to do with her overwhelming need for somebody to take care of her. For somebody to love her. It made me wonder if there was anybody out there who did. I suspected not. Or at least not in the way she needed them to. A less-than-ideal childhood? Perhaps. Ultimately, it didn't matter. You can't really blame someone for something that's not their fault—even if they do annoy the crap out of you.

So I rolled out of bed that morning prepared to have another talk with her before I headed out to the Regent mine again. A kinder, gentler sort of talk. Only trouble was, I couldn't find her.

"I haven't seen her," Jocelyn told me when I wandered into the Cabin.

"She's not in her tent, either."

"I have no idea where she is, then." Jocelyn's tone was clipped.

I slid onto a stool. "What's up?" I asked her. "You seem a bit . . ."

"Annoyed?" she suggested. "Irritated? Pissed off? Stressed? I am. A little. Ed never showed up for dinner last night." She gestured toward a Saran-wrapped plate on the counter.

I crinkled my brow. "Oh. That's weird."

"What's weird?" asked Paul, stepping into the room.

In a few terse words, Jocelyn explained about Ed. I got the impression that she was really annoyed with Paul, though he seemed oblivious to it if she was.

"I think he went back out," Paul said mildly. "I saw him hiking off with a giant backpack early this morning—or late last night, depending on your point of view."

Jocelyn made a frustrated noise. "Sometimes those scientists . . ." she began, then caught herself and slid me a contrite look. "I mean . . ."

"Don't worry," I laughed, waving it off. "I know exactly what you mean."

"All I want is to be kept informed," Jocelyn sighed. "Is that too much to ask for? The tourists know when mealtimes are and *they're* always back in time for them. Ed told me he'd be here for supper. I set some aside for him. Put it together on a nice plate." She picked up the plastic covered plate and started scraping the contents into the garbage. "And now here I am wasting good food. He told me he'd be here for breakfast too—so did Michele, for that matter—and now you say he's gone back into the field, and she's nowhere to be found."

Thoroughly worked up now, she slapped the plate on the counter beside the sink. Her lips were thin and tight. Paul looked like he wanted to be anywhere but here. "So do I cook for them or not?"

It was meant as a rhetorical question, but I answered it promptly.

"I wouldn't."

She paused and glanced over at me, one eyebrow raised quizzically.

"Rules of the house," I told her with a shrug. "If they can't follow 'em, too bad. If they come looking for breakfast, toss them a box of Corn Flakes or something."

"They're paying for room and board."

"So? At field camp, if you miss meals, you go without or you make something yourself. I realize you probably don't want a bunch of scientists dicking around in your kitchen, so give 'em a cold breakfast if they wander in. Personally, I'd give them bread crusts and water and make them do their own dishes too, but you're probably too nice for that."

Jocelyn's expression eased. "Don't be too sure of that," she said, a smile lurking in her eyes.

I didn't have much of an appetite (for several days now, I hadn't felt like eating in the morning), but Jocelyn mixed up a small batch of pancakes and, despite feeling slightly nauseated, I managed to eat a couple of them. Surprisingly, I felt better for it afterwards.

It was a nice morning. Quiet and relaxed now that Jocelyn's temper had improved. Bright rays of sunshine beamed light and warmth into the room and it seemed like nothing bad had ever or could ever happen here. The three of us (four, if you counted Karma) lounged around on the couches, sipping coffee as we chatted about the small things that people talk about early in the morning when the sun is shining in a clear aquamarine sky and nobody has anything particularly pressing to do. Despite my earlier resolve to find Michele and go out to Regent and collect more samples, I felt remarkably unambitious.

Then, of course, I started to feel guilty.

"You know, I should really head out to Regent again," I said. Reluctantly.

"Our lives are too heavy with *should*," Paul admonished, wagging his finger at me.

I smiled crookedly. "Tell me about it. Most of the time, I try to avoid the *should*s, but in this case . . . "

Jocelyn was stroking Karma. "When are you going back out to Pika Camp?"

I knew she was only asking out of idle curiosity, but I wished she hadn't brought it up. It wasn't that I didn't *want* to see Kelt again. I did. I was missing him again already—even if we had done nothing but argue since I'd come up north. But I knew I should talk to him. Should sit him down and tell him there was a distinct possibility he was going to be a father. Another *should*—and one I wouldn't be able to avoid for much longer, no matter how much we were fighting or how many toxic ptarmigan were poking around the Regent Mine.

Not that I could tell Jocelyn and Paul any of this.

"Soon," I said evasively. "I've got to go back to Regent first."

"Are you going to catch more ptarmigan?" she asked.

"I'm going to try. I'd like to get a few more samples.

And then I can send the lot of them down to Edmonton for testing."

"And that will tell you if the arsenic is leaking?"

"Yeah," I nodded.

"And then what?" Jocelyn asked.

I still hadn't figured that part out. "I'm not sure," I admitted. "In terms of the site itself, whoever gets the contract to clean it up is going to find the same thing and draw the same conclusions and maybe even conduct the same tests."

"Maybe?"

"It depends. Usually in a case like this, you look at the regulatory requirements. The Fisheries Act is the most important. If the fish are being affected, then something has to be done."

"Wouldn't the government care about the mammals and birds?"

"Oh, they might *care*," I said. "But there aren't any regulatory acts protecting them—except the Migratory Birds Act, but ptarmigan aren't migratory, so it isn't applicable. Ultimately, I don't know if anyone's going to be interested in what I've collected."

"But what you're doing, it's not really about Regent, is it?" Paul said.

I shook my head slowly. "No. No, it's not."

Jocelyn sat up straighter. "Selena?" she asked point-blank.

I met her eyes steadily. "I don't know," I told her. "But yes. It's quite possible her death is connected to the mine."

Jocelyn looked down at Karma again. "They've officially cleared that tourist, you know," she said after a moment. "They're saying it was somebody from here—someone we *know*." She raised her eyes to meet mine. The lines on her face had deepened. Her dark eyes reflected fear, anger, and a deep, underlying hurt. "But now you think it had something to do with Regent?" A cautious note of hope had entered her voice.

"It's *possible*." I emphasized the word.

Jocelyn thought about it for a moment, then her shoulders slumped. "It wouldn't make sense," she said. "Regent's a horrible mess, I grant you, but it's been that way for a long, long time. What about how strange she'd been getting?" she lowered her voice. "What about her *pregnancy*?" There was an odd note in her voice. Envy? Yearning? All of a sudden I remembered that she and Paul were trying to have kids. Unsuccessfully, so far. The news of Selena's pregnancy must have hurt.

"Strange?" I latched onto the word. "In what way?"

Jocelyn glanced at Paul.

"She just wasn't herself," Paul explained. "She almost seemed paranoid at times."

"And depressed," Jocelyn added. "Willa was having a terrible time with her moods."

"Willa wasn't exactly helping!" Paul said.

Jocelyn glared at him and he backed down.

"They were having some difficulties," Jocelyn conceded. "But something sure wasn't right with Selena. Sometimes she seemed confused too. Like she wasn't sure what she was doing. Or even who she was talking to."

My frown deepened. "When did all this start?"

Jocelyn considered the question. "About three months ago," she answered finally. "Maybe less."

I fell silent for a moment. Arsenic poisoning was the first thing that jumped to mind. But confusion, paranoia, and depression? Those were symptoms that manifested after years of chronic exposure—unless the poisoning was acute. She'd been in the Yukon only a couple of years, and the field season was only a few months long. Short of taking a dip in a barrel of arsenic trioxide, there was no way she could have ingested that much of it in so short a period of time. Not from Regent.

"Maybe she was just going through a bad spell," I said finally. "Happens to all of us at some point. And you say she and Willa were having problems. If she was depressed, I mean clinically depressed, it could certainly manifest itself like that."

"And her pregnancy?" Jocelyn asked.

I pulled my mouth to one side. "I couldn't even *begin* to speculate on that. You've no idea, um . . ."

"Who the father was?" Jocelyn shook her head. "Not even a clue. All the men around here were pretty quick to deny any involvement," she said, carefully not looking at Paul.

I saw a slow flush creep up his cheeks, and I felt suddenly uncomfortable. All was not well with this couple. Was it possible Paul had had the affair with Selena? *Paul?* He didn't seem like the type. Although . . . he certainly seemed sympathetic to Selena. And he shared her interest in the mine. And hadn't Willa mentioned a love poem?

"Well," I continued after an uneasy silence. "I . . . I don't know how all that fits in with what happened to her—or even if it does. What I do know is there are way too many questions about her work. First and foremost is why she didn't tell anyone that she was working at Regent. Not even Willa knew about it. The state of Regent isn't exactly a secret up here."

"Everybody knows it's a mess," Paul agreed.

"Exactly." I nodded. "So why keep her work there a secret? If anything, you'd think people would be happy she was out there. Happy that somebody was doing something about the problem. I find that very odd. The second odd thing is her field notes and why she would leave them to a complete stranger. Which brings me to the oddest thing of all." I paused. "Selena's notes were stolen out of my tent. Notes that were presumably about this work, because the other stuff—the stuff I had a chance to read—was all pretty standard. I can't imagine why someone would go to the trouble of stealing field notes about the impact of climate change on ptarmigan. Stealing them and then destroying them in the cabin fire, which is what the RCMP think happened."

Jocelyn's eyes had gone round.

"You know, I hadn't really put it together like that," Paul said slowly.

"The biggest question for me is, why she was out at Regent in the first place. It just doesn't make sense."

There was a lengthy pause, then Paul spoke. "I . . . I might be able to shed some light on that," he said, almost unwillingly.

"What?" Jocelyn sat up and stared at him. "What are you talking about? You knew Selena was working out there?"

"I *suspected* it," he told her. He turned to me to

explain. "It's all because of my interest in the mine," he said. "I told you yesterday that I've been working on a cycle of poems about it."

I nodded.

"Well, while I was doing the research, I spoke to Bruce Dyer."

"Who's Bruce Dyer?" Jocelyn demanded.

"The Public Health official who headed up the task force. The one that eventually recommended the drums be stored underground." Paul paused again. "The thing is," he continued more slowly, "I went and saw him when I was in Vancouver last year. He remembered everything about the Regent mine. He was open enough to share a lot of information with me—things about the mine and Della James that I'd never read or heard anywhere else. And he was honest enough to admit that he hadn't acted quickly enough. He told me his research assistant had recognized the situation was urgent long before he did. She tried to warn him, but she was just some kid. A grad student from Australia working for him for the summer. And he didn't pay enough attention to what she was telling him."

"Until Terry's children died," Jocelyn said in disgust.

"Until they died," Paul agreed.

"Who was the grad student?" I asked, already knowing what the answer would be.

Paul saw it in my eyes. He nodded. "Selena Barry," he said.

"*What?*" Jocelyn exploded. "My god, Paul! How could you keep this to yourself? My god!"

"It wasn't mine to share," Paul said defensively.

"Selena never said a word about it. She didn't even tell us she was working out at Regent. Nobody here knew about a second study site."

"But you guessed," I said.

Paul looked at me and nodded once. "Yeah. I guessed. Last winter she had me searching the Internet—she wasn't good with computers—she was trying to find some journal article about cadmium toxicity in willow ptarmigan. I wondered at the time why she was after it."

"You didn't ask?"

"I did. She blew off the question." He rubbed his forehead. "I think she felt responsible for what happened—maybe even for what's happening to the place now. I think she was trying to find a way to get the site cleaned up the only way she knew how."

"Expiating her guilt? But nobody was charged. Didn't you tell me the deaths were ruled accidental?"

Paul nodded. "They were, for a lot of different reasons. That doesn't mean Selena or Bruce Dyer or any halfway sensitive human being wouldn't feel responsible. Guilty."

I conceded the point.

"I can't believe you never told me this!" Jocelyn's eyes were sparking. "How could you keep this to yourself?"

Paul didn't answer her. Wouldn't look at her. I wondered again about the nature of his relationship with Selena.

"Did you say anything to Terry?" I asked as the thought occurred to me. "Anything that might have clued him in."

Paul stared at me, understanding all too well the reason for the question. "Never," he said decisively.

"There's no way on earth he could have known. Selena's name was never on the report. Nobody knew who she was. And Bruce Dyer died a month after I spoke him. Besides, I've been very careful not to breathe a word of it to anyone—not even Selena suspected I knew anything about it."

"Not even your wife knew." Jocelyn's tone was pure venom.

"It wasn't my place," he told her again. "Besides, I didn't know for sure she was out at Regent until Robyn found out yesterday."

"Have you told the RCMP?" I asked.

Paul shook his head uncomfortably. "No. No, I . . . I need to, I guess."

I didn't bother stating the obvious.

Jocelyn had retreated into icy silence.

"It was Selena's information, to share or not," he told her. Pleading for understanding.

Jocelyn wouldn't even look at him

Oblivious to human tensions, Karma stretched and rolled over to expose her belly to the sun. I reached over and gave her a last pat before pushing myself off the couch.

I didn't feel like going out to Regent. Didn't feel like thinking about secrets and murder and leaking toxins. All I really wanted to do was sun my own belly and pretend everything in the world was all right. But Paul and Jocelyn were in obvious need of some privacy, a woman was dead, ptarmigan were dying, and I might be pregnant. Few things in my world were "right." And at the moment, I could do something about only one of them.

"I'm going to need more samples," I told them. "I'm going to Regent."

But I wasn't.

*"Excuse me?"*

"I think someone dumped sugar in your gas tank," Terry repeated the words.

He was standing beside my SUV, which had made a horrible grinding, choking sort of noise when I'd tried to start it up. Terry was telling me why.

"Look," he said, pointing to the ground. "You can see where they spilled some of it."

I got out and bent down to inspect the tiny white crystals. My mouth hung slack in surprise.

"It's an urban legend," Terry assured me softly. His tone was sympathetic even if his eyes wouldn't meet mine.

"What?"

"It's not true what they say about sugar ruining an engine."

I turned and stared at him.

"Popular belief has it that if you pour sugar in the gas tank, you'll ruin the engine," he told my knees earnestly. "The sugar dissolves in gasoline, travels along the fuel lines, and turns into a sludgy kind of liquid cement in your engine. The engine seizes and when everything cools, the sludge hardens and you have to replace the entire engine."

"But . . ."

"It's not true," he said again, mistaking my concern. "A researcher at Berkeley proved it. Sugar doesn't actually dissolve in gasoline, so it won't caramelize or turn into cement or any of that stuff."

"But the engine won't start."

"Oh, it's clogged your fuel filters. And possibly your injectors," Terry said. "You'll have to change the filters. You may even have to take the gas tank out and dump it, depending on how much sugar's in there. But it's not that big a deal."

I didn't really give a rat's ass about the engine or the gas tank at the moment, though that would probably change when the car rental agency handed me my bill. Right now, I had a more pressing question.

"But . . . who would do something like that?"

Terry shut his mouth with an audible snap and shrugged at his feet. Unable to answer.

I didn't need him to. Pieces of the puzzle were starting to form a definite picture—one that had Regent Mine painted all over it. Someone had seen me out at Regent yesterday. Had circled round my vehicle. There was only one reason someone would try to sabotage my SUV. Clearly whoever had done it didn't want me going back to the mine.

Maybe I didn't need any more samples to send off. Maybe I didn't even need to get the ones I had collected analyzed. Something wasn't right at Regent and it was looking more and more like Selena Barry might have been murdered because of it.

It was past time to find Inspector Chesnut.

## August 2

Willa is back. At first she seemed happy to see me, throwing her arms around me. Kissing me with a warmth and passion that have been all too rare lately in our relationship. Then we closed the door to our little cabin and I realized she is still angry with me. Full of exuberant affection in front of the others. Full of sharp words and cold comments in the privacy of our home.

Her anger was born weeks ago. In the fires of our previous disagreements. She does not know about Ed—will not, if I can help it. I sit in guilty silence and let her bitterness etch scars across my psyche. It is my punishment. My penance.

The chicks need to be checked. Counted. But I can see I will not be going out in the field tomorrow. Or the next day. This, too, is my penance.

## August 5

I still haven't been out to count the chicks and I'm finding it difficult to care. Even the names of the dead, dutifully recited before sleep, are losing their impact. Is this what giving up feels like?

All I want to do is sleep. And I'm dreaming so much lately. Strange, disjointed, disturbing images. I'm so tired I feel like my eyes are perpetually crossed. Why does it seem like my life is falling apart?

## August 7

And then, the icing on the cake . . . I have apparently picked up some kind of computer virus. Diana just called to tell me the virus has been busily sending out part of an old message to everyone in my address book. I didn't even realize my virus definitions were out of date. Now I have to warn everyone not to open any e-mail attachments from me and figure out a way to clean the damn thing off my system. Hope Paul will help me.

## August 9

How strange to read the last few entries I wrote here. Two days ago, I felt tired. Used up. Old. Today I feel . . . so many things. Shocked. Scared. Young.

I am pregnant.

I never thought I'd write those words. Never thought I'd experience that aspect of life. When I chose Willa as my life partner, it was with the full knowledge that in gaining a lover, I was closing the door on other opportunities. Heather Has Two Mommies is all very well and good, and there are many lesbian couples who choose to have children. For myself, I've always found the concept of artificial insemination distasteful. I knew that when I embraced the so-called alternative life, I was saying goodby to any chance I had of being a parent. And now, I'm pregnant.

I suspected it days ago when the time for my period came and went with no sign of it. And I felt . . . different. Full somehow. It's hard to explain. But the test kit I bought in Dawson yesterday confirms it. The blue line doesn't lie.

A baby!

Obviously I won't tell Ed, but oh god, how am I going to tell Willa?

# 31

"She's not here," Constable Matas informed me when I rapped on the RV's door.

"Not . . . here?" The words hit me like the proverbial eighteen-wheeler.

"Inspector Chesnut had to go down to Whitehorse for a few days," he said with a smirky smile. He seemed unusually pleased with himself. Almost smug.

I wondered what was going on.

"Please sit down," he motioned me over to the small kitchen area. "Can I help you with anything?"

I hesitated, unwilling to confide my suspicions.

"Is this about Michele Thorpe?"

"Uh . . ." Startled by the question, I sank down onto one of the benches. "Michele?"

He slid onto the opposite bench and leaned forward slightly. "I heard your fight with her last night," he said. Softly. Intimately. As if we were sharing a dirty secret. "I heard her trying to turn you." His upper lip curled in disgust. "Trying to pervert you."

I was speechless.

"We know she had an affair with the Barry woman—your friend Kelt told us that. We know she's trouble." His eyes betrayed his eagerness as he leaned closer. "We can charge her with harassment," he told me. "That wouldn't be a problem. We can even take out a restraining order if she doesn't want to abide by the law."

"Harassment? Restraining order? Wait a minute . . . this isn't about *Michele*."

His eyelids drooped down, hooding his eyes.

"It was quite a fight you had."

"It was a *discussion*," I told him. Flatly. "And it's over. It wasn't important. I don't want to charge her with harassment and I don't want to take out a restraining order."

"Then what *do* you want, Ms Devara?" he sneered.

I stood up. "Nothing," I told him. Acidly polite. "It can wait until Inspector Chesnut is back."

"Intolerant son of a bitch!" I muttered under my breath as I stalked back to my tent. I slammed the tent door behind me, wishing it were heavier. Then I kicked off my boots. One thudded against the other with a satisfying thump.

"Homophobic bastard," I swore again. Wasn't the RCMP supposed to have tolerance training? I snorted inelegantly. Matas must've missed that day at the academy.

I finished blowing off steam with a few more well-chosen phrases. But once I'd calmed down, I didn't know what to do with myself. I needed to talk to Inspector Chesnut, but she was down in Whitehorse for gods knew how long. I needed to go back out to Regent and collect more samples, but with my SUV sugared out of commission, that wasn't going to happen, either.

Most of all, I needed to see Kelt again. To tell him about the second study site. To share my suspicions about Regent. And to finally confide my deepest fears—regardless of what I thought his reaction might be. I was through with waiting for the universe to unfold. I was ready to pull the sucker flat myself. But I couldn't go back to Pika Camp yet. Not without first telling the inspector about Regent.

I sighed heavily and stared around the tent. It was a mess. I'd been here for a few days now and it showed. Shirts and socks were strewn about. A pair of pants hung over Kelt's milk carton bookcase. There was underwear on the foot of the bed. Maybe I should clean up.

I found the book under a flannel shirt.

*Birds of the Yukon Territory.*

Selena Barry's book. I sank onto the bed. Remembering all over again how much I didn't want it. I ran my fingers over the cover photo of a raven against a blue sky. It did look like a beautiful book. I opened it to the first pages.

It was a lovely thing. Attractive layout. Good maps. Gorgeous photos. For each species, there was even a section on their place in First Nations culture and history. Impressive.

So when I came to the first pages of handwritten scrawl, I almost gasped at the desecration. Who would scribble on the appendices in a book like this? Then I realized the words had been written on onionskin. The thin paper tucked between the glossier pages of the book. I flipped past it. More onionskin. Pages and pages of it. I knew what it was. Knew what it had to be. Slowly, I turned back to the first page and started reading.

## March 19

Whenever I read a novel—one that really captures my interest—I find myself speeding through the pages. Sprinting past each cluster of black markings. Past each line and paragraph and chapter. They say that it's the journey that matters, not the destination. But that's not how I read a book . . .

# 32

I read until the sun had arced across the sky. Until my shoulder muscles burned from holding up the heavy book and my eyes ached from deciphering Selena's scrawl. Some of the entries had been written neatly. Carefully. Much like her field notes. But others, the more disturbing sections, were barely legible. As if another hand had formed the letters.

I finally closed the book and put it down. Then I took a deep breath and held it for a long, long time.

There was much about this diary that was disturbing. More than just Selena's clear mental decline. The confusion and depression that Jocelyn and Paul had noticed were all too evident in these pages. But it went beyond that. Selena had also been hallucinating. Had been experiencing memory loss. And there had been physical changes too. Rashes, dry hair and nails. All, if I wasn't mistaken, classic symptoms of arsenic poisoning. There were two possibilities. Either Regent was a whole lot worse than I'd thought, or she'd been ingesting arsenic.

I knew which possibility my money was on. The mine site was a horrific mess, but it wasn't acutely toxic. And her symptoms had been too pronounced, their onset too sudden to be caused by any sort of chronic exposure. A thought occurred to me. I hefted the book back to my lap and skimmed the pages again, stopping to reread certain passages in more detail.

Yes. I was right. Selena's worst moments seemed to occur when she was staying at the retreat. She always felt better once she'd been out in the field for a while. There was no question in my mind. Someone had been poisoning Selena Barry before she was stabbed to death. And after reading her diary, I was left with two suspects. Ed and Terry.

Two men.

Two very different motives.

The fact that Ed had had an affair with Selena was surprising, but at least he hadn't known about his impending fatherhood. Her death had had nothing to do with her pregnancy. Still, it was clear from what I'd read that Ed had more than a small stake in keeping any eyes away from the Regent Mine. He'd encouraged Selena to keep her work there a secret. Less for the reasons he gave her, I suspected, and more because he'd found himself a kimberlite pipe. Or maybe some of those rare blue beryls he'd told me about. Whatever. He'd obviously discovered something out there and didn't want anybody nosing around until he'd staked the area.

Ed must have stolen Selena's notes, I realized. Must have destroyed them in the cabin fire. And it must have been Ed who had seen me out at Regent the other day. Who had circled around my vehicle and ducked out of

sight when I returned to it. He was protecting something, all right. Likely some kind of strike. But did that
make him a murderer?

And what about Terry? It was his children who had
died all those years ago. The last name was different, but
perhaps they'd had their mother's name. If so, Selena
could not have realized it had been Terry's children
whose deaths haunted her. Killed because of bureau-
cratic inaction and someone else's negligence. It was
cruel irony that the one person Selena had confided in
about the tragedy had been exactly the wrong person
to tell. Personally I thought she'd assumed far too much
blame, but Terry may have thought otherwise.

Could Terry really have murdered Selena for revenge?
Terry? The guy barely looked you in the face when he
spoke to you. He barely spoke, for that matter, and when
he did, it was in a whisper.

But did Ed make any more sense as a suspect? I liked
Ed. And just because he wanted to protect his stakes
didn't make him a killer. But, as he'd said himself, the
mining industry was all about publicity. All about raising interest in buying a company's stock. The Regent
Mine site was a public relations disaster waiting to happen. No matter how valuable it might be, a strike close
to Regent would be affected by the mine's bad publicity.
If nothing else, any company looking to develop a new
mine would probably have to assume some liability for
the old one.

Ed had told me the chance of having a developed
mine was very low, but the chance of people making
money from the *possibility* of a mine was much higher.
He couldn't have believed that he'd be able to keep the

location of his find secret for very long. But maybe he thought he could keep it quiet long enough to make a fortune. People had killed for money before. How far would Ed go to make a fortune?

There was also the manner of Selena's death to consider. She had been stabbed. Multiple times. There had been an awful lot of blood. Blood everywhere, Kelt said. Terry had gone pale and shaky at the sight of a splinter in my finger. Had his reaction been real, or a put-on?

I took another deep breath. The tent's walls were starting to close in on me. There had been too many revelations in too short a time. And there were too many as yet unanswered questions. I felt like there wasn't enough air to breathe.

Jocelyn. I had to find Jocelyn.

She was the next best thing to Inspector Chesnut. Selena had been depressed for months, haunted by what she was finding at Regent. But the really strange behavior—the confusion and hallucinations—had started about two months ago. It must have been then that the poisoning had begun. I didn't know how long Ed had been at Willow Creek, but Jocelyn would know. And she would know if Terry's reaction to blood was real.

I had to find Jocelyn.

I found much more.

**33**

It had grown cooler and the wind had come up again. Dampening the whining buzz of insects. Whispering secrets through the black spruce trees.

Her hair undulated across the rippling water like knots of writhing black snakes. Her skin was ice white. In stark contrast to the wine-dark water around her. How much blood was in the human body? Enough so that it seemed the hot tub was filled with it. Enough to have spilled over the edge. Violent crimson puddles on the ground.

One arm stuck up unnaturally over the wooden rim, the fingers rigid as if to ward off what had already taken place. I took an unwilling step towards the tub. Towards that arm. Those fingernails. Those short, short fingernails. I knew those nails. She'd talked about them just the other day. Waved them in my face. I felt my gorge rising.

*Oh gods.*
Michele.

I'd completely forgotten about her. About my intention to apologize. And now it was far too late.

I didn't throw up, though it took every ounce of willpower I possessed. I clenched my teeth hard against it. Struggled to swallow it down.

Michele was dead in the hot tub.

I steeled myself against another surge of nausea and stepped closer. Her face was submerged just beneath the surface of the red-tinted water. Her eyes were hidden by the seaweed masses of her hair. But her neck was visible. The wound across it gaping open like an unbuttoned shirt. The edges pale and loose.

"Gods," I breathed. Half prayer, half curse.

Someone had slit her throat.

I did throw up then. Staggering to one side. Collapsing on the ground. Vomiting up shock. Horror. Guilt. Fear.

It was a long time before I could get up again.

I found Jocelyn first. She was coming around the side of the Cabin when I stumbled up. She took one look at me and dropped the basket of laundry she'd been carrying.

I blurted out my story. I'm not sure how coherent I was. Probably not very. Jocelyn closed her eyes as if in prayer, then promptly took my arm and hustled me over to the RCMP's van.

Constable Matas was less than impressed to see me again, but he straightened up—all professional concern—as soon as he heard what I'd found.

"Wait in your tent," he instructed after I spilled the words out. "I'll have some questions for you later."

"I'm coming with you," Jocelyn told him.

He turned and looked at her, fully prepared to refuse. But she stood her ground. The quintessential immovable force. His eyes were unreadable, but he nodded once. Acknowledging her right. Her need.

I had no desire to join them and every desire to comply with Matas' instructions. My back ached, I was shivering, and my stomach wasn't at all sure it was finished being sick. All I wanted to do was go back to my tent and cocoon myself in my sleeping bag. But first I had to find the satellite phone. I needed to talk to Kelt.

I got Stavros instead.

"He's not here," he told me. "I am not expecting them back until late this evening."

I swallowed and tried not to cry.

"It's an emergency," I told him. "Michele—" I gulped and tried again. "Michele's been killed."

Stavros was shocked. He let loose a stream of Greek.

"Look," I cut him off. "Are they in range of the walkie-talkies?"

He paused. Then, "I am not certain. I will try."

"Good. Tell him . . . tell him I'm okay," I said. "But I think he should come back."

"Yes, of course. Um . . . how did she . . .?"

"Somebody cut her throat."

I heard him gasp.

"Stav, I don't want to stay here any longer than I have to. It's just . . . tell Kelt to hurry, okay?"

"I will. And you. You will be careful, yes?"

My throat closed up a bit at his concern. "Yes," I managed to squeeze out. "I'm going to be very, very careful."

# 34

I was shivering even under several layers of blankets and sleeping bags. My stomach was cramping, my lower back ached, and I wanted desperately to be anywhere but here.

Michele's wasn't the first dead body I'd stumbled across, but it sure didn't get any easier with repetition. And this time, I'd known the victim personally. Had interacted with her. Spoken to her. I squirmed, remembering the last words I'd said to her. Implacable, angry words. Spoken out of irritation and frustration, granted, but still harsh. Unwarranted. I wasn't proud of them. I'd even intended to find her the next day. To apologize for them.

And now I never could.

Who would want to kill Michele? Who wouldn't, asked a small voice in the back of my mind, reminding me of her aggravating manner. But that wasn't entirely fair. Michele *had* been a difficult personality. Pushy. Exasperating. But people didn't usually get their throats cut because they were irritating. Not in real life. They just got voted off the island. So what was it about Michele that had pushed someone into casting the final vote?

She'd known Selena Barry. Had wanted to know her a whole lot better. Kelt even thought she'd had an affair with her and he was usually pretty clued out when it came to that sort of thing. What if Willa had discovered something about Michele? Something that led her to believe Michele had been the poem-writing lover. A distinct possibility, given that Willa didn't know about Ed.

Ed. How did he fit into all this? And Regent? Before today, I was so sure that Selena's death had had something to do with the old mine. Had Michele known about it too? If she and Selena had been friends, then maybe Selena had confided in Michele about her work. But Selena hadn't said anything about it in her diary. In fact, the only mention she'd made of Michele had to do with how much of a nuisance she was.

It just didn't make sense. None of it made sense.

It was the shouting that roused me. I felt like I'd been sitting here for hours. I looked up and blinked at the little travel clock. I *had* been sitting here for hours! Two hours, to be exact. What was going on? Why hadn't Constable Matas come to ask his questions?

More shouting.

I pushed my hair behind my ears and listened hard. I couldn't make out the words. I threw off my blanket cocoon and jumped to my feet. It sounded like a fight. But before I could fling open the tent door, I heard the slam of another door and the retreat went silent again.

Cautiously, I poked my head out and looked around. Nothing moved.

I threw on my coat and made my way over to the RCMP's camper. The retreat was quiet. Almost eerily quiet. I rapped softly on the door.

"Come in."

I opened the door. Frank Matas was standing in the center of the van, buckling on his gun holster. I swallowed and tried not to look at it.

"I was . . ." I began.

He looked at me. Unhelpfully.

"I was . . . um, wondering if you wanted to ask those questions," I stuttered.

"Ah." He rolled his shoulders back. "No, I think I've got everything I need."

"But . . . you didn't even ask me about finding her. Or if I saw anything suspicious. Or if—"

"Please," he interrupted coldly. "Don't embarrass yourself by pretending to be a cop. If anyone can be considered 'suspicious' in this situation, Ms Devara, it's you."

"Me!"

His eyes glinted at me. "You did have a—how did you put it?—*discussion* with the deceased," he reminded me. "A rather . . . vocal discussion. Overheard by everyone here at the retreat."

"You don't seriously think . . ." I broke off. Appalled by the implication.

He let me stew for a full minute before shaking his head.

"I don't," he told me.

I felt my muscles relax, though I hadn't been consciously aware of the tension.

"Which is why I've arrested Mr. Theriault."

I opened my mouth. Closed it.

"Terry?" I squeaked finally. "You arrested *Terry*?"

He put his fingertips together. Reminding me of a movie villain. Under other circumstances, I would have laughed at the sight. Not now.

"It appears Mr. Theriault has been experimenting with CCA," he told me. "Chromated copper arsenate."

I stared at him. CCA. Arsenic.

"Wood preservative," he explained, misinterpreting my reaction. "No doubt left over from his construction activities. The thing is, Selena Barry's system was rife with the stuff."

The brightness of his eyes belied his cool tone. He was *excited* by this. I felt a surge of revulsion.

"And it turns out," he lowered his voice almost conspiratorially, "Mr. Theriault had a motive. A very *compelling* motive."

I knew all about Terry's motive but I didn't want to tell Matas that.

"But Selena was stabbed," I pointed out. "Not poisoned! And Michele had her throat cut. Terry's *afraid* of blood. He almost passed out when I got a splinter in my hand."

I wasn't sure why I was defending Terry so vigorously. He'd been high on my own suspect list. And if what Matas had told me about the arsenic was true, it was certainly damning. But this arrest seemed far too rushed. Matas' pleasure in it too pronounced. All my internal alarm bells were going off.

"An act," Matas waved off my objections.

"But what about Ed?" I demanded.

That stopped him for a moment. "Ed Farrell?" He raised his eyebrows.

"There's something going on at Regent," I said, quietly intense, willing him to listen to me. "Something not right. Ed's been hanging around there. I don't know if it has anything to do with these murders but Selena was working out there and her notes were stolen and—"

"Ms Devara." His tone, icily polite, brought me up short. "You are a biologist. A scientist. I respect that. But as far as I know, you are not a law enforcement officer. Or an investigator. You have no training or skill along those lines."

"But why would Terry kill Michele?" I tried another tack.

Matas shrugged, unconcerned. "I'm sure we'll find out in due course," he said. "Now, if you'll excuse me, I need to take Mr. Theriault down to Whitehorse. It's already late and it's a long drive. I don't much relish the idea of stopping along the way with a murderer in my back seat."

He took a step towards the door. Towards me. I stood my ground for a few seconds, unable to believe he'd ignore what I had to say. His eyes hardened. I turned and stumbled out of the camper. I looked around, blinking rapidly in the afternoon light, noticing Matas' SUV only now. It was parked beside my own decommissioned SUV. Terry was locked in the back seat.

He was sitting quietly. Face drained of all color. Cheeks sunken. Eyes huge. Haunted and scared. I met his gaze and he stared at me. As I walked away, I could feel his eyes searing the skin from my back.

# 35

The Cabin was deserted when I burst through the door.

"Jocelyn!" I called. "Paul! Willa?"

No answer.

I was about to turn around when I spied the satellite phone sitting on its cradle.

Inspector Chesnut. She was the one I really needed to talk to.

I fumbled in my coat pocket. She'd given me her card . . . Yes. There it was. Inspector Gaylene Chesnut. Complete with phone number and e-mail address. I snatched up the phone and punched in the numbers.

Inspector Chesnut would know what to do, would listen to what I had to say. The more I thought about what had just happened, the more uncomfortable I was with it. Matas was completely ignoring any other possible angle. Hell, he hadn't even interviewed me and *I*'d found Michele's body. Surely that went against his much-vaunted training. If Terry was guilty, then Matas had the right man in custody and that was fine. But if

Terry was innocent? Then the real killer was still out there. Still *here*.

"You've reached the voice mail of Inspector Chesnut. I'm not available to take your call right now, but if you leave a message, I'll get back to you as soon as possible. If this is an emergency situation—"

"Shit, shit, shit," I cursed under my breath. Then I left her a message to call me at the retreat as soon as possible.

Paul slammed through the door just as I was hanging up.

"Robyn! Did you hear about Terry?" His cheeks were flushed from exertion. Sweat was streaming down his face.

"I heard. Where's Jocelyn?"

"I don't know. I've been trying to find her. I can't find Willa, either." He sank onto a chair. "I just can't believe it. There's a mistake. There has to be a mistake. Oh my god, what have I done?"

"What do you mean?"

"I told Frank about Selena this morning. About how she blamed herself for what happened to Terry's kids."

"You told Frank?"

Paul nodded. "This morning. After I told you about it. You . . . your reaction made me realize that it might be relevant.  But how could Terry have known? The only reason I knew is because I spoke to Bruce Dyer in person."

"Maybe Terry did too, at some point."

"Frank's saying that Terry was poisoning her."

"I know."

He scrubbed at his forehead.

"But Selena was stabbed!" he said, echoing my own reaction. "And Michele—"

"I know."

"But Terry can't stand the sight of blood!" he cried.

"Are you *sure*?" I demanded intently. "How do you know?"

"*How do I know?* I know because I helped him build all these cabins. I know because the day I fell and sliced my leg open, he passed out cold and Jocelyn had to take me into Dawson to get it stitched up. You can't fake that. And why would he try? That was way before Selena ever showed up. I tried to tell Frank, but he wouldn't listen."

I swore again.

Paul leaned forward urgently. "Robyn, Terry couldn't have killed Selena. Or Michele."

"No," I agreed. Thinking hard.

"Look, Paul," I began. "Something's not right here. You haven't seen Ed, have you?"

"Ed? No. I haven't seen anybody since Jocelyn told me about Michele." His voice started to rise.

"Okay, calm down. I think, at the very least, Constable Matas jumped the gun. We need to get in touch with Inspector Chesnut."

"She's gone down to Whitehorse."

"I know. I just tried phoning her. She's not at her desk. I had to leave a voice mail. But I don't know when she'll get it. I've got her e-mail address too, but Kelt's laptop is buggered up."

"So are all the rest of the computers."

"Yeah, I heard. Paul, I'd really like to e-mail her. Sometimes people will check their e-mail before their phone messages." I always did.

Paul perked up. Still worried but hopeful. "I can try to fix them," he told me. "It's a virus, but I should be able to clean it off. I've been meaning to, Jocelyn keeps bugging me about it. She leaves all the computer stuff up to me. But I just haven't had the time and—"

I gave him a look that brought him up short. "Now would be a *really* good time."

I handed Kelt's black laptop over to Paul before sliding into the chair beside him. My stomach still hurt and my legs were feeling rubbery. I felt my forehead. Maybe I was coming down with something.

"Selena got it," Paul said as the computer booted up. "The virus, I mean. She didn't know that much about computers. She opened an e-mail attachment she shouldn't have and her system got infected with it. It's called bugbear. It's a mass-mailing worm."

"Lovely."

"Yeah," Paul agreed. "It really screws up a system. The cursor starts doing weird stuff, and it terminates your antivirus software. Okay, let me see . . . oh, right. I got as far as downloading the removal tool, but I need to run it. And clean off the infected message."

He launched the e-mail program. The cursor was jumping all over the screen. Just like it had done the other day.

"And . . . there's where the problem started." He hit the "enter" button and an e-mail message popped up on the screen.

It was a message sent by Selena. But it wasn't for Kelt.

My dear Liane,

I know, honey. I know how hard it is. But you've got to hang in there. It will get better, I promise you that. We've all been through it in our own way. For both Willa and myself, the outcome was much the same as your own. It's part of the price you pay for walking a different path. You must concentrate on the good things in life and accept the rest. The loss. Family, I have discovered, is entirely what you make it. Beth sounds like a rare gem. Focus on that. On your relationship with her. It will see you through the bad times.

The text broke off then, followed by several lines of garbled text.

"Liane." I muttered. Wondering why the name sounded familiar. "Who's Liane? And why was Selena sending Kelt a message for her?"

"It's the way bugbear works," Paul explained. "It picks up an old undeleted message from your e-mail program and sends it out to everyone in your address book, along with copy of itself for the ride. It has a better chance of infecting more systems if the message sounded legit." He tapped the screen. "It doesn't mean anything. We all got the same message."

He closed the window and prepared to delete the file. "I was surprised to get it myself," he said as tapped out a sequence of keystrokes. "I didn't even know Selena was still in touch with her. It's been ages since Liane left."

All of a sudden, it clicked.

"Liane." I said out loud. "Liane *Matas*?"

Paul stared at me. "That's right," he said, puzzled by my tone. "Frank's daughter."

Frank Matas' daughter.
Oh.
*Oh.*

# 36

"*Stop!*" I shouted. "Don't delete that message!"

Paul's jumped. His mouth hung open in surprise.

"Open it up again. What's the date on it? When did Selena send that to Liane?"

Paul stared at me for a second before turning back to the keyboard. His finger still hovered over the "delete" key. "Um . . . I don't know. A couple of months ago, it looks like."

"And when did this virus hit? When did this message go out to everybody else?"

Paul glanced back at the screen. "August third."

"August third," I repeated. "And she was killed on what? The tenth?"

Paul nodded. Still mystified.

*Oh gods.*

Not Ed at all. And not Terry, either. I jumped to my feet.

"You have to go after them," I told Paul.

He blinked at me.

"Frank Matas killed Selena," I told him.

"*What?*"

"Because of Liane. Because she's gay and so was Selena."

"But—"

"Look, Jocelyn told me that nobody had heard from Liane in over a year, but this message was sent two months ago! All you have to do is read it. Selena wasn't just in contact with Liane, she was *helping* her. Helping her adapt to an alternative lifestyle. A *same-sex* relationship!"

Pure anathema to someone with Matas' prejudices.

I stopped and sucked in a shaky breath, thinking it through. "Frank must have gotten a copy of this message. When the virus hit. If Selena was as clued-out about computers as you say she was, she probably never cleaned out her address book. I bet you anything there was an old address of Liane's sitting there."

Paul was struggling with it. "But . . ."

"Oh gods," I groaned as the second revelation hit me. "And Michele!"

"Michele?"

"She was bisexual. Frank overheard her hitting on me. He thinks she had the affair with Selena."

*Because of me. Because I was the one who had encouraged Kelt to share his camp gossip with the RCMP.*

"He told me she was trouble," I said. "A pervert. He wanted me to file a complaint and take out a restraining order against her." I scrubbed my forehead, remembering his look of revulsion. Had he slept with Michele? I was willing to bet that he had. "He's got a hate on for anybody gay," I told Paul.

"But he arrested *Terry*."

"I know." I took a deep breath and tried to explain. Speaking slowly as it all fell into place in my mind. "I think he's trying to use Terry as a scapegoat. But his case won't stand up. All anyone has to do is flash Terry a paper cut and that'll be it. Matas' case falls apart. And then there'll be an investigation into why he was so damn eager to haul Terry away." I met Paul's eyes. Shock and horror mirroring what was in my own. "He's not rational. I'm afraid Terry's not going to make it to Whitehorse. Paul, you've got to go after them."

Paul mastered his shock with a visible effort. "I don't drive," he reminded me miserably. "I never learned. I just . . . I get too distracted. I—"

There was no choice. "Then I'll have to go," I interrupted. "But I need your car."

"The keys are on the hook," he said. "It's the orange pickup truck. And I'm coming with you."

"No! You need to keep trying Inspector Chesnut. And let the others know. Kelt—" *oh gods, Kelt!* "Kelt's on his way here right now. He knows about Michele, but that's it. Someone's got to be here to tell him."

"You want me to tell him you've gone chasing after a murderer?" Paul asked incredulously. "He'll *kill* me."

"He won't kill you," I assured him. Hoping it was true. "Besides, we don't have a choice. You don't drive and we can't wait for Jocelyn or Willa to come back. There isn't anybody else. I've got to go, Paul. They've already got almost an hour on me."

**37**

I blasted down the Dempster as if the Black Riders were on my tail. Breaking every speed limit in the territory and probably the rest of the country. There was no sign of Matas' SUV. The sky was cloudless, the sun directly overhead, banishing any illusion of soft edges from the harsh landscape. The highway was dry and very, very empty. Not even a wisp of a dust cloud on the horizon.

My stomach was still cramping. I pressed down hard on the gas pedal, doubt assailing me from all sides. I was a biologist, not an investigator. Was I right about this? Instinct told me I was, but instincts could be wrong. What about the arsenic in Selena's system, for example? I'd realized myself that she was being poisoned, had concluded that somebody from the retreat was doing it. And Terry had access to and knowledge of CCA. He also had a motive. Had it been poetic justice? To poison Selena with arsenic like his children had been poisoned?

The soy milk, I realized belatedly. He must have put it in the soy milk. Selena had been lactose-intolerant, she was the only person who drank the vile stuff—until

Jocelyn had used up the last of it in her coffee cake. Terry had been incensed when he found out. Incensed? Or horrified that Jocelyn was about to serve an arsenic-laced dessert to a bunch of innocent people?

Yes, Terry fit the profile of poisoner all too well.

But Selena didn't die of arsenic poisoning. I had to keep reminding myself of that. She'd been very sick from it, granted, but ultimately it hadn't killed her. And Terry's reaction to blood was real. He couldn't have killed her. Not with a knife.

I was coming up on Tombstone now. Still no sign of any other vehicles. But I thought I could see the ghost of a dust cloud in the distance. I clutched the steering wheel and sped on.

What about Regent? And its contaminated ptarmigan? What about Ed and his claim staking and his affair with Selena? What about the conveniently missing, presumably destroyed field notes? All of which appeared damning when taken into account with Selena's murder. Had Ed killed her and destroyed evidence of her work at Regent to ensure Regent's "secrets" remained quietly obscure? A distinct possibility, though it wouldn't have lasted for long—not with INAC putting out a request for proposals to clean the place up.

Ed made a very convincing suspect when you considered Selena's death. But Michele's death simply did not fit that scenario. Michele hadn't worked with Selena. She wasn't a prospector, or an environmental activist, or even a consultant. The Regent Mine was completely out of her purview. In fact the only connection between the two dead women was their lifestyle—a way of life that Frank Matas despised.

I kept thinking about his comments. His unveiled disgust when he'd uttered the word *dyke*. As if his mouth had been polluted by the very syllable. What would such an intolerant man do if he found out his daughter—the daughter that was lost to him, the daughter who had *left* him—had chosen that path? Was being helped along it by one of the very women he hated?

I clenched my teeth and pressed harder on the gas pedal.

There! There was a dust cloud. Just ahead.

I blasted around a couple of curves and suddenly there in front of me was the SUV. I breathed a sigh of relief. Two figures were visible. Terry was still okay.

Frank Matas wasn't sane, I was convinced of that. But despite what Kelt might think, I wasn't stupid enough to interfere. I didn't intend to cut Frank off or confront him in any way. I'd just follow along behind him. Just a friendly little shadow all the way to Whitehorse. An orange guardian angel.

But Frank had other ideas.

He must have spotted me as soon as I'd come around the bend. He started to speed up. Ninety klicks. 100. 120.

There was nowhere for him to go. No side streets to turn on to. Not even a shadow to hide in.

One hundred and thirty.

I cursed as I matched him. The speed limit on the Dempster was eighty. For good reason.

Dust billowed up behind him, like a bomb's aftermath. Blocking the sun. Obscuring my vision.

Quickly, I glanced down at my speedometer. I was doing 140 now.

I swore again, gripping the steering wheel as I rounded another curve. I could feel the tires slide on the broken shale. My stomach cramped.

*Son of a bitch!*

Visibility was down. I could barely see the road. I eased off the gas pedal.

It was the only thing that saved my life.

I was already starting to slow down when I came around a sharp curve in the road. And there, right in front of me, was Frank's SUV, sideways in the middle of the narrow highway.

I didn't have time to swear. I didn't even have time to scream. I stomped on the brakes with both feet. There was a squeal of protest. The truck skidded sideways across the road. Desperately I pumped the brakes, trying to stop the momentum. But I'd been going too fast. The truck lurched crazily, shale spraying out from under the tires. It kept sliding. And with a sickening crunch, dropped off the side of the highway and started to roll.

Thank the gods for airbags.

The white bag smashed me back against my seat. The seat belt cut a slash across my shoulder.

The truck rolled once.

Metal shrieking.

Twice.

Crumpling under its own weight.

I felt something smack against my cheekbone. Something else sliced fire across the bridge of my nose. I cried out and threw my hands up over my face. Protecting my eyes.

The truck scraped across the tussock tundra, tearing a wide gash in the moss. Crushing all the delicate alpine plants, before finally coming to a rocking halt on the passenger's side.

My door was dented inwards, the metal touching my hip. The airbag had started to deflate, the windshield was smashed. Small crystals of tempered glass twinkled around me. I could smell the sharp, sweetish smell of gas. And then, I heard the crunch of tires on the road. I looked up. Frank's SUV was backing up toward me.

For moment—a very brief moment—I thought he was coming to help. To pull me out of the wreckage.

Fat chance.

As soon as his face came into view, peering out the passenger window, I could see the cruel smirk dancing on his mouth. I closed my eyes, trying to prepare myself for whatever was coming next. I had a feeling he wasn't going to leave me like this. Then there was a spray of gravel. My eyes flew open to see his SUV peeling away.

As I hung, suspended from my seat belt, taking stock, I suddenly felt a familiar warmth on my thighs. I almost laughed. Almost cried. The thought washed over me with a wave composed equally of relief and surprising regret.

Not pregnant after all.

And then, I checked out of reality for a while.

# 38

Frank left me there. Left me bleeding in the crumpled wreckage. Bastard. He no doubt hoped I'd died in the crash. The only reason he hadn't stuck around to make sure of it was because of the eighteen-wheeler coming up behind him. The dust plume must have warned him of its approach.

It was the truck driver who pulled me carefully out of the wreck. Who listened to my frantic story. Who settled me in his passenger seat and had the presence of mind to radio the RCMP detachment in Dawson City.

As soon as he told the dispatcher about the crash, he passed the radio over to me. "Best if you explain things," he said with an encouraging nod.

I accepted the radio, surprised to see my hand shaking. Well, maybe not that surprised.

"Hello? Are you there?" The dispatcher's calm voice crackled over the radio.

I took a deep breath (also shaky) then pressed the button and began to speak. "Hi. My name's Robyn Devara," I said. "And I know this is going to sound whacked, but please, just hear me out. I've been staying up at Willow Creek and—"

The radio crackled and a new voice suddenly came on.

"Robyn? Is that you?"

A voice I recognized.

"Inspector Chesnut? Gaylene?"

"What's going on?" she demanded, not bothering to confirm her identity.

"It's Frank!" I burst out. "He killed Selena! And Michele's dead. I think he killed her too. I know it sounds crazy but—"

"We know," she interrupted. "We know all about Frank. I've been in Vancouver talking to his daughter."

Gaylene had been talking to Liane? I didn't have time to think about that.

"He's got Terry," I told her succinctly. And then the whole story came spilling out. Selena's e-mail to Liane. Terry's arrest. The chase. The crash.

Gaylene cut me off before I finished. "How long ago?" she asked intently. "How long since he forced you off the road?"

I hesitated. Uncertain.

"Not long," the trucker answered the question.

I glanced over at him.

"Saw the dust in the distance," he explained. "Couldn't have been that long since it happened."

I relayed the information to Gaylene. I heard her speaking rapidly to someone in the background. Then she was back.

"Look Robyn, I've got to go. We had a detachment

all ready to go up to Willow Creek and arrest Frank. He's probably off the Dempster and on the Klondike by now. We're heading out. Can you get yourself to the Dawson medi-clinic?"

"I'll take you," the trucker volunteered.

"Yes," I told her.

"Good. Go there. Make sure you're okay. And don't worry about Terry. Frank has nowhere to go."

She signed off and I passed the radio back to the truck driver. All of a sudden I was crushingly, unbearably tired.

"You just sit there and close your eyes," the trucker told me kindly. "We'll be in Dawson before you know it."

"Thanks," I said, managing a grateful smile. "Thanks for everything."

"No worries," he told me. "Got to watch out for each other up here. Besides, I got a daughter a little younger than you. I'd like to think that if she was in the same kinda pickle, there'd be somebody around to give her a hand."

I lay on a narrow bed in a darkened room at the clinic. Blinking back tears as I thought about the trucker's kindness. He hadn't saved my life—beyond a few cuts and bruises, I hadn't been injured that badly—but he'd certainly saved me from an unpleasant situation. And he'd saved Terry's life.

The nurse at the clinic had finally called the RCMP to find out what had happened. I'd been quite insistent about it (read: a pain in the ass). They'd caught Frank.

It sounded like things had gotten a bit hairy, but they'd stopped him in the end. Terry was alive. Badly frightened, but alive. Frank had been arrested.

All because of an anonymous trucker. I'd been so shaken by the crash, I hadn't even asked his name.

There was a light tap at the door.

"Come in," I called.

The door cracked open. A line of light in the dimness. And Kelt slipped into the room.

I heard his breath explode out with relief.

Wordlessly, I sat up and held out my arms. It took a long time to reassure him that I was okay. To reassure us both.

I would have been quite happy to continue this all afternoon. To hug and be hugged. Kiss and be kissed. Reassure and be reassured. I would have been quite happy to do without the explaining part of the thing. I'd survived a crash. Had walked away with nothing but a few cuts (though the gash across my nose would probably leave a scar). I was lucky, but I owed him the explanation.

Kelt stared down at his shoes for the whole time it took me to cover everything. His hands were clasped tightly in his lap. All I could see was the top of his head, I couldn't see his face at all and I found myself speaking nervously. In jerky, clipped sentences. More than anything else, I wished he would look at me. Then I might have an idea of how he was feeling.

When I finally ran out of words, we sat in silence for a long time.

"Why didn't you tell me?" he asked finally.

"There wasn't time. Frank was taking Terry away and I was afraid—"

"Why didn't you tell me you thought you were pregnant?" he interrupted my explanation.

I shut my mouth.

Oh. That.

He looked at me then. Finally. And I suddenly wished he were staring at his shoes again. The top of his head was a lot easier to look at than green eyes darkened by hurt.

*Oh gods, I've lost him.*

"I . . . I wasn't sure . . ."

"So?"

"So, I didn't know how to tell you."

"You could have tried!"

"But all we were doing was fighting. It seems like we've been fighting ever since I got here."

Kelt sighed. Shoulders slumping. "I know."

There was a silence then, "I was afraid," I admitted in a small voice. "I didn't want to lose you."

"Lose me!" Kelt stared at me. Incredulous. "Did you honestly think—?"

"No!" I cried miserably. "Yes. I don't know." I scrubbed at my face. My eyes were unaccountably wet. "Maybe."

I couldn't look at him. Couldn't stand to see the hurt anymore.

*Oh gods, I've lost him.*

Then I felt his arms go around me.

"Robyn," he said. His voice was softer than I'd ever heard it. "I love you. That's a forever thing. It's not going to change. It doesn't matter if I'm stressed out and crabby. It doesn't matter if we're apart from each other for months on end. Or arguing incessantly with each other. I want my life to be with you. Working. Playing. Arguing. Growing gray hairs. All that stuff. With you."

I hesitated before I asked it. "Just . . . me?"

He squeezed tighter. He didn't answer right away. "Not necessarily," he said finally. "You surprised me with this, you really did. But I guess . . . I guess I've always thought that someday I'd like to be a dad—as long as you want to be a mum."

He made it a question.

I thought about it. About the sleep deprivation. The late-night feedings. The constant work. About essentially becoming a secondary life form for a creature that would demand everything from me and more—and then one day grow up and leave me behind.

Then I thought about showing a small person a pika on its haypile, a cat, toasting its belly in the sun, fish swimming over a coral reef. I thought about teaching a daughter about birds and plants and squishy things that live in the mud. And reading to her about hobbits and velveteen rabbits and fruit bats pretending to be birds. She would leave me one day, yes, but all creatures fledged eventually. She would leave to find her own path. And that was okay.

That was life.

"I think," I said into Kelt's shirt. "I think someday I'd like that."

# 39

Kelt and I were lying on the couch in the Cabin. Sunning our bellies. Still recovering from the events of two days ago. Karma was on her back in between us, toasting her own tummy. We'd be going back to Pika Camp—it was almost time to start shutting things down for the season—but we needed to rest first. Recover and regroup.

"Why was Michele back at the retreat?" I asked, trying to take my mind off various aches and pains.

Kelt didn't answer right away. I lifted my head off his chest and looked at him.

"I sent her home," he admitted, not meeting my eyes. "I had to! She wasn't pulling her own weight anymore. And things were getting pretty heated with the others. She didn't leave me much of a choice." His voice was tight, like he was trying to justify it to himself.

I covered his hand with mine. "No," I sighed. "She really didn't."

He hesitated, then, "I didn't tell her mum," he said

quietly. "About sending her home, I mean. She . . . didn't need to know that about her daughter. Not now."

"Oh." I squeezed his hand. "That was nice of you."

"But if I hadn't told her to leave—"

I cut him off. "Don't even go there. If Frank hadn't killed her that night, he would have found some other time to do it. The man is insane, Kelt."

He nodded glumly. "I know, I know." He rolled his shoulders. "I still feel guilty. I just wish . . . " His voice trailed off.

I waited.

"I guess I wish she'd found whatever it was she was looking for. Before she died. I think she had a sad life." He paused again, then, "I wish it could have been different for her," he said so softly, I almost missed it.

"Yeah," I said. Remembering. "Me too."

It was Dwayne who told us what Ed had been looking for.

"Emeralds," he said succinctly. "Seems he found himself a right promising bunch of rocks just east of the old Regent gold mine. Shocked the pantyhose off the entire mining community when the news broke."

I raised my eyebrows. The Band-Aid across my nose pulled at the skin. Emeralds! Not a kimberlite pipe. Not diamonds at all. It seemed that Ed was just as duplicitous as the prospectors he'd described to Selena. Somehow, it didn't surprise me.

"I mean, everybody pretty much knew there had to be kimberlite north of Dawson," Dwayne was saying. "They keep finding diamonds in placer deposits. But nobody figured on emeralds. Only place emeralds have ever been found in the Yukon is away down in the southeast part of the territory."

"Didn't they do a mineral survey when the gold mine was operating?" Kelt asked. "It's hard to believe nobody knew they were there."

"Not really," Dwayne disagreed. "Hell, back then, nobody even knew there were diamonds in Canada, let alone emeralds." He seemed vastly entertained by it all. "I tell ya, every prospector in Dawson's seein' green. He's been a busy boy, our Ed. Seems he's registered some twenty thousand acres already and now the cat's outta the bag. He's got me and my chopper booked solid for the next three weeks." Dwayne rubbed his hands gleefully. "Should be able to stake five times that before we're through. I think I'm gonna buy me some shares in an emerald mine."

Dwayne's eyes were shining. Sparkling like the gems to come.

"Be careful," I warned him. "Don't lose your shirt."

He grinned boyishly. Still full of bright excitement. "I got lots of shirts," he assured me before pushing himself to his feet. "Well, gotta blast. There's a million things to do."

"Dwayne," I touched his arm gently. "Just . . . be careful who you trust, okay?"

"No problemo," he said, though he shot me an odd look. "And you. You just be careful in general, you hear? No more car chases."

"I promise," I said holding my right hand up. "Got no vehicle anyways and you know, I won't get far on foot."

Dwayne was still chuckling as he left.

I wanted to say more. To tell him about Ed. But what was there to tell? That I could prove, that is.

Frank Matas had confessed to both murders. He was also under investigation for the disappearance of his wife. Inspector Chesnut had come out to the retreat earlier in the day to tell us the news. She'd been suspicious of Frank early on, she told us. He had ignored some fairly basic procedures during the course of their investigation and, when she realized he had such close ties to the people at the retreat, she'd decided to dig a little further. His daughter, she added, had been very helpful.

Matas apparently saw himself as a kind of avenging angel. Purging the unclean. Saving the world from sin. Totally deluded, in other words. I could see why his daughter had needed to run away. I, for one, was immensely glad he was behind bars.

So Ed was off the hook for murder. But that still left a lot of questions. Who had stolen Selena's notes? Who had destroyed them? Who had been watching me at Regent? Who had sabotaged my SUV? There was only one person who had a vested interest in keeping Selena's work secret—and it wasn't Terry and it wasn't Frank Matas. And now that I'd had some time to think about it, I found myself also questioning Ed's reasons for having an affair with Selena. She had been beautiful, yes. It could have been an honest attraction. Or it might have been a calculated attempt to control her—to keep her quiet—until he'd finished staking his claims. According to her diary (which I'd dutifully handed over to Gaylene), he hadn't paid her much attention until she'd spotted him hanging around Regent.

Maybe I just had a nasty, suspicious mind. Maybe. But I was just as glad Ed was still away in the field. I really didn't care to see him at the moment.

I just hoped Dwayne would take my advice.

The field season was almost over for the year. Kelt would be coming back again next year. With any luck so would I, if the government decided it was time to clean up Regent. And if Woodrow got the contract to do it. And if Ed's emerald strike didn't interfere with the process. A lot of *if*s. I was trying not to think too much about them. *Que será* and all that.

It was a sentiment echoed by Jocelyn. For different reasons.

For Willow Creek Wilderness and Adventure Retreat, the tourist season had ended decisively with Michele's death. It was a blow to Jocelyn and Paul.

"But we'll weather it," Jocelyn assured me. "It'll be tough, but we'll get through it. The universe will unfold as it should."

I looked at her in surprise and wondered if she'd ever been to Nepal.

"What's Willa going to do now?" Kelt asked.

"Spend some time in Edmonton," Jocelyn replied. "But she'll be back," she added quickly. Too quickly. "This *is* where she belongs." I wondered if she was trying to convince us or herself.

"And Terry?" I asked. Surprised that I'd spoken the words aloud.

"Terry will come back here," Jocelyn answered after a pause so long, I was beginning to doubt that I'd actually asked the question. "Eventually. We still don't know if the RCMP will charge him. But Paul and I have talked about it. If he wants to, he can keep working for us. Get some counseling. And try to forgive himself."

She paused again. "You know he stopped poisoning Selena. Just before she died. He couldn't go through with it. I don't think he realized until then how far he'd fallen."

I didn't say anything.

Jocelyn chewed the inside of her cheek for a moment. "He's been so damaged for so long. It's time he healed. His best chance of finding peace is up here."

"Where there's room," I said, recalling some of her first words to me.

"Room to breathe deep," she agreed.

## August 9

Being pregnant has changed everything. It used to be that I could predict the future. There is a certain security in the knowledge that you know approximately what will happen next week and the week after and the months and years after that. Now, the future is hidden in a fog of uncertainty. And maybe that's a good thing.

Already I love this little being, this tiny water creature, with a fierceness that astonishes me. I must tell Willa, I know. But not quite yet. I want to savor this feeling. This wonder. And I must come up with a way of telling her. A way in which the hurt will not consume the love. A way in which she'll want to stay and raise this child with me. I want that more than anything.

I'm feeling younger now, not so old and used-up. The role of mother is a youthful one. Not the mantle of a woman who has seen too many years and made too many mistakes. I feel young and . . . hopeful, I think. It's been so long since I had any hope, I've almost forgotten what it feels like.

The cotton grass is blooming, carpeting the land in tiny, white Truffula Trees. I will go out to Regent tomorrow. The chicks will have left their feather-lined nests by now. I will go and count them and determine if the ptarmigan breeding success has been compromised. I will gather up all my data and do whatever it is I need to do to get Regent cleaned up. I will continue to fight the good fight. For the Yukon. For Jeff and Kyle Starr. And for the person-to-be growing inside me who will fall in love with the harsh, uncompromising beauty of this land as much as I have.

How do we live? How should we live? Simple questions. A simple answer.

With hope.

## ACKNOWLEDGEMENTS

When I first started working on Ptarmageddon, the only responsibility I had was to my three sardine-loving cats. I had time. I had focus. I had a book to write. And then my husband and I adopted a beautiful baby girl. Suddenly, I had no time. No focus. And pretty much no sleep. I still had a book to write, though.

It has taken me a long time to get this one out. And the fact that I did has much to do with many different people. First off, I am grateful to my publishers, Todd Besant and Sharon Caseburg, who watched several deadlines come and go without a manuscript to be seen—and without saying anything about it (well, not too much). Thanks to Pat Sanders for her thoughtful edit (and for being a pleasure to work with). I am also exceedingly grateful to Ethel Woods, who came and looked after my daughter so I could get some writing done (or just get a little sleep!) and Rachel Van Caeseele, who let me use her flat so I had a place to go and write (or sleep). They are the best neighbours I've ever known. My parents and in-laws came through with flying colours on the grandparent support front, and Jennifer and Tom Carter provided the "Australianisms" for which I am very thankful. And Jamis Paulson from the Manitoba Writers' Guild came to my aid most gallantly with a loaner when my computer monitor gave up the ghost in the last couple of weeks before my deadline.

On the scientific side of things, I'd like to thank Dr. Susan Hannon for discussing her work with ptarmigan, Dr. David Hik for information about pikas (and the tall tales of field camps). Richard Kellett and Pam Scowen, so fortuitously encountered on the Dempster Highway, provided much of the geological information. Lisette Ross explained the details of radio-tagging, Dave Hubert told me about working at abandoned mine sites, and Mack Hislop opened my eyes to the world of mineral prospecting. All crucial sources when writing a book of this nature.

I'd like to thank my dad, my friend Kaye, and (always and for everything, including the title!) my husband Michael. They are my first readers and sometimes (despite the fact that they're supposed to love me) my harshest critics. Essential, in other words.

And finally, I must thank those un-nameable people who irritate me, thus unwittingly providing me with inspiration for the book. What, after all, is a mystery without a murder?

## ABOUT THE AUTHOR

*Ptarmageddon* is Karen Dudley's fourth Robyn Devara mystery. Born in France, Dudley has worked in field biology, production art, photo research, paleo-environmental studies, editing, and archaeology. She lives in Winnipeg.